Isaac Asimov, world maestro of science fiction, was [illegible] Russia near Smolensk in 1920 and brought to the United States by his parents three years later. He grew up in Brooklyn where he went to grammar school and at the age of eight he gained his citizen papers. A remarkable memory helped him finish high school before he was sixteen. He then went on to Columbia University and resolved to become a chemist rather than follow the medical career his father had in mind for him. He graduated in chemistry and after a short spell in the Army he gained his doctorate in 1949 and qualified as an instructor in biochemistry at Boston University School of Medicine where he became Associate Professor in 1955, doing research in nucleic acid. Increasingly, however, the pressures of chemical research conflicted with his aspirations in the literary field, and in 1958 he retired to full-time authorship while retaining his connection with the University.

Asimov's fantastic career as a science fiction writer began in 1939 with the appearance of a short story, *Marooned Off Vesta*, in *Amazing Stories*. Thereafter he became a regular contributor to the leading SF magazines of the day including *Astounding*, *Astonishing Stories*, *Super Science Stories* and *Galaxy*. He won the Hugo Award four times and the Nebula Award once. With nearly five hundred books to his credit and several hundred articles, Asimov's output was prolific by any standards. Apart from his many world-famous science fiction works, Asimov also wrote highly successful detective mystery stories, a four-volume *History of North America*, a two-volume *Guide to the Bible*, a biographical dictionary, encyclopaedias, textbooks and an impressive list of books on many aspects of science, as well as two volumes of autobiography.

Isaac Asimov died in 1992 at the age of 72.

BY THE SAME AUTHOR

The Foundation Saga

Prelude to Foundation
Foundation
Foundation and Empire
Second Foundation
Foundation's Edge
Foundation and Earth

Galactic Empire Novels

The Currents of Space
Pebble in the Sky

Earth is Room Enough
The Martian Way
The End of Eternity
The Winds of Change

Asimov's Mysteries
The Gods Themselves
Nightfall One
Nightfall Two
Buy Jupiter
The Bicentennial Man
Nine Tomorrows

Robot Stories and Novels

I, Robot
The Rest of the Robots
The Complete Robot
The Caves of Steel
The Naked Sun
The Robots of Dawn
Robots and Empire

The Early Asimov: Volume 1
The Early Asimov: Volume 2
The Early Asimov: Volume 3

Nebula Award Stories 8 (editor)
The Science Fictional Solar System (editor, with Martin Harry Greenberg and Charles G. Waugh)

Non-fiction

The Stars in their Courses
The Left Hand of the Electron
Asimov on Science Fiction
The Sun Shines Bright
Counting the Eons
Far As Human Eye Could See

Detection

Tales of the Black Widowers
More Tales of the Black Widowers
Casebook of the Black Widowers
Authorised Murder
The Union Club Mysteries

Voyager

ISAAC ASIMOV

Foundation

HarperCollins*Publishers*

HarperCollins *Publishers* India
a joint venture with
The India Today Group
by arrangement with
HarperCollins *Publishers* Limited

Voyager
An imprint of HarperCollins *Publishers*
77-85 Fulham Palace Road,
Hammersmith, London W6 8JB

www.voyager-books.com

This paperback edition 1995
3 5 7 9 8 6 4

Previously published in paperback by
HarperCollins Science Fiction and Fantasy 1994, reprinted once
and by Grafton 1960 reprinted thirty-nine times

First published in Great Britain by
Weidenfeld & Nicolson Ltd 1953

ISBN 978-0-00-727042-2

Set in Plantin

HarperCollins Publishers
A-53, Sector 57, NOIDA, Uttar Pradesh - 201301, India
77-85 Fulham Palace Road, London W6 8JB, United Kingdom
Hazelton Lanes, 55 Avenue Road, Suite 2900, Toronto, Ontario M5R 3L2
and 1995 Markham Road, Scarborough, Ontario M1B 5M8, Canada
25 Ryde Road, Pymble, Sydney, NSW 2073, Australia
31 View Road, Glenfield, Auckland 10, New Zealand
10 East 53rd Street, New York NY 10022, USA

Printed and bound at
Gopsons Papers Ltd., Noida

FOUNDATION

Part I

THE PSYCHOHISTORIANS

1

HARI SELDON ... *born in the 11,988th year of the Galactic Era: died 12,069. The dates are more commonly given in terms of the current Foundational Era as –79 to the year 1 F.E. Born to middle-class parents on Helicon, Arcturus sector (where his father, in a legend of doubtful authenticity, was a tobacco grower in the hydroponic plants of the planet), he early showed amazing ability in mathematics. Anecdotes concerning his ability are innumerable, and some are contradictory. At the age of two, he is said to have ...*

... Undoubtedly his greatest contributions were in the field of psychohistory. Seldon found the field little more than a set of vague axioms; he left it a profound statistical science ...

... The best existing authority we have for the details of his life is the biography written by Gaal Dornick who, as a young man, met Seldon two years before the great mathematician's death. The story of the meeting ...

'ENCYCLOPEDIA GALACTICA*'

His name was Gaal Dornick and he was just a country boy who had never seen Trantor before. That is, not in real life. He *had* seen it many times on the hyper-video, and occasionally in tremendous three-dimensional newscasts covering an Imperial Coronation or the opening of a Galactic Council. Even though he had lived all his life on the world of Synnax, which circled a star at the edges of the Blue Drift, he was not cut off from civilization, you see. At that time, no place in the Galaxy was.

There were nearly twenty-five million inhabited planets in

* All quotations from the *Encyclopedia Galactica* here reproduced are taken from the 116th Edition published in 1020 F.E. by the Encyclopedia Galactica Publishing Co., Terminus, with permission of the publishers.

the Galaxy then, and not one but owed allegiance to the Empire whose seat was on Trantor. It was the last half-century in which that could be said.

To Gaal, this trip was the undoubted climax of his young, scholarly life. He had been in space before so that the trip, as a voyage and nothing more, meant little to him. To be sure, he had travelled previously only as far as Synnax's only satellite in order to get the data on the mechanics of meteor driftage which he needed for his dissertation, but space-travel was all one whether one travelled half a million miles, or as many light years.

He had steeled himself just a little for the Jump through hyper-space, a phenomenon one did not experience in simple interplanetary trips. The Jump remained, and would probably remain for ever, the only practical method of travelling between the stars. Travel through ordinary space could proceed at no rate more rapid than that of ordinary light (a bit of scientific knowledge that belonged among the few items known since the forgotten dawn of human history), and that would have meant years of travel between even the nearest of inhabited systems. Through hyper-space, that unimaginable region that was neither space nor time, matter nor energy, something nor nothing, one could traverse the length of the Galaxy in the intervals between two neighbouring instants of time.

Gaal had waited for the first of those Jumps with a little dread curled gently in his stomach, and it ended in nothing more than a trifling jar, a little internal kick which ceased an instant before he could be sure he had felt it. That was all.

And after that, there was only the ship, large and glistening; the cool production of 12,000 years of Imperial progress; and himself, with his doctorate in mathematics freshly obtained and an invitation from the great Hari Seldon to come to Trantor and join the vast and somewhat mysterious Seldon Project.

What Gaal was waiting for after the disappointment of the

Jump was that first sight of Trantor. He haunted the View-room. The steel shutter-lids were rolled back at announced times and he was always there, watching the hard brilliance of the stars, enjoying the incredible hazy swarm of a star cluster, like a giant conglomeration of fire-flies caught in mid-motion and stilled forever. At one time there was the cold, blue-white smoke of a gaseous nebula within five light years of the ship, spreading over the window like distant milk, filling the room with an icy tinge, and disappearing out of sight two hours later, after another Jump.

The first sight of Trantor's sun was that of a hard, white speck all but lost in a myriad such, and recognizable only because it was pointed out by the ship's guide. The stars were thick here at the Galactic centre. But with each Jump, it shone more brightly, drowning out the rest, paling them and thinning them out.

An officer came through and said, 'View-room will be closed for the remainder of the trip. Prepare for landing.'

Gaal had followed after, clutching at the sleeve of the white uniform with the Spaceship-and-Sun of the Empire on it.

He said, 'Would it be possible to let me stay? I would like to see Trantor.'

The officer smiled and Gaal flushed a bit. It occurred to him that he spoke with a provincial accent.

The officer said, 'We'll be landing on Trantor by morning.'

'I mean I want to see it from space.'

'Oh. Sorry, my boy. If this were a space-yacht we might manage it. But we're spinning down, sunside. You wouldn't want to be blinded, burnt, and radiation-scarred all at the same time, would you?'

Gaal started to walk away.

The officer called after him, 'Trantor would only be grey blur anyway, Kid. Why don't you take a space-tour once you hit Trantor. They're cheap.'

Gaal looked back, 'Thank you very much.'

It was childish to feel disappointed, but childishness comes almost as naturally to a man as to a child, and there was a lump in Gaal's throat. He had never seen Trantor spread out in all its incredibility, as large as life, and he hadn't expected to have to wait longer.

2

The ship landed in a medley of noises. There was the far-off hiss of the atmosphere cutting and sliding past the metal of the ship. There was the steady drone of the conditioners fighting the heat of friction, and the slower rumble of the engines enforcing deceleration. There was the human sound of men and women gathering in the debarkation rooms and the grind of the hoists lifting baggage, mail, and freight to the long axis of the ship, from which they would be later moved to the unloading platform.

Gaal felt the slight jar that indicated the ship no longer had an independent motion of its own. Ship's gravity had been giving way to planetary gravity for hours. Thousands of passengers had been sitting patiently in the debarkation rooms which swung easily on yielding force-fields to accommodate its orientation to the changing direction of the gravitational forces. Now they were crawling down curving ramps to the large, yawning locks.

Gaal's baggage was minor. He stood at a desk, as it was quickly and expertly taken apart and put together again. His visa was inspected and stamped. He himself paid no attention.

This was Trantor! The air seemed a little thicker here, the gravity a bit greater, than on his home planet of Synnax, but he would get used to that. He wondered if he would get used to immensity.

Debarkation Building was tremendous. The roof was almost lost in the heights. Gaal could almost imagine that clouds could form beneath its immensity. He could see no opposite wall; just men and desks and converging floor till it faded out in haze.

The man at the desk was speaking again. He sounded annoyed. He said, 'Move on, Dornick.' He had to open the visa, look again, before he remembered the name. Gaal said, 'Where – where—'

The man at the desk jerked a thumb, 'Taxis to the right and third left.'

Gaal moved, seeing the glowing twists of air suspended high in nothingness and reading, 'TAXIS TO ALL POINTS.'

A figure detached itself from anonymity and stopped at the desk, as Gaal left. The man at the desk looked up and nodded briefly. The figure nodded in return and followed the young immigrant.

He was in time to hear Gaal's destination.

Gaal found himself hard against a railing.

The small sign said, 'Supervisor.' The man to whom the sign referred did not look up. He said, 'Where to?'

Gaal wasn't sure, but even a few seconds' hesitation meant men queueing in line behind him.

The Supervisor looked up, 'Where to?'

Gaal's funds were low, but there was only this one night and then he would have a job. He tried to sound nonchalant, 'A good hotel, please.'

The Supervisor was unimpressed, 'They're all good. Name one.'

Gaal said, desperately, 'The nearest one, please.'

The Supervisor touched a button. A thin line of light formed along the floor, twisting among others which brightened and dimmed in different colours and shades. A ticket was shoved into Gaal's hands. It glowed faintly.

The Supervisor said, 'One point twelve.'

Gaal fumbled for the coins. He said, 'Where do I go?'

'Follow the light. The ticket will keep glowing as long as you're pointed in the right direction.'

Gaal looked up and began walking. There were hundreds creeping across the vast floor, following their individual trails, sifting and straining themselves through intersection points to arrive at their respective destinations.

His own trail ended. A man in glaring blue-and-yellow uniform, shining and new in unstainable plasto-textile, reached for his two bags.

'Direct line to the Luxor,' he said.

The man who followed Gaal heard that. He also heard Gaal say, 'Fine,' and watched him enter the blunt-nosed vehicle.

The taxi lifted straight up. Gaal stared out the curved, transparent window, marvelling at the sensation of air-flight within an enclosed structure and clutching instinctively at the back of the driver's seat. The vastness contracted and the people became ants in random distribution. The scene contracted further and began to slide backward.

There was a wall ahead. It began high in the air and extended upward out of sight. It was riddled with holes that were the mouths of tunnels. Gaal's taxi moved toward one, then plunged into it. For a moment, Gaal wondered idly how his driver could pick out one among so many.

There was now only blackness, with nothing but the past-flashing of a coloured signal light to relieve the gloom. The air was full of a rushing sound.

Gaal leaned forward against deceleration then and the taxi popped out of the tunnel and descended to ground level once more.

'The Luxor Hotel,' said the driver, unnecessarily. He helped Gaal with his baggage, accepted a tenth-credit tip with a business-like air, picked up a waiting passenger, and was rising again.

In all this, from the moment of debarkation, there had been no glimpse of sky.

3

TRANTOR ... *At the beginning of the thirteenth millennium, this tendency reached its climax. As the centre of the Imperial Government for unbroken hundreds of generations and located, as it was, in the central regions of the Galaxy among the most densely populated and industrially advanced worlds of the system, it could scarcely help being the densest and richest clot of humanity the Race had ever seen.*

Its urbanization, progressing steadily, had finally reached the ultimate. All the land surface of Trantor, 75,000,000 square miles in extent, was a single city. The population, at its height, was well in excess of forty billions. This enormous population was devoted almost entirely to the administrative necessities of Empire, and found themselves all to few for the complications of the task. (It is to be remembered that the impossibility of proper administration of the Galactic Empire under the uninspired leadership of the later Emperors was a considerable factor in the Fall.) Daily, fleets of ships in the tens of thousands brought the produce of twenty agricultural worlds to the dinner tables of Trantor...

Its dependence upon the outer worlds for food and, indeed, for all necessities of life, made Trantor increasingly vulnerable to conquest by siege. In the last millennium of the Empire, the monotonously numerous revolts made Emperor after Emperor conscious of this, and Imperial policy became little more than the protection of Trantor's delicate jugular vein ...

ENCYCLOPEDIA GALACTICA

Gaal was not certain whether the sun shone, or, for that matter, whether it was day or night. He was ashamed to ask. All the planet seemed to live beneath metal. The meal of which he had just partaken had been labelled luncheon, but there were many planets which lived a standard time-scale that took no account of the perhaps inconvenient alteration of day and night. The rate of planetary turnings differed, and he did not know that of Trantor.

At first, he had eagerly followed the signs to the 'Sun Room' and found it but a chamber for basking in artificial radiation. He lingered a moment or two, then returned to the Luxor's main lobby.

He said to the room clerk, 'Where can I buy a ticket for a planetary tour?'

'Right here.'

'When will it start?'

'You just missed it. Another one tomorrow. Buy a ticket now and we'll reserve a place for you.'

'Oh.' Tomorrow would be too late. He would have to be at the University tomorrow. He said, 'There wouldn't be an observation tower – or something? I mean, in the open air.'

'Sure! Sell you a ticket for that, if you want. Better let me check if it's raining or not.' He closed a contact at his elbow and read the flowing letters that raced across a frosted screen. Gaal read with him.

The room clerk said, 'Good weather. Come to think of it, I do believe it's the dry season now.' He added, conversationally, 'I don't bother with the outside myself. The last time I was in the open was three years ago. You see it once, you know, and that's all there is to it – here's your ticket. Special elevator in the rear. It's marked "To the Tower". Just take it.'

The elevator was of the new sort that ran by gravitic repulsion. Gaal entered and others flowed in behind him. The operator closed a contact. For a moment, Gaal felt suspended in space as gravity switched to zero, and then he had weight again in small measure as the elevator accelerated upward. Deceleration followed and his feet left the floor. He squawked against his will.

The operator called out, 'Tuck your feet under the railing. Can't you read the sign?'

The others had done so. They were smiling at him as he madly and vainly tried to clamber back down the wall. Their shoes pressed upward against the chromium of the railings that stretched across the floor in parallels set two feet apart. He had noticed those railings on entering and had ignored them.

Then a hand reached out and pulled him down.

He gasped his thanks as the elevator came to a halt.

He stepped out upon an open terrace bathed in a white brilliance that hurt his eyes. The man, whose helping hand he had just now been the recipient of, was immediately behind him.

The man said, kindly, 'Plenty of seats.'

Gaal closed his mouth, he had been gaping, and said, 'It certainly seems so.' He started for them automatically, then stopped.

He said, 'If you don't mind, I'll just stop a moment at the railing. I – I want to look a bit.'

The man waved him on, good-naturedly, and Gaal leaned out over the shoulder-high railing and bathed himself in all the panorama.

He could not see the ground. It was lost in the ever-increasing complexities of man-made structures. He could see no horizon other than that of metal against sky, stretching out to almost uniform greyness, and he knew it was so over all the land-surface of the planet. There was scarcely any motion to be seen – a few pleasure-craft lazed against the sky – but all the busy traffic of billions of men were going on, he knew, beneath the metal skin of the world.

There was no green to be seen; no green, no soil, no life other than man. Somewhere on the world, he realized vaguely, was the Emperor's palace, set amid one hundred square miles of natural soil, green with trees, rainbowed with flowers. It was a small island amid an ocean of steel, but it wasn't visible from where he stood. It might be ten thousand miles away. He did not know.

Before very long, he must have his tour!

He sighed noisily, and realized finally that he was on Trantor at last; on the planet which was the centre of all the Galaxy and the kernel of the human race. He saw none of its weaknesses. He saw no ships of food landing. He was not aware of a jugular vein delicately connecting the forty billion of Trantor with the rest of the Galaxy. He was conscious only of the mightiest deed of man; the complete and almost contemptuously final conquest of a world.

He came away a little blank-eyed. His friend of the elevator was indicating a seat next to himself and Gaal took it.

The man smiled, 'My name is Jerril. First time on Trantor?'

'Yes, Mr Jerril.'

'Thought so. Jerril's my first name. Trantor gets you if you've got the poetic temperament. Trantorians never come up here, though. They don't like it. Gives them nerves.'

'Nerves! – my name's Gaal, by the way. Why should it give them nerves? It's glorious.'

'Subjective matter of opinion, Gaal. If you're born in a cubicle and grow up in a corridor, and work in a cell, and vacation in a crowded sun-room, then coming up into the open with nothing but sky over you might just give you a nervous breakdown. They make the children come up here once a year, after they're five. I don't know if it does any good. They don't get enough of it, really, and the first few times they scream themselves into hysteria. They ought to start as soon as they're weaned and have the trip once a week.'

He went on, 'Of course, it doesn't really matter. What if they never come out at all? They're happy down there and they run the Empire. How high up do you think we are?'

He said, 'Half a mile?' and wondered if that sounded naïve.

It must have, for Jerril chuckled a little. He said, 'No. Just five hundred feet.'

'What? But the elevator took about—?'

'I know. But most of the time it was just getting up to ground level. Trantor is tunnelled over a mile down. It's like an iceberg. Nine-tenths of it is out of sight. It even works itself out a few miles into the sub-ocean soil at the shore-lines. In fact, we're down so low that we can make use of the temperature difference between ground level and a couple of miles under to supply us with all the energy we need. Did you know that?'

'No, I thought you used atomic generators.'

'Did once. But this is cheaper.'

'I imagine so.'

'What do you think of it all?' For a moment, the man's good nature evaporated into shrewdness. He looked almost sly.

Gaal fumbled. 'Glorious,' he said, again.

'Here on vacation? Travelling? Sightseeing?'

'Not exactly. At least, I've always wanted to visit Trantor but I came here primarily for a job.'

'Oh?'

Gaal felt obliged to explain further, 'With Dr Seldon's project at the University of Trantor.'

'Raven Seldon?'

'Why, no. The one I mean is Hari Seldon – the psychohistorian Seldon. I don't know of any Raven Seldon.'

'Hari's the one I mean. They call him Raven. Slang, you know. He keeps predicting disaster.'

'He does?' Gaal was genuinely astonished.

'Surely, you must know.' Jerril was not smiling. 'You're coming to work for him, aren't you?'

'Well, yes, I'm a mathematician. Why does he predict disaster? What kind of disaster?'

'What kind would you think?'

'I'm afraid I wouldn't have the least idea. I've read the papers Dr Seldon and his group have published. They're on mathematical theory.'

'Yes, the ones they publish.'

Gaal felt annoyed. He said, 'I think I'll go to my room now. Very pleased to have met you.'

Jerril waved his arm indifferently in farewell.

Gaal found a man waiting for him in his room. For a moment, he was too startled to put into words the inevitable, 'What are you doing here?' that came to his lips.

The man rose. He was old and almost bald and he walked with a limp, but his eyes were very bright and blue.

He said, 'I am Hari Seldon,' an instant before Gaal's befuddled brain placed the face alongside the memory of the many times he had seen it in pictures.

4

PSYCHOHISTORY ... *Gaal Dornick, using non-mathematical concepts, has defined psychohistory to be that branch of mathematics which deals with the reactions of human conglomerates to fixed social and economic stimuli . . .*

. . . Implicit in all these definitions is the assumption that the human conglomerate being dealt with is sufficiently large for valid statistical treatment. The necessary size of such a conglomerate may be determined by Seldon's First Theorem which . . . A further necessary assumption is that the human conglomerate be itself unaware of psychohistoric analysis in order that its reactions be truly random . . .

The basis of all valid psychohistory lies in the development of the Seldon Functions which exhibit properties congruent to those of such social and economic forces as . . .

ENCYCLOPEDIA GALACTICA

'Good afternoon, sir,' said Gaal. 'I— I—'

'You didn't think we were to meet before tomorrow? Ordinarily, we would not have. It is just that if we are to use your services, we must work quickly. It grows continually more difficult to obtain recruits.'

'I don't understand, sir.'

'You were talking to a man on the observation tower, were you not?'

'Yes. His first name is Jerril. I know no more about him.'

'His name is nothing. He is an agent of the Commission of Public Safety. He followed you from the space-port.'

'But why? I am afraid I am very confused.'

'Did the man on the tower say nothing about me?'

Gaal hesitated, 'He referred to you as Raven Seldon.'

'Did he say why?'

'He said you predict disaster.'

'I do. What does Trantor mean to you?'

Everyone seemed to be asking his opinion of Trantor. Gaal felt incapable of response beyond the bare word, 'Glorious.'

'You say that without thinking. What of psychohistory?'

'I haven't thought of applying it to the problem.'

'Before you are done with me, young man, you will learn to apply psychohistory to all problems as a matter of course – observe.' Seldon removed his calculator pad from the pouch at his belt. Men said he kept one beneath his pillow for use in moments of wakefulness. Its grey, glossy finish was slightly worn by use. Seldon's nimble fingers, spotted now with age, played along the hard plastic that rimmed it. Red symbols glowed out from the grey.

He said, 'That represents the condition of the Empire at present?'

He waited.

Gaal said finally, 'Surely that is not a complete representation.'

'No, not complete,' said Seldon. 'I am glad you do not accept my word blindly. However, this is an approximation which will serve to demonstrate the proposition. Will you accept that?'

'Subject to my later verification of the derivation of the function, yes.' Gaal was carefully avoiding a possible trap.

'Good. Add to this the known probability of Imperial assassination, viceregal revolt, the contemporary recurrence of periods of economic depression, the declining rate of planetary explorations, the ...'

He proceeded. As each item was mentioned, new symbols sprang to life at his touch, and melted into the basic function which expanded and changed.

Gaal stopped him only once. 'I don't see the validity of that set-transformation.'

Seldon repeated it more slowly.

Gaal said, 'But that is done by way of a forbidden socio-operation.'

'Good. You are quick, but not yet quick enough. It is not forbidden in this connection. Let me do it by expansions.'

The procedure was much longer and at its end, Gaal said, humbly, 'Yes, I see now.'

Finally, Seldon stopped. 'This is Trantor five centuries from now. How do you interpret that? Eh?' He put his head to one side and waited.

Gaal said, unbelievingly, 'Total destruction! But – but that is impossible. Trantor has never been—'

Seldon was filled with the intense excitement of a man whose body only had grown old. 'Come, come. You saw how the result was arrived at. Put it into words. Forget the symbolism for a moment.'

Gaal said, 'As Trantor becomes more specialized, it becomes more vulnerable, less able to defend itself. Further, as it becomes more and more the administrative centre of Empire, it becomes a greater prize. As the Imperial succession becomes more and more uncertain, and the feuds among the great families more rampant, social responsibility disappears.'

'Enough. And what of the numerical probability of total destruction within five centuries?'

'I couldn't tell.'

'Surely you can perform a field-differentation?'

Gaal felt himself under pressure. He was not offered the calculator pad. It was held a foot from his eyes. He calculated furiously and felt his forehead grow slick with sweat.

He said, 'About 85 per cent?'

'Not bad,' said Seldon, thrusting out a lower lip, 'but not

good. The actual figure is 92.5 per cent.'

Gaal said, 'And so you are called Raven Seldon? I have seen none of this in the journals.'

'But of course not. This is unprintable. Do you suppose the Imperium could expose its shakiness in this manner? That is a very simple demonstration in psychohistory. But some of our results have leaked out among the aristocracy.'

'That's bad.'

'Not necessarily. All is taken into account.'

'But is that why I'm being investigated?'

'Yes. Everything about my project is being investigated.'

'Are you in danger, sir?'

'Oh, yes. There is a probability of 1.7 per cent that I will be executed, but of course that will not stop the project. We have taken that into account as well. Well, never mind. You will meet me, I suppose, at the University tomorrow?'

'I will,' said Gaal.

5

COMMISSION OF PUBLIC SAFETY . . . *The aristocratic coterie rose to power after the assassination of Cleon I, last of the Entuns. In the main, they formed an element of order during the centuries of instability and uncertainty in the Imperium. Usually under the control of the great families of the Chens and the Divarts, it degenerated into a blind instrument for maintenance of the status quo . . . They were not completely removed as a power in the state until after the accession of the last strong Emperor, Cleon II. The first Chief Commissioner . . .*

. . . In a way, the beginning of the Commission's decline can be traced to the trial of Hari Seldon two years before the beginning of the Foundational Era. That trial is described in Gaal Dornick's biography of Hari Seldon . . .

ENCYCLOPEDIA GALACTICA

Gaal did not carry out his promise. He was awakened the next morning by a muted buzzer. He answered it, and the voice of the desk clerk, as muted, polite and deprecating as it well might be, informed him that he was under detention at the order of the Commission for Public Safety.

Gaal sprang to the door and found it would no longer open. He could only dress and wait.

They came for him and took him elsewhere, but it was still detention. They asked him questions most politely. It was all very civilized. He explained that he was a provincial of Synnax; that he had attended such and such schools and obtained a Doctor of Mathematics degree on such and such a date. He had applied for a position on Dr Seldon's staff and had been accepted. Over and over again he gave these details; and over and over again they returned to the question of his joining the Seldon Project. How had he heard of it; what were to be his duties; what secret instructions had he received; what was it all about?

He answered that he did not know. He had no secret instructions. He was a scholar and a mathematician. He had no interest in politics.

And finally the gentle inquisitor asked, 'When will Trantor be destroyed?'

Gaal faltered, 'I could not say of my own knowledge.'

'Could you say of anyone's?'

'How could I speak for another?' He felt warm; over-warm.

The inquisitor said, 'Has anyone told you of such destruction; set a date?' And, as the young man hesitated, he went on, 'You have been followed, doctor. We were at the airport when you arrived; on the observation tower when you waited for your appointment; and, of course, we were able to overhear your conversation with Dr Seldon.'

Gaal said, 'Then you know his views on the matter.'

'Perhaps. But we would like to hear them from you.'

'He is of the opinion that Trantor would be destroyed within five centuries.'

'He proved it – uh – mathematically?'

'Yes, he did' – defiantly.

'You maintain the – uh – mathematics to be valid, I suppose?'

'If Dr Seldon vouches for it, it is valid.'

'Then we will return.'

'Wait. I have a right to a lawyer. I demand my rights as an Imperial citizen.'

'You shall have them.'

And he did.

It was a tall man that eventually entered, a man whose face seemed all vertical lines and so thin that one could wonder whether there was room for a smile.

Gaal looked up. He felt dishevelled and wilted. So much had happened, yet he had been on Trantor not more than thirty hours.

The man said, 'I am Lors Avakim. Dr Seldon has directed me to represent you.'

'Is that so? Well, then, look here. I demand an instant appeal to the Emperor. I'm being held without cause. I'm innocent of anything, of *anything*.' He slashed his hands outwards, palms down. 'You've got to arrange a hearing with the Emperor, instantly.'

Avakim was carefully emptying the contents of a flat folder on to the floor. If Gaal had had the stomach for it, he might have recognized Cellomet legal forms, metal thin and tapelike, adapted for insęrtion within the smallness of a personal capsule. He might also have recognized a pocket recorder.

Avakim, paying no attention to Gaal's outburst, finally looked up. He said, 'The Commission will, of course, have a spy beam on our conversation. This is against the law, but they will use one nevertheless.'

Gaal ground his teeth.

'However,' and Avakim seated himself deliberately, 'the recorder I have on the table – which is a perfectly ordinary recorder to all appearances and performs its duties well – has the additional property of completely blanketing the spy beam. This is something they will not find out at once.'

'Then I can speak.'

'Of course.'

'Then I want a hearing with the Emperor.'

Avakim smiled frostily, and it turned out that there was room for it on his thin face after all. His cheeks wrinkled to make the room. He said, 'You are from the provinces.'

'I am none the less an Imperial citizen. As good a one as you or as any of this Commission of Public Safety.'

'No doubt; no doubt. It is merely that, as a provincial, you do not understand life on Trantor as it is. There are no hearings before the Emperor.'

'To whom else would one appeal from this Commission? Is there other procedure?'

'None. There is no recourse in a practical sense. Legalistically, you may appeal to the Emperor, but would get no hearing. The Emperor today is not the Emperor of an Entun dynasty, you know. Trantor, I am afraid, is in the hands of the aristocratic families, members of which compose the Commission of Public Safety. This is a development which is well predicted by psychohistory.'

Gaal said, 'Indeed? In that case, if Dr Seldon can predict the history of Trantor five hundred years into the future—'

'He can predict it fifteen hundred years into the future.'

'Let it be fifteen thousand. Why couldn't he yesterday have predicted the events of this morning and warned me? – no, I'm sorry.' Gaal sat down and rested his head in one sweating palm. 'I quite understand that psychohistory is a statistical science and cannot predict the future of a single man with any accuracy. You'll understand that I'm upset.'

'But you are wrong. Dr Seldon was of the opinion that you would be arrested this morning.'

'What!'

'It is unfortunate, but true. The Commission has been more and more hostile to his activities. New members joining the group have been interfered with to an increasing extent. The graphs showed that for our purposes, matters might best be brought to a climax now. The Commission of itself was moving somewhat slowly so Dr Seldon visited you yesterday for the purpose of forcing their hand. No other reason.'

Gaal caught his breath. 'I resent—'

'Please. It was necessary. You were not picked for any personal reasons. You must realize that Dr Seldon's plans, which are laid out with the developed mathematics of over eighteen years, include all eventualities with significant probabilities. This is one of them. I've been sent here for no other purpose than to assure you that you need not fear. It will end well; almost certainly so for the project; and with reasonable probability for you.'

'What are the figures?' demanded Gaal.

'For the project, over 99.9 per cent.'

'And for myself?'

'I am instructed that this probability is 77.2 per cent.'

'Then I've got better than one chance in five of being sentenced to prison or to death.'

'The last is under one per cent.'

'Indeed. Calculations upon one man mean nothing. You send Dr Seldon to me.'

'Unfortunately, I cannot. Dr Seldon is himself arrested.'

The door was thrown open before the rising Gaal could do more than utter the beginning of a cry. A guard entered, walked to the table, picked up the recorder, looked upon all sides of it and put it in his pocket.

Avakim said quietly, 'I will need that instrument.'

'We will supply you with one, Counsellor, that does not cast a static field.'

'My interview is done, in that case.'

Gaal watched him leave and was alone.

6

The trial (Gaal supposed it to be one, though it bore little resemblance legalistically to elaborate trial techniques Gaal had read of) had not lasted long. It was in its third day. Yet already, Gaal could no longer stretch his memory back far enough to embrace its beginning.

He himself had been but little pecked at. The heavy guns were trained on Dr Seldon himself. Hari Seldon, however, sat there unperturbed. To Gaal, he was the only spot of stability remaining in the world.

The audience was small and drawn exclusively from among the Barons of the Empire. Press and public were excluded and it was doubtful that any significant number of outsiders even knew that a trial of Seldon was conducted. The atmosphere was one of unrelieved hostility toward the defendants.

Five of the Commission of Public Safety sat behind the raised desk. They wore scarlet and gold uniforms and the shining, close-fitting plastic caps that were the sign of their judicial function. In the centre was the Chief Commissioner Linge Chen. Gaal had never before seen so great a Lord and he watched him with fascination. Chen, throughout the trial, rarely said a word. He made it quite clear that much speech was beneath his dignity.

The Commission's Advocate consulted his notes and the examination continued, with Seldon still on the stand:

Q. Let us see, Dr Seldon. How many men are now engaged in the project of which you are head?

A. Fifty mathematicians.

Q. Including Dr Gaal Dornick?

A. Dr Dornick is the fifty-first.

Q. Oh, we have fifty-one then? Search your memory, Dr Seldon. Perhaps there are fifty-two or fifty-three? Or perhaps even more?

A. Dr Dornick has not yet formally joined my organization. When he does, the membership will be fifty-one. It is now fifty, as I have said.

Q. Not perhaps nearly a hundred thousand?

A. Mathematicians? No.

Q. I did not say mathematicians. Are there a hundred thousand in all capacities?

A. In all capacities, your figure may be correct.

Q. *May* be? I say it *is*. I say that the men in your project number ninety-eight thousand, five hundred and seventy-two.

A. I believe you are counting women and children.

Q. (raising his voice) Ninety-eight thousand five hundred and seventy-two individuals is the intent of my statement. There is no need to quibble.

A. I accept the figures.

Q. (referring to his notes) Let us drop that for a moment, then, and take up another matter which we have already discussed at some length. Would you repeat, Dr Seldon your thoughts concerning the future of Trantor?

A. I have said, and I say again, that Trantor will lie in ruins within the next five centuries.

Q. You do not consider your statement a disloyal one?

A. No, sir. Scientific truth is beyond loyalty and disloyalty.

Q. You are sure that your statement represents scientific truth?

A. I am.

Q. On what basis?

A. On the basis of the mathematics of psychohistory.

Q. Can you prove that this mathematics is valid?

A. Only to another mathematician.

Q. (with a smile) Your claim then, is that your truth is of so esoteric a nature that it is beyond the understanding of a plain man. It seems to me that truth should be clearer than that, less mysterious, more open to the mind.

A. It presents no difficulties to some minds. The physics of energy transfer, which we know as thermodynamics, has been clear and true through all the history of man since the mythical ages, yet there may be people present who would find it impossible to design a power engine. People of high intelligence, too. I doubt if the learned Commissioners—

At this point, one of the Commissioners leaned toward the Advocate. His words were not heard but the hissing of the voice carried a certain asperity. The Advocate flushed and interrupted Seldon.

Q. We are not here to listen to speeches, Dr Seldon. Let us assume that you have made your point. Let me suggest to you that your predictions of disaster might be intended to destroy public confidence in the Imperial Government for purposes of your own.

A. That is not so.

Q. Let me suggest that you intend to claim that a period of time preceding the so-called ruin of Trantor will be filled with unrest of various types.

A. That is correct.

Q. And that by the mere prediction thereof, you hope to bring it about, and to have then an army of a hundred thousand available.

A. In the first place, that is not so. And if it were, investigation will show you that barely ten thousand are men of military age, and none of these has training in arms.

Q. Are you acting as an agent for another?

A. I am not in the pay of any man, Mr. Advocate.

Q. You are entirely disinterested? You are serving science?

A. I am.

Q. Then let us see how. Can the future be changed, Dr Seldon?

A. Obviously. This court-room may explode in the next few

hours, or it may not. If it did, the future would undoubtedly be changed in some minor respects.

Q. You quibble, Dr Seldon. Can the overall history of the human race be changed?

A. Yes.

Q. Easily?

A. No. With great difficulty.

Q. Why?

A. The psychohistoric trend of a planetful of people contains a huge inertia. To be changed it must be met with something possessing a similar inertia. Either as many people must be concerned, or if the number of people be relatively small, enormous time for change must be allowed. Do you understand?

Q. I think I do. Trantor need not be ruined, if a great many people decide to act so that it will not.

A. That is right.

Q. As many as a hundred thousand people?

A. No, sir. That is far too few.

Q. You are sure?

A. Consider that Trantor has a population of over forty billions. Consider further that the trend leading to ruin does not belong to Trantor alone but to the Empire as a whole and the Empire contains nearly a quintillion human beings.

Q. I see. Then perhaps a hundred thousand people can change the trend, if they and their descendants labour for five hundred years.

A. I'm afraid not. Five hundred years is too short a time.

Q. Ah! In that case, Dr Seldon, we are left with this deduction to be made from your statements. You have gathered one hundred thousand people within the confines of your project. These are insufficent to change the history of Trantor within five hundred years. In other words, they cannot prevent the destruction of Trantor no matter what they do.

A. You are unfortunately correct.

Q. And on other hand, your hundred thousand are intended for no illegal purpose.

A. Exactly.

Q. (slowly and with satisfaction) In that case, Dr Seldon – now attend, sir, most carefully, for we want a considered answer. What is the purpose of your hundred thousand?

The Advocate's voice had grown strident. He had sprung his trap; backed Seldon into a corner; driven him astutely from any possibility of answering.

There was a rising buzz of conversation at that which swept the ranks of the peers in the audience and invaded even the row of Commissioners. They swayed toward one another in their scarlet and gold, only the Chief remaining uncorrupted.

Hari Seldon remained unmoved. He waited for the babble to evaporate.

A. To minimize the effects of that destruction.

Q. And exactly what do you mean by that?

A. The explanation is simple. The coming destruction of Trantor is not an event in itself, isolated in the scheme of human development. It will be the climax to an intricate drama which was begun centuries ago and which is accelerating in pace continuously. I refer, gentlemen, to the developing decline and fall of the Galactic Empire.

The buzz now became a dull roar. The Advocate, unheeded, was yelling, 'You are openly declaring that—' and stopped because the cries of 'Treason' from the audience showed that the point had been made without any hammering.

Slowly, the Chief Commissioner raised his gavel once and let it drop. The sound was that of a mellow gong. When the reverberations ceased, the gabble of the audience also did. The Advocate took a deep breath.

Q. (theatrically) Do you realize, Dr Seldon, that you are

speaking of an Empire that has stood for twelve thousand years, through all the vicissitudes of the generations, and which has behind it the good wishes and love of a quadrillion human beings?

A. I am aware both of the present status and the past history of the Empire. Without disrespect, I must claim a far better knowledge of it than any in this room.

Q. And you predict its ruin?

A. It is a prediction which is made by mathematics. I pass no moral judgements. Personally, I regret the prospect. Even if the Empire were admitted to be a bad thing (an admission I do not make), the state of anarchy which would follow its fall would be worse. It is that state of anarchy which my project is pledged to fight. The fall of Empire, gentlemen, is a massive thing, however, and not easily fought. It is dictated by a rising bureaucracy, a receding initiative, a freezing of caste, a damming of curiosity – a hundred other factors. It has been going on, as I have said, for centuries, and it is too majestic and massive a movement to stop.

Q. Is it not obvious to anyone that the Empire is as strong as it ever was?

A. The appearance of strength is all about you. It would seem to last for ever. However, Mr. Advocate, the rotten tree-trunk, until the very moment when the storm-blast breaks it in two, has all the appearance of might that it ever had. The storm-blast whistles through the branches of the Empire even now. Listen with the ears of psychohistory, and you will hear the creaking.

Q. (uncertainly) We are not here, Dr Seldon, to lis—

A. (firmly) The Empire will vanish and all its good with it. Its accumulated knowledge will decay and the order it has imposed will vanish. Interstellar wars will be endless; interstellar trade will decay; population will decline; worlds will lose touch with the main body of the Galaxy – and so matters will remain.

Q. (a small voice in the middle of a vast silence) For ever?

A. Psychohistory, which can predict the fall, can make statements concerning the succeeding dark ages. The Empire, gentlemen, as has just been said, has stood twelve thousand years. The dark ages to come will endure not twelve, but *thirty* thousand years. A Second Empire will rise, but between it and our civilization will be one thousand generations of suffering humanity. We must fight that.

Q. (recovering somewhat) You contradict yourself. You said earlier that you could not prevent the destruction of Trantor; hence, presumably, the fall - the *so-called* fall of the Empire.

A. I do not say now that we can prevent the fall. But it is not yet too late to shorten the interregnum which will follow. It is possible, gentlemen, to reduce the duration of anarchy to a single millennium, if my group is allowed to act now. We are at a delicate moment in history. The huge, onrushing mass of events must be deflected just a little - just a little— It cannot be much, but it may be enough to remove twenty-nine thousand years of misery from human history.

Q. How do you propose to do this?

A. By saving the knowledge of the race. The sum of human knowing is beyond any one man; any thousand men. With the destruction of our social fabric, science will be broken into a million pieces. Individuals will know much of the exceedingly tiny facets of which there is to know. They will be helpless and useless by themselves. The bits of lore, meaningless, will not be passed on. They will be lost through the generations. *But*, if we now prepare a giant summary of *all* knowledge, it will never be lost. Coming generations will build on it, and will not have to rediscover it for themselves. One millennium will do the work of thirty thousand.

Q. All this—

A. All my project; my thirty thousand men with their wives and children, are devoting themselves to the preparation of an *Encyclopedia Galactica*. They will not complete it in their lifetimes. I will not even live to see it fairly begun. But by the time Trantor falls, it will be complete and copies will exist in every major library in the Galaxy.

The Chief Commissioner's gavel rose and fell. Hari Seldon left the stand and quietly took his seat next to Gaal.

He smiled and said, 'How did you like the show?'

Gaal said, 'You stole it. But what will happen now?'

'They'll adjourn the trial and try to come to a private agreement with me.'

'How do you know?'

Seldon said, 'I'll be honest. I don't know. It depends on the Chief Commissioner. I have studied him for years. I have tried to analyse his workings, but you know how risky it is to introduce the vagaries of an individual in the psychohistoric equations. Yet I have hopes.'

7

Avakim approached, nodded to Gaal, leaned over to whisper to Seldon. The cry of adjournment rang out, and guards separated them. Gaal was led away.

The next day's hearings were entirely different. Hari Seldon and Gaal Dornick were alone with the Commission. They were seated at a table together, with scarcely a separation between the five judges and the two accused. They were even offered cigars from a box of iridescent plastic which had the appearance of water, endlessly flowing. The eyes were fooled into seeing the motion although the fingers reported it to be hard and dry.

Seldon accepted one; Gaal refused.

Seldon said, 'My lawyer is not present.'

A Commissioner replied, 'This is no longer a trial, Dr Seldon. We are here to discuss the safety of the State.'

Linge Chen said, '*I* will speak,' and the other Commissioners sat back in their chairs, prepared to listen. A silence formed about Chen into which he might drop his words.

Gaal held his breath. Chen, lean and hard, older in looks than in fact, was the actual Emperor of all the Galaxy. The child who bore the title itself was only a symbol manufactured by Chen, and not the first such, either.

Chen said, 'Dr Seldon, you disturb the peace of the Emperor's realm. None of the quadrillions living now among all the stars of the Galaxy will be living a century from now. Why, then, should we concern ourselves with events of five centuries distance?'

'I shall not be alive half a decade hence,' said Seldon, 'and yet it is of overpowering concern to me. Call it idealism. Call it an identification of myself with that of mystical generalization to which we refer by the term, "man".'

'I do not wish to take the trouble to understand mysticism. Can you tell me why I may not rid myself of yourself and of an uncomfortable and unneccessary five-century future which I will never see by having you executed tonight?'

'A week ago,' said Seldon, lightly, 'you might have done so and perhaps retained a one in ten probability of yourself remaining alive at year's end. Today, the one in ten probability is scarcely one in ten thousand.'

There were expired breaths in the gathering and uneasy stirrings. Gaal felt the short hairs prickle on the back of his neck. Chen's upper eyelids dropped a little.

'How so?' he said.

'The fall of Trantor,' said Seldon, 'cannot be stopped by any conceivable effort. It can be hastened easily, however. The tale of my interrupted trial will spread through the Galaxy. Frustration of my plans to lighten the disaster will convince people that the future holds no promise to them. Already they recall the lives of their grandfathers with envy. They will see that political revolutions and trade stagnations will increase. The feeling will pervade the Galaxy that only what a man can grasp for himself at that moment will be of any account. Ambitious men will not wait and unscrupulous men will not hang back. By their every action they will hasten the decay of the worlds. Have me killed and Trantor will fall not within five centuries but within fifty years and you, yourself, within a single year.'

Chen said, 'These are words to frighten children, and yet your death is not the only answer which will satisfy us.'

He lifted his slender hand from the papers on which it rested, so that only two fingers touched lightly upon the topmost sheet.

'Tell me,' he said, 'will your only activity be that of preparing this encyclopedia you speak of?'

'It will.'

'And need that be done on Trantor?'

'Trantor, my lord, possesses the Imperial Library, as well as the scholarly resources of the University of Trantor.'

'And yet if you were located elsewhere; let us say upon a planet where the hurry and distractions of a metropolis will not interfere with scholastic musings; where your men may devote themselves entirely and single-mindedly to their work – might not that have advantages?'

'Minor ones, perhaps.'

'Such a world has been chosen, then. You may work, doctor, at your leisure, with your hundred thousand about you. The Galaxy will know that you are working and fighting the Fall. They will even be told that you will prevent the Fall.' He smiled. 'Since I do not believe in so many things, it is not difficult for me to disbelieve in the Fall as well, so that I am entirely convinced I will be telling the truth to the people. And meanwhile, doctor, you will not trouble Trantor and there will be no disturbance of the Emperor's peace.

'The alternative is death for yourself and for as many of your followers as will seem necessary. Your earlier threats I disregard. The opportunity for choosing between death and exile is given you over a time period stretching from this moment to one five minutes hence.'

'Which is the world chosen, my lord?' said Seldon.

'It is called, I believe, Terminus,' said Chen. Negligently, he turned the papers upon his desk with his finger-tips so that they faced Seldon. 'It is uninhabited, but quite habitable, and can be moulded to suit the necessities of scholars. It is somewhat secluded—'

Seldon interrupted, 'It is at the edge of the Galaxy, sir.'

'As I have said, somewhat secluded. It will suit your needs for concentration. Come, you have two minutes left.'

Seldon said, 'We will need time to arrange such a trip. There are twenty thousand families involved.'

'You will be given time.'

Seldon thought a moment, and the last minute began to die. He said, 'I accept exile.'

Gaal's heart skipped a beat at the words. For the most part, he was filled with a tremendous joy for who would not be, to escape death. Yet in all his vast relief, he found space for a little regret that Seldon had been defeated.

8

For a long while, they sat silently as the taxi whined through the hundreds of miles of worm-like tunnels toward the University. And then Gaal stirred. He said:

'Was what you told the Commissioner true? Would your execution have really hastened the Fall?'

Seldon said, 'I never lie about psychohistoric findings. Nor would it have availed me in this case. Chen knew I spoke the truth. He is a very clever politician and politicians by the very nature of their work must have an instinctive feeling for the truths of psychohistory.'

'Then need you have accepted exile?' Gaal wondered, but Seldon did not answer.

When they burst out upon the University grounds, Gaal's muscles took action of their own; or rather, inaction. He had to be carried, almost, out of the taxi.

All the University was a blaze of light. Gaal had almost

forgotten that a sun could exist. Nor was the University in the open. Its buildings were covered by a monstrous dome of glass-and-yet-not-glass. It was polarized; so that Gaal could look directly upon the blazing star above. Yet its light was undimmed and it glanced off the metal buildings as far as the eye could see.

The University structures themselves lacked the hard steel-grey of the rest of Trantor. They were silvery, rather. The metallic lustre was almost ivory in colour.

Seldon said, 'Soldiers, it seems.'

'What?' Gaal brought his eyes to the prosaic ground and found a sentinel ahead of them.

They stopped before him, and a soft-spoken captain materialized from a near-by doorway.

He said, Dr Seldon?'

'Yes.'

'We have been waiting for you. You and your men will be under martial law henceforth. I have been instructed to inform you that six months will be allowed you for preparations to leave for Terminus.'

'Six months!' began Gaal, but Seldon's fingers were upon his elbow with gentle pressure.

'These are my instructions,' repeated the captain.

He was gone, and Gaal turned to Seldon, 'Why, what can be done in six months? This is but slower murder.'

'Quietly. Quietly. Let us reach my office.'

It was not a large office, but it was quite spy-proof and quite undetectably so. Spy-beams trained upon it received neither a suspicious silence nor an even more suspicious static. They received, rather, a conversation constructed at random out of a vast stock of innocuous phrases in various tones and voices.

'Now,' said Seldon, at his ease, 'six months will be enough.'

'I don't see how.'

'Because, my boy, in a plan such as ours, the actions of others are bent to our needs. Have I not said to you already that Chen's temperamental make-up has been subjected to greater scrutiny than that of any other single man in history. The trial was not allowed to begin until the time and circumstances were right for the ending of our own choosing.'

'But could you have arranged—'

'– to be exiled to Terminus? Why not?' He put his fingers on a certain spot on his desk and a small section of the wall behind him slid aside. Only his own fingers could have done so, since only his particular print-pattern could have activated the scanner beneath.

'You will find several microfilms inside,' said Seldon. 'Take the one marked with the letter T.'

Gaal did so and waited while Seldon fixed it within the projector and handed the young man a pair of eyepieces. Gaal adjusted them, and watched the film unroll before his eyes.

He said, 'But then—'

Seldon said, 'What surprises you?'

'Have you been preparing to leave for two years?'

'Two and a half. Of course, we could not be certain that it would be Terminus he would choose, but we hoped it might be and we acted upon that assumption—'

'But why, Dr Seldon? If you arranged the exile, why? Could not events be far better controlled here on Trantor?'

'Why, there are some reasons. Working on Terminus, we will have Imperial support without ever rousing fears that we would endanger Imperial safety.'

Gaal said, 'But you aroused those fears only to force exile. I still do not understand.'

'Twenty thousand families would not travel to the end of the Galaxy of their own will perhaps.'

'But why should they be forced there?' Gaal paused. 'May I not know?'

Seldon said, 'Not yet. It is enough for the moment that you know that a scientific refuge will be established on Terminus. And another will be established at the other end of the Galaxy, let us say,' and he smiled, 'at Star's End. And as for the rest, I will die soon, and you will see more than I – no, no. Spare me your shock and good wishes. My doctors tell me that I cannot live longer than a year or two. But then, I have accomplished in life what I have intended and under what circumstances may one better die?'

'And after you die, sir?'

'Why, there will be successors – perhaps even yourself. And these successors will be able to apply the final touch in the scheme and instigate the revolt on Anacreon at the right time and in the right manner. Thereafter, events may roll unheeded.'

'I do not understand.'

'You will.' Seldon's lined face grew peaceful and tired, both at once. 'Most will leave for Terminus, but some will stay. It will be easy to arrange. But as for me,' and he concluded in a whisper, so that Gaal could scarcely hear him, 'I am finished.'

Part II

THE ENCYCLOPEDISTS

1

TERMINUS . . . *Its location (see map) was an odd one for the role it was called upon to play in Galactic history, and yet as many writers have never tired of pointing out, an inevitable one. Located on the very fringe of the Galactic spiral, an only planet of an isolated sun, poor in resources and negligible in economic value, it was never settled in the five centuries after its discovery, until the landing of the Encyclopedists . . .*

It was inevitable that as a new generation grew, Terminus would become something more than an appendage of the psychohistorians of Trantor. With the Anacreonian revolt and the rise to power of Salvor Hardin, first of the great line of . . .

ENCYCLOPEDIA GALACTICA

Lewis Pirenne was busily engaged at his desk in the one well-lit corner of the room. Work had to be co-ordinated. Effort had to be organized. Threads had to be woven into a pattern.

Fifty years now; fifty years to establish themselves and set up Encyclopedia Foundation Number One into a smoothly working unit. Fifty years to gather the raw material. Fifty years to prepare.

It had been done. Five more years would see the publication of the first volume of the most monumental work the Galaxy had ever conceived. And then at ten-year intervals – regularly – like clockwork – volume after volume. And with them there would be supplements; special articles on events of current interest, until—

Pirenne stirred uneasily, as the muted buzzer upon his desk muttered peevishly. He had almost forgotten the appointment. He shoved the door release and out of an abstracted corner of one eye saw the door open and the broad figure of

Salvor Hardin enter. Pirenne did not look up.

Hardin smiled to himself. He was in a hurry, but he knew better than to take offence at Pirenne's cavalier treatment of anything or anyone that disturbed him at his work. He buried himself in the chair on the other side of the desk and waited.

Pirenne's stylus made the faintest scraping sound as it raced across paper. Otherwise, neither motion nor sound. And then Hardin withdrew a two-credit coin from his vest pocket. He flipped it and its stainless-steel surface caught flitters of light as it tumbled through the air. He caught it and flipped it again, watching the flashing reflections lazily. Stainless steel made good medium of exchange on a planet where all metal had to be imported.

Pirenne looked up and blinked. 'Stop that!' he said querulously.

'Eh?'

'That infernal coin tossing. Stop it.'

'Oh.' Hardin pocketed the metal disc. 'Tell me when you're ready, will you? I promised to be back at the City Council meeting before the new aqueduct project is put to a vote.'

Pirenne sighed and shoved himself away from the desk. 'I'm ready. But I hope you aren't going to bother me with city affairs. Take care of that yourself, please. The Encyclopedia takes up all my time.'

'Have you heard the news?' questioned Hardin, phlegmatically.

'What news?'

'The news that the Terminus City ultrawave set received two hours ago. The Royal Governor of the Prefect of Anacreon has assumed the title of king.'

'Well? What of it?'

'It means,' responded Hardin, 'that we're cut off from the inner regions of the Empire. We've been expecting it but that doesn't make it any more comfortable. Anacreon stands square across what was our last remaining trade route to Santanni and to Trantor and to Vega itself! Where is our metal to come from?

We haven't managed to get a steel or aluminium shipment through in six months and now we won't be able to get any at all, except by grace of the King of Anacreon.'

Pirenne tch-tched impatiently. 'Get them through him, then.'

'But can we? Listen, Pirenne, according to the charter which established this Foundation, the Board of Trustees of the Encyclopedia Committee has been given full administrative powers. I, as Mayor of Terminus City, have just enough power to blow my own nose and perhaps to sneeze if you countersign an order giving me permission. It's up to you and your Board then. I'm asking you in the name of the City, whose prosperity depends upon uninterrupted commerce with the Galaxy, to call an emergency meeting—'

'Stop! A campaign speech is out of order. Now, Hardin, the Board of Trustees has not barred the establishment of a municipal government on Terminus. We understand one to be necessary because of the increase in population since the Foundation was established fifty years ago, and because of the increasing number of people involved in non-Encyclopedia affairs. *But* that does not mean that the first and *only* aim of the Foundation is no longer to publish the definitive Encyclopedia of all human knowledge. We are a State-supported, scientific institution, Hardin. We cannot - must not - *will* not interfere in local politics.'

'Local politics! By the Emperor's left big toe, Pirenne, this is a matter of life and death. The planet, Terminus, by itself cannot support a mechanized civilization. It lacks metals. You know that. It hasn't a trace of iron, copper, or aluminium in the surface rocks, and precious little of anything else. What do you think will happen to the Encyclopedia if this watchamacallum King of Anacreon clamps down on us?'

'On *us*? Are you forgetting that we are under the direct control of the Emperor himself? We are not part of the Prefect of Anacreon or of any other prefect. Memorize that! We are part of the Emperor's personal domain, and no one touches us.

The Empire can protect its own.'

'Then why didn't it prevent the Royal Governor of Anacreon from kicking over the traces? And only Anacreon? At least twenty of the outermost prefects of the Galaxy, the entire Periphery as a matter of fact, have begun steering things their own way. I tell you I feel darned uncertain of the Empire and its ability to protect us.'

'Hokum! Royal Governors, Kings – what's the difference? The Empire is always shot through with a certain amount of politics and with different men pulling this way and that. Governors have rebelled, and, for that matter, Emperors have been deposed, or assassinated before this. But what has that to do with the Empire itself? Forget it, Hardin. It's none of our business. We are first of all and last of all – scientists. And our concern is the Encyclopedia. Oh, yes, I'd almost forgotten. Hardin!'

'Well?'

'Do something about that paper of yours!' Pirenne's voice was angry.

'The Terminus City *Journal*? It isn't mine; it's privately owned. What's it been doing?'

'For weeks now it has been recommending that the fiftieth anniversary of the establishment of the Foundation be made the occasion for public holidays and quite inappropriate celebrations.'

'And why not? The radium clock will open the First Vault in three months. I would call this a big occasion, wouldn't you?'

'Not for silly pageantry, Hardin. The First Vault and its opening concern the Board of Trustees alone. Anything of importance will be communicated to the people. That is final and please make it plain in the *Journal*.'

'I'm sorry, Pirenne, but the City Charter guarantees a certain minor matter known as freedom of the press.'

'It may. But the Board of Trustees does not. I am the Emperor's representative on Terminus, Hardin, and have full powers in this respect.'

Hardin's expression became that of a man counting to ten, mentally. He said, grimly: 'In connection with your status as Emperor's representative, then, I have a final piece of news to give you.'

'About Anacreon?' Pirenne's lips tightened. He felt annoyed.

'Yes. A special envoy will be sent to us from Anacreon. In two weeks.'

'An envoy? Here? From Anacreon?' Pirenne chewed that. 'What for?'

Hardin stood up, and shoved his chair back up against the desk. 'I give you one guess.'

And he left – quite unceremoniously.

2

Anselm haut Rodric – 'haut' itself signifying noble blood – Sub-prefect of Pluema and Envoy Extraordinary of his Highness of Anacreon – plus half a dozen other titles – was met by Salvor Hardin at the space-port with all the imposing ritual of a state occasion.

With a tight smile and a low bow, the sub-prefect had flipped his blaster from its holster and presented it to Hardin butt first. Hardin returned the compliment with a blaster specifically borrowed for the occasion. Friendship and goodwill were thus established, and if Hardin noted the barest bulge at haut Rodric's shoulder, he prudently said nothing.

The ground car that received them then – preceded, flanked, and followed by the suitable cloud of minor functionaries – proceeded in a slow, ceremonious manner to Cyclopedia Square, cheered on its way by a properly enthusiastic crowd.

Sub-prefect Anselm received the cheers with the complaisant indifference of a soldier and a nobleman.

He said to Hardin, 'And this city is all your world?'

Hardin raised his voice to be heard above the clamour. 'We are a young world, your eminence. In our short history we have had but few members of the higher nobility visiting our poor planet. Hence our enthusiasm.'

It is certain that 'higher nobility' did not recognize irony when he heard it.

He said thoughtfully: 'Founded fifty years ago. Hm-m-m! You have a great deal of unexploited land here, mayor. You have never considered dividing it into estates?'

'There is no necessity as yet. We're extremely centralized; we have to be, because of the Encyclopedia. Some day, perhaps, when our population has grown—'

'A strange world! You have no peasantry?'

Hardin reflected that it didn't require a great deal of acumen to tell that his eminence was indulging in a bit of fairly clumsy pumping. He replied casually: 'No – nor nobility.'

Haut Rodric's eyebrows lifted. 'And your leader – the man I am to meet?'

'You mean Dr Pirenne? Yes! He is the Chairman of the Board of Trustees – and a personal representative of the Emperor.'

'*Doctor*? No other title? A *scholar*? And he rates above the civil authority?'

'Why, certainly,' replied Hardin, amiably. 'We're all scholars more or less. After all, we're not so much a world as a scientific foundation – under the direct control of the Emperor.'

There was a faint emphasis upon the last phrase that seemed to disconcert the sub-prefect. He remained thoughtfully silent during the rest of the slow way to Cyclopedia Square.

If Hardin found himself bored by the afternoon and evening that followed, he had at least the satisfaction of realizing that Pirenne and haut Rodric – having met with loud and mutual protestations of esteem and regard – were detesting each other's company a good deal more.

Haut Rodric had attended with glazed eye to Pirenne's

lecture during the 'inspection tour' of the Encyclopedia Building. With polite and vacant smile, he had listened to the latter's rapid patter as they passed through the vast storehouses of reference films and the numerous projection rooms.

It was only after he had gone down level by level into and through the composing departments, editing departments, publishing departments, and filming departments that he made the first comprehensive statement.

'This is all very interesting,' he said, 'but it seems a strange occupation for grown men. What good is it?'

It was a remark, Hardin noted, for which Pirenne found no answer, though the expression of his face was most eloquent.

The dinner that evening was much the mirror image of the events of that afternoon, for haut Rodric monopolized the conversation by describing – in minute technical detail and with incredible zest – his own exploits as battalion head during the recent war between Anacreon and the neighbouring newly proclaimed Kingdom of Smyrno.

The details of the sub-prefect's account were not completed until dinner was over and one by one the minor officials had drifted away. The last bit of triumphant description of mangled space-ships came when he had accompanied Pirenne and Hardin on to the balcony and relaxed in the warm air of the summer evening.

'And now,' he said, with a heavy joviality, 'to serious matters.'

'By all means,' murmured Hardin, lighting a long cigar of Vegan tobacco – not many left, he reflected – and teetering his chair back on two legs.

The Galaxy was high in the sky and its misty lens shape stretched lazily from horizon to horizon. The few stars here at the very edge of the universe were insignificant twinkles in comparison.

'Of course,' said the sub-prefect, 'all the formal discussions – the paper signing and such dull technicalities, that is – will take place before the— What is it you call your Council?'

'The Board of Trustees,' replied Pirenne, coldly.

'Queer name! Anyway, that's for tomorrow. We might as well clear some of the underbrush, man to man, right now, though. Hey?'

'And this means—' prodded Hardin.

'Just this. There's been a certain change in the situation out here in the Periphery and the status of your planet has become a trifle uncertain. It would be very convenient if we succeeded in coming to an unerstanding as to how the matter stands. By the way, mayor, have you another one of those cigars?'

Hardin started and produced one reluctantly.

Anselm haut Rodric sniffed at it and emitted a clucking sound of pleasure. 'Vegan tobacco! Where did you get it?'

'We received some last shipment. There's hardly any left. Space knows when we'll get more – if ever.'

Pirenne scowled. He didn't smoke – and, for that matter, detested the odour. 'Let me understand this, your eminence. Your mission is merely one of clarification?'

Haut Rodric nodded through the smoke of his first lusty puffs.

'In that case, it is soon over. The situation with respect to Encyclopedia Foundation Number One is what it always has been.'

'Ah! And what is it that it always has been?'

'Just this: a State-supported scientific institution and part of the personal domain of his august majesty, the Emperor.'

The sub-prefect seemed unimpressed. He blew smoke rings. 'That's a nice theory, Dr Pirenne. I imagine you've got charters with the Imperial Seal upon it – but what's the actual situation? How do you stand with respect to Smyrno? You're not fifty parsecs from Smyrno's capital, you know. And what about Konom and Daribow?'

Pirenne said: 'We have nothing to do with any prefect. As part of the Emperor's—'

'They're not prefects,' reminded haut Rodric; 'they're kingdoms now.'

'Kingdoms then. We have nothing to do with them. As a scientific institution—'

'Science be dashed!' swore the other, via a bouncing soldierly oath that ionized the atmosphere. 'What the devil has that got to do with the fact that we're liable to see Terminus taken over by Smyrno at any time?'

'And the Emperor? He would just sit by?'

Haut Rodric calmed down and said: 'Well, now, Dr Pirenne, you respect the Emperor's property and so does Anacreon, but Smyrno might not. Remember, we've just signed a treaty with the Emperor – I'll present a copy to that Board of yours tomorrow – which places upon us the responsibility of maintaining order within the borders of the old Prefect of Anacreon on behalf of the Emperor. Our duty is clear, then, isn't it?'

'Certainly. But Terminus is not part of the Prefect of Anacreon.'

'And Smyrno—'

'Nor is it part of the Prefect of Smyrno. It's not part of any prefect.'

'Does Smyrno know that?'

'I don't care what it knows.'

'*We* do. We've just finished a war with her and she still holds two stellar systems that are ours. Terminus occupies an extremely strategic spot between the two nations.'

Hardin felt weary. He broke in: 'What is your proposition, your eminence?'

The sub-prefect seemed quite ready to stop fencing in favour of more direct statements. He said briskly: 'It seems perfectly obvious that, since Terminus cannot defend itself, Anacreon must take over the job for its own sake. You understand we have no desire to interfere with internal administration—'

'Uh-huh,' grunted Hardin dryly.

'—but we believe that it would be best for all concerned to have Anacreon establish a military base upon the planet.'

'And that is all you would want – a military base in some of the vast unoccupied territory – and let it go at that?'

'Well, of course, there would be the matter of supporting the protecting forces.'

Hardin's chair came down on all fours, and his elbows went forward on his knees. 'Now we're getting to the nub. Let's put it into language. Terminus is to be a protectorate and to pay tribute.'

'Not tribute. Taxes. We're protecting you. You pay for it.'

Pirenne banged his hand on the chair with sudden violence. 'Let me speak, Hardin. Your eminence, I don't care a rusty half-credit coin for Anacreon, Smyrno, or all your local politics and petty wars. I tell you this is a State-supported tax-free institution.'

'State-supported? But *we* are the State, Dr Pirenne, and we're not supporting.'

Pirenne rose angrily. 'Your eminence, I am the direct representative of—'

'– his august majesty, the Emperor,' chorused Anselm haut Rodric sourly, 'and I am the direct representative of the King of Anacreon. Anacreon is a lot nearer, Dr Pirenne.'

'Let's get back to business,' urged Hardin. 'How would you take these so-called taxes, your eminence? Would you take them in kind; wheat, potatoes, vegetables, cattle?'

The sub-prefect stared. 'What the devil? What do we need with those? We've got hefty surpluses. Gold, of course. Chromium or vanadium would be even better, incidentally, if you have it in quantity.'

Hardin laughed. 'Quantity! We haven't even got iron in quantity. Gold! Here, take a look at our currency.' He tossed a coin to the envoy.

Haut Rodric bounced it and stared. 'What is it? Steel?'

'That's right.'

'I don't understand.'

'Terminus is a planet practically without metals. We import it all. Consequently, we have no gold, and nothing to pay unless you want a few thousand bushels of potatoes.'

'Well – manufactured goods.'

'Without metal? What do we make our machines out of?'

There was a pause and Pirenne tried again. 'This whole discussion is wide of the point. Terminus is not a planet, but a scientific foundation preparing a great encyclopedia. Space, man, have you no respect for science?'

'Encyclopedias don't win wars.' Haut Rodric's brows furrowed. 'A completely unproductive world, then – and practically unoccupied at that. Well, you might pay with land.'

'What do you mean?' asked Pirenne.

'This world is just about empty and the unoccupied land is probably fertile. There are many of the nobility on Anacreon that would like an addition to their estates.'

'You can't propose any such—'

'There's no necessity for looking so alarmed, Dr Pirenne. There's plenty for all of us. If it comes to what it comes, and you co-operate, we could probably arrange it so that you lose nothing. Titles can be conferred and estates granted. You understand me, I think.'

Pirenne sneered: 'Thanks!'

And then Hardin said ingenuously: 'Could Anacreon supply us with adequate quantities of plutonium for our atomic-power plant? We've only a few years' supply left.'

There was a gasp from Pirenne and then a dead silence for minutes. When haut Rodric spoke it was in a voice quite different from what it had been till then:

'You have atomic power?'

'Certainly. What's unusual in that? I imagine atomic power is fifty thousand years old now. Why shouldn't we have it? Except that it's a little difficult to get plutonium.'

'Yes ... yes.' The envoy paused and added uncomfortably: 'Well, gentlemen, we'll pursue the subject tomorrow. You'll excuse me—'

Pirenne looked after him and gritted through his teeth: 'That insufferable, dull-witted donkey! That—'

Hardin broke in: 'Not at all. He's merely the product of his environment. He doesn't understand much except that "I got a gun and you ain't".'

Pirenne whirled on him in exasperation. 'What in Space did you mean by the talk about military bases and tribute? Are you crazy?'

'No. I merely gave him rope and let him talk. You'll notice that he managed to stumble out with Anacreon's real intentions – that is, the parcelling up of Terminus into landed estates. Of course, I don't intend to let that happen.'

'*You* don't intend. *You* don't. And who are you? And may I ask what you meant by blowing off your mouth about our atomic-power plant? Why, it's just the thing that would make us a military target.'

'Yes,' grinned Hardin. 'A military target to stay away from. Isn't it obvious why I brought the subject up? It happened to confirm a very strong suspicion I had.'

'And that was what?'

'That Anacreon no longer has an atomic-power economy. If they had, our friend would undoubtedly have realized that plutonium, except in ancient tradition is not used in power plants. And therefore it follows that the rest of the Periphery no longer has atomic power either. Certainly Smyrno hasn't, or Anacreon wouldn't have won most of the battles in their recent war. Interesting, wouldn't you say?'

'Bah!' Pirenne left in fiendish humour, and Hardin smiled gently.

He threw his cigar away and looked up at the outstretched Galaxy. 'Back to oil and coal, are they?' he murmured – and what the rest of his thoughts were he kept to himself.

3

When Hardin denied owning the *Journal*, he was perhaps technically correct, but no more. Hardin had been the leading spirit in the drive to incorporate Terminus into an autonomous municipality – he had been elected its first mayor – so it was not surprising that, though not a single share of *Journal* stock was in his name, some 60 per cent was controlled by him in more devious fashions.

There were ways.

Consequently, when Hardin began suggesting to Pirenne that he be allowed to attend meetings of the Board of Trustees, it was not quite coincidence that the *Journal* began a similar campaign. And the first mass meeting in the history of the Foundation was held, demanding representation of the City in the 'national' government.

And, eventually, Pirenne capitulated with ill grace.

Hardin, as he sat at the foot of the table, speculated idly as to just what it was that made physical scientists such poor administrators. It might be merely that they were too used to inflexible fact and far too unused to pliable people.

In any case, there was Tomaz Sutt and Jord Fara on his left; Lundin Crast and Yate Fulham on his right; with Pirenne, himself, presiding. He knew them all, of course, but they seemed to have put on an extra special bit of pomposity for the occasion.

Hardin half dozed through the initial formalities and then perked up when Pirenne sipped at the glass of water before him by way of preparation and said:

'I find it very gratifying to be able to inform the Board that since our last meeting, I have received word that Lord Dorwin, Chancellor of the Empire, will arrive at Terminus in two weeks. It may be taken for granted that our relations with Anacreon will be smoothed out to our complete satisfaction as soon as the Emperor is informed of the situation.'

He smiled and addressed Hardin across the length of the table. 'Information to this effect has been given to the *Journal*.'

Hardin snickered below his breath. It seemed evident that Pirenne's desire to strut this information before him had been one reason for his admission into the sacrosanctum.

He said evenly: 'Leaving vague expressions out of account, what do you expect Lord Dorwin to do?'

Tomaz Sutt replied. He had a bad habit of addressing one in the third person when in his more stately moods.

'It is quite evident,' he observed, 'that Mayor Hardin is a professional cynic. He can scarcely fail to realize that the Emperor would be most unlikely to allow his personal rights to be infringed.'

'Why? What would he do in case they were?'

There was an annoyed stir. Pirenne said, 'You are out of order,' and, as an afterthought, 'and are making what are near-treasonable statements, besides.'

'Am I to consider myself answered?'

'Yes! If you have nothing further to say—'

'Don't jump to conclusions. I'd like to ask a question. Besides this stroke of diplomacy – which may or may not prove to mean anything – has anything concrete been done to meet the Anacreonic menace?'

Yate Fulham drew one hand along his ferocious red moustache. 'You see a menace there, do you?'

'Don't you?'

'Scarcely' – this with indulgence. 'The Emperor—'

'Great Space!' Hardin felt annoyed. 'What is this? Every once in a while someone mentions "Emperor" or "Empire" as if it were a magic word. The Emperor is fifty thousand parsecs away, and I doubt whether he gives a damn about us. And if he does, what can he do? What there was of the imperial navy in these regions is in the hands of the four kingdoms now and Anacreon has its share. Listen, we have to fight with guns, not with words.

'Now, get this. We've had two months' grace so far, mainly because we've given Anacreon the idea that we've got atomic weapons. Well, we all know that there's a little white lie. We've got atomic power, but only for commercial uses, and darn little at that. They're going to find that out soon, and if you think they're going to enjoy being jollied along, you're mistaken.'

'My dear sir—'

'Hold on: I'm not finished.' Hardin was warming up. He liked this. 'It's all very well to drag chancellors into this, but it would be much nicer to drag a few great big siege guns fitted for beautiful atomic bombs into it. We've lost two months, gentlemen, and we may not have another two months to lose. What do you propose to do?'

Said Lundin Crast, his long nose wrinkling angrily: 'If you're proposing the militarization of the Foundation, I won't hear a word of it. It would mark our open entrance into the field of politics. We, Mr Mayor, are a scientific foundation and nothing else.'

Added Sutt: 'He does not realize, moreover, that building armaments would mean withdrawing men – valuable men – from the Encyclopedia. That cannot be done, come what may.'

'Very true,' agreed Pirenne. 'The Encyclopedia first – always.'

Hardin groaned in spirit. The Board seemed to suffer violently from Encyclopedia on the brain.

He said icily: 'Has it ever occurred to this Board that it is barely possible that Terminus may have interests other than the Encyclopedia?'

Pirenne replied: 'I do not conceive, Hardin, that the Foundation can have *any* interest other than the Encyclopedia.'

'I didn't say the Foundation; I said *Terminus*. I'm afraid you don't understand the situation. There's a good million of us here on Terminus, and not more than a hundred and fifty thousand are working directly on the Encyclopedia. To the rest of us, this is *home*. We were born here. We're living here. Compared with our farms and our homes and our factories, the Encyclopedia means little to us. We want them protected—'

He was shouted down.

'The Encyclopedia first,' ground out Crast. 'We have a mission to fulfil.'

'Mission, hell,' shouted Hardin. 'That might have been true fifty years ago. But this is a new generation.'

'That has nothing to do with it,' replied Pirenne. 'We are scientists.'

And Hardin leaped through the opening. 'Are you, though? That's a nice hallucination, isn't it? Your bunch here is a perfect example of what's been wrong with the entire Galaxy for thousands of years. What kind of science is it to be stuck out here for centuries classifying the work of scientists of the last millennium? Have you ever thought of working onward, extending their knowledge and improving upon it? No! You're quite happy to stagnate. The whole Galaxy is, and has been for Space knows how long. That's why the Periphery is revolting; that's why communications are breaking down; that's why petty wars are becoming eternal; that's why whole systems are losing atomic power and going back to barbarous techniques of chemical power.

'If you ask me,' he cried, '*the Galaxy is going to pot!*'

He paused and dropped into his chair to catch his breath, paying no attention to the two or three that were attempting simultaneously to answer him.

Crast got the floor. 'I don't know what you're trying to gain by your hysterical statements, Mr Mayor. Certainly, you are adding nothing constructive to the discussion. I move, Mr Chairman, that the speaker's remarks be placed out of order and the discussion be resumed from the point where it was interrupted.'

Jord Fara bestirred himself for the first time. Up to this point

Fara had taken no part in the argument even at its hottest. But now his ponderous voice, every bit as ponderous as his three-hundred-pound body, burst its bass way out.

'Haven't we forgotten something, gentlemen?'

'What?' asked Pirenne, peevishly.

'That in a month we celebrate our fiftieth anniversary.' Fara had a trick of uttering the most obvious platitudes with great profundity.

'What of it?'

'And on that anniversary,' continued Fara, placidly, 'Hari Seldon's Vault will open. Have you ever considered what might be in the Vault?'

'I don't know. Routine matters. A stock speech of congratulations, perhaps. I don't think any significance need be placed on the Vault – though the *Journal*' – and he glared at Hardin, who grinned back – 'did try to make an issue of it. I put a stop to that.'

'Ah,' said Fara, 'but perhaps you are wrong. Doesn't it strike you' – he paused and put a finger to his round little nose – 'that the Vault is opening at a very convenient time?'

'Very *in*convenient time, you mean,' muttered Fulham. 'We've got some other things to worry about.'

'Other things more important than a message from Hari Seldon? I think not.' Fara was growing more pontifical than ever, and Hardin eyed him thoughtfully. What was he getting at?

'In fact,' said Fara, happily, 'you all seem to forget that Seldon was the greatest psychologist of our time and that he was the founder of our Foundation. It seems reasonable to assume that he used his science to determine the probable course of the history of the immediate future. If he did, as seems likely, I repeat, he would certainly have managed to find a way to warn us of danger and, perhaps, to point out a solution. The Encyclopedia was very dear to his heart, you know.'

An aura of puzzled doubt prevailed. Pirenne hemmed. 'Well, now, I don't know. Psychology is a great science, but –

there are no psychologists among us at the moment, I believe. It seems to me we're on uncertain ground.'

Fara turned to Hardin. 'Didn't you study psychology under Alurin?'

Hardin answered, half in reverie: 'Yes, I never completed my studies, though. I got tired of theory. I wanted to be a psychological engineer, but we lacked the facilities, so I did the next best thing – I went into politics. It's practically the same thing.'

'Well, what do you think of the Vault?'

And Hardin replied cautiously, 'I don't know.'

He did not say a word for the remainder of the meeting – even though it got back to the subject of the Chancellor of the Empire.

In fact, he didn't even listen. He'd been put on a new track and things were falling into place – just a little. Little angles were fitting together – one or two.

And psychology was the key. He was sure of that.

He was trying desperately to remember the psychological theory he had once learned – and from it he got one thing right at the start.

A great psychologist such as Seldon could unravel human emotions and human reactions sufficiently to be able to predict broadly the historical sweep of the future.

And that meant – hm-m-m!

4

Lord Dorwin took snuff. He also had long hair, curled intricately and, quite obviously, artificially, to which were added a pair of fluffy, blond sideburns, which he fondled affectionately. Then, too, he spoke in overprecise statements and left out all the r's.

At the moment, Hardin had no time to think of more of the reasons for the instant detestation in which he had held the noble chancellor. Oh, yes, the elegant gestures of one hand with which he accompanied his remarks and the studied condescension with which he accompanied even a simple affirmative.

But, at any rate, the problem now was to locate him. He had disappeared with Pirenne half an hour before – passed clean out of sight, blast him.

Hardin was quite sure that his own absence during the preliminary discussions would quite suit Pirenne.

But Pirenne had been seen in this wing and on this floor. It was simply a matter of trying every door. Half-way down, he said, 'Ah!' and stepped into the darkened room. The profile of Lord Dorwin's intricate hair-do was unmistakable against the lighted screen.

Lord Dorwin looked up, and said: 'Ah, Hahdin. You ah looking foah us, no doubt?' He held out his snuff-box – over-adorned and poor workmanship at that, noted Hardin – and was politely refused whereat he helped himself to a pinch and smiled graciously.

Pirenne scowled and Hardin met that with an expression of blank indifference.

The only sound to break the short silence that followed was the clicking of the lid of Lord Dorwin's snuff-box. And then he put it away and said:

'A gweat achievement, this Encyclopedia of yoahs, Hahdin. A feat, indeed, to rank with the most majestic accomplishments of all time.'

'Most of us think so, milord. It's an accomplishment not quite accomplished as yet, however.'

'Fwom the little I have seen of the efficiency of yoah Foundation, I have no feahs on that scoah.' And he nodded to Pirenne, who responded with a delighted bow.

Quite a love feast, thought Hardin. 'I wasn't complaining about the lack of efficiency, milord, as much as of the definite excess of efficiency on the part of the Anacreonians – though in another and more destructive direction.'

'Ah, yes, Anacweon.' A negligent wave of the hand. 'I have just come from theah. Most bahbawous planet. It is thowoughly inconceivable that human beings could live heah in the Periphewy. The lack of the most elementawy wequiahments of a cultuahed gentleman; the absence of the most fundamental necessities foah comfoht and convenience – the uttah desuetude into which they—'

Hardin interrupted dryly: 'The Anacreonians, unfortunately, have all the elementary requirements for warfare and all the fundamental necessities for destruction.'

'Quite, quite.' Lord Dorwin seemed annoyed, perhaps at being stopped midway in his sentence. 'But we ahn't to discuss business now, y'know. Weally, I'm othahwise concuhned. Doctah Piwenne, ahn't you going to show me the second volume? Do, please.'

The lights clicked out and for the next half-hour Hardin might as well have been on Anacreon for all the attention they paid him. The book upon the screen made little sense to him, nor did he trouble to make the attempt to follow, but Lord Dorwin became quite humanly excited at times. Hardin noticed that during these moments of excitement the chancellor pronounced his r's.

When the lights went on again, Lord Dorwin said: 'Mahvelous. Twuly mahvelous. You ah not, by chance, intewested in ahchaeology, ah you, Hahdin?'

'Eh?' Hardin shook himself out of an abstracted reverie. 'No, milord, can't say I am. I'm a psychologist by original intention and a politician by final decision.'

'Ah! No doubt intewesting studies. I, myself, y'know' – he helped himself to a giant pinch of snuff – 'dabble in ahchaeology.'

'Indeed?'

'His lordship,' interrupted Pirenne, 'is most thoroughly acquainted with the field.'

'Well, p'haps I am, p'haps I am,' said his lordship complacently. 'I *have* done an awful amount of wouk in the science. Extwemely well-wead, in fact. I've gone thwough all of Jawdun, Obijasi, Kwomill ... oh, all of them y'know.'

'I've heard of them, of course,' said Hardin, 'but I've never read them.'

'You should some day, my deah fellow. It would amply repay you. Why, I cutainly considah it well wuhth the twip heah to the Pewiphewy to see this copy of Lameth. Would you believe it, my libwawy totally lacks a copy. By the way, Doctah Piwenne, you have not fohgotten yoah pwomise to twans-develop a copy foah me befoah I leave?'

'Only too pleased.'

'Lameth, you must know,' continued the chancellor, pontifically, 'pwesents a new and most intewesting addition to my pwevious knowledge of the "Owigin Question".'

'Which question?' asked Hardin.

'The "Owigin Question". The place of the owigin of the human species, y'know. Suahly you must know that it is thought that owiginally the human wace occupied only one planetawy system.'

'Well, yes, I know that.'

'Of cohse, no one knows exactly which system it is – lost in the mists of atiquity. Theah ah theawies, howevah, Siwius, some say. Othahs insist on Alpha Centauwi, oah on Sol, oah on 61 Cyngi – all in the Siwius sectah, you see.'

'And what does Lameth say?'

'Well, he goes off along a new twail completely. He twies to show that ahchaeological wemains on the thuhd planet of the Ahctuwian System show that humanity existed theah befoah theah wah any indications of space-twavel.'

'And that means it was humanity's birth planet?'

'P'haps. I must wead it closely and wigh the evidence befoah I can say foah cuhtain. One must see just how weliable his obsuhvations ah.'

Hardin remained silent for a short while. Then he said,

'When did Lameth write his book?'

'Oh – I should say about eight hundwed yeahs ago. Of cohse, he has based it lahgely on the pwevious wuhk of Gleen.'

'Then why rely on him? Why not go to Arcturus and study the remains for yourself?'

Lord Dorwin raised his eyebrows and took a pinch of snuff hurriedly. 'Why, whatevah foah, my deah fellow?'

'To get the information first hand, of course.'

'But wheah's the necessity? It seems an uncommonly wound-about and hopelessly wigmawolish method of getting anyweahs. Look heah, now, I've got the wuhks of all the old mastahs – the gweat ahchaeologists of the past. I wigh them against each othah – balance the disagweements – analyse the conflicting statements – decide which is pwobably cowwect – and come to a conclusion. That is the scientific method. At least' – patronizingly – 'as *I* see it. How insuffewably cwude it would be to go to Ahctuwus, oah to Sol, foah instance, and blundah about, when the old mastahs have covahed the gwounds so much moah effectively than we could possibly hope to do.'

Hardin murmured politely, 'I see.'

Scientific method, hell! No wonder the Galaxy was going to pot.

'Come, milord,' said Pirenne, 'I think we had better be returning.'

'Ah, yes. P'haps we had.'

As they left the room, Hardin said suddenly, 'Milord, may I ask a question?'

Lord Dorwin smiled blandly and emphasized his answer with a gracious flutter of the hand. 'Cuhtainly, my deah fellow. Only too happy to be of suhvice. If I can help you in any way fwom my pooah stoah of knowledge—'

'It isn't exactly about archaeology, milord.'

'No?'

'No. It's this: last year we received news here in Terminus about the explosion of a power plant on Planet V of Gamma

Andromeda. We got the barest outline of the accident – no details at all. I wonder if you could tell me exactly what happened.'

Pirenne's mouth twisted. 'I wonder you annoy his lordship with questions on totally irrelevant subjects.'

'Not at all, Doctah Piwenne,' interceded the chancellor. 'It is quite all wight. Theah isn't much to say concuhning it in any case. The powah plant did explode and it was quite a catastwophe, y'know. I believe sevewal million people wah killed and at least half the planet was simply laid in wuins. Weally, the govuhnment is sewiously considewing placing seveah westwictions upon the indiscwiminate use of atomic powah – though that is not a thing for general publication, y'know.'

'I understand,' said Hardin. 'But what was wrong with the plant?'

'Well, weally,' replied Lord Dorwin indifferently, 'who knows? It had bwoken down some yeahs pweviously and it is thought that the weplacements and wepaiah wuhk wuh most infewiah. It is *so* difficult these days to find men who *weally* undahstand the moah technical details of ouah powah systems.' And he took a sorrowful pinch of snuff.

'You realize,' said Hardin, 'that the independent kingdoms of the Periphery have lost atomic power altogether?'

'Have they? I'm not at all suhpwised. Bahbawous planets— Oh, but my deah fellow, don't call them independent. They ahn't y'know. The tweaties we've made with them ah pwoof positive of that. They acknowledge the soveweignty of the Empewah. They'd have to, of cohse, oah we wouldn't tweat with them.'

'That may be so, but they have considerable freedom of action.'

'Yes, I suppose so. Considewable. But that scahcely mattahs. The Empiah is fah bettah off, with the Pewiphewy twown upon its own wesoahces – as it is, moah oah less. They ahn't any good to us, y'know. *Most* bahbawous planets. Scahcely civilized.'

'They were civilized in the past. Anacreon was one of the richest of the outlying provinces. I understand it compared favourably with Vega itself.'

'Oh, but, Hahdin, that was centuwies ago. You can scahcely dwaw conclusions fwom that. Things wah diffewent in the old gweat days. We ahn't the men we used to be, y'know. But, Hahdin, come, you ah a most puhsistent chap. I've told you I simply won't discuss business today. Doctah Piwenne did pwepayah me foah you. He told me you would twy to badgah me, but I'm fah too old a hand foah that. Leave it foah next day.'

And that was that.

5

This was the second meeting of the Board that Hardin had attended, if one were to exclude the informal talks the Board members had had with the now-departed Lord Dorwin. Yet the mayor had a perfectly definite idea that at least one other, and possibly two or three, had been held, to which he had somehow never received an invitation.

Nor, it seemed to him, would he have received notification of this one had it not been for the ultimatum.

At least, it amounted to an ultimatum, though a superficial reading of the visigraphed document would lead one to suppose that it was a friendly interchange of greetings between two potentates.

Hardin fingered it gingerly. It started off floridly with a salutation from 'His Puissant Majesty, the King of Anacreon, to his friend and brother, Dr Lewis Pirenne, Chairman of the Board of Trustees, of the Encyclopedia Foundation Number One,' and it ended even more lavishly with a gigantic, multi-coloured seal of the most involved symbolism.

But it was an ultimatum just the same.

Hardin said: 'It turned out that we didn't have much time after all – only three months. But little as it was, we threw it away unused. This thing here gives us a week. What do we do now?'

Pirenne frowned worriedly. 'There must be a loophole. It is absolutely unbelievable that they would push matters to extremities in the face of what Lord Dorwin has assured us regarding the attitude of the Emperor and the Empire.'

Hardin perked up. 'I see. You have informed the King of Anacreon of this alleged attitude?'

'I did – after having placed the proposal to the Board for a vote and having received unanimous consent.'

'And when did this vote take place?'

Pirenne climbed on to his dignity. 'I do not believe I am answerable to you in any way, Mayor Hardin.'

'All right. I'm not that vitally interested. It's just my opinion that it was your diplomatic transmission of Lord Dorwin's valuable contribution to the situation' – he lifted the corner of his mouth in a sour half-smile – 'that was the direct cause of this friendly little note. They might have delayed longer otherwise – though I don't think the additional time would have helped Terminus any, considering the attitude of the Board.'

Said Yate Fulham: 'And just how do you arrive at that remarkable conclusion, Mr Mayor?'

'In a rather simple way. It merely required the use of that much-neglected commodity – common sense. You see, there is a branch of human knowledge known as symbolic logic, which can be used to prune away all sorts of clogging deadwood that clutters up human language.'

'What about it?' said Fulham.

'I applied it. Among other things, I applied it to this document here. I didn't really need to for myself because I knew what it was all about, but I think I can explain it more easily to five physical scientists by symbols rather than by words.'

Hardin removed a few sheets of paper from the pad under his

arm and spread them out. 'I didn't do this myself, by the way,' he said. 'Muller Holk of the Division of Logic has his name signed to the analyses, as you can see.'

Pirenne leaned over the table to get a better view and Hardin continued: 'The message from Anacreon was a simple problem, naturally, for the men who wrote it were men of action rather than men of words. It boils down easily and straightforwardly to the unqualified statement, when in symbols is what you see, and which in words, roughly translated, is, "You give us what we want in a week, or we beat the hell out of you and take it anway".'

There was silence as the five members of the Board ran down the line of symbols, and then Pirenne sat down and coughed uneasily.

Hardin said, 'No loophole, is there, Dr Pirenne?'

'Doesn't seem to be.'

'All right.' Hardin replaced the sheets. 'Before you now you see a copy of the treaty between the Empire and Anacreon – treaty, incidentally, which is signed on the Emperor's behalf by the same Lord Dorwin who was here last week – and with it a symbolic analysis.'

The treaty ran through five pages of fine print and the analysis was scrawled out in just under half a page.

'As you see, gentlemen, something like 90 per cent of the treaty boiled right out of the analysis as being meaningless, and what we end up with can be described in the following interesting manner:

'Obligations of Anacreon to the Empire: *None!*

'Powers of the Empire over Anacreon: *None!*'

Again the five followed the reasoning anxiously, checking carefully back to the treaty, and when they were finished, Pirenne said in a worried fashion, 'That seems to be correct.'

'You admit, then, that the treaty is nothing but a declaration of total independence on the part of Anacreon and a recognition of that status by the Empire?'

'It seems so.'

'And do you suppose that Anacreon doesn't realize that, and is not anxious to emphasize the position of independence - so that it would naturally tend to resent any appearance of threats from the Empire? Particularly when it is evident that the Empire is powerless to fulfil any such threats, or it would never have allowed independence.'

'But then,' interposed Sutt, 'how would Mayor Hardin account for Lord Dorwin's assurances of Empire support? They seemed—' He shrugged. 'Well, they seemed satisfactory.'

Hardin threw himself back in the chair. 'You know, that's the most interesting part of the whole business. I'll admit I had thought his Lordship a most consummate donkey when I first met him - but it turned out that he was actually an accomplished diplomat and a most clever man. I took the liberty of recording all his statements.'

There was a flurry, and Pirenne opened his mouth in horror.

'What of it?' demanded Hardin. 'I realize it was a gross breach of hospitality and a thing no so-called gentleman would do. Also, that if his lordship had caught on, things might have been unpleasant; but he didn't, and I have the record, and that's that. I took that record, had it copied and sent that to Holk for analysis, also.'

Lundin Crast said, 'And where is the analysis?'

'That,' replied Hardin, 'is the interesting thing. The analysis was the most difficult of the three by all odds. When Holk, after two days of steady work, succeeded in eliminating meaningless statements, vague gibberish, useless qualifications - in short, all the goo and dribble - he found he had nothing left. Everything cancelled out.'

'Lord Dorwin, gentlemen, in five days of discussion *didn't say* one *damned thing*, and said it so you never noticed. *There* are the assurances you had from your precious Empire.'

Hardin might have placed an actively working stench bomb on the table and created no more confusion than existed after his last statement. He waited, with weary patience, for it to die down.

'So,' he concluded, 'when you sent threats – and that's what they were – concerning Empire action to Anacreon, you merely irritated a monarch who knew better. Naturally, his ego would demand immediate action, and the ultimatum is the result – which brings me to my original statement. We have one week left and what do we do now?'

'It seems,' said Sutt, 'that we have no choice but to allow Anacreon to establish military bases on Terminus.'

'I agree with you there,' replied Hardin, 'but what do we do toward kicking them off again at the first opportunity?'

Yate Fulham's moustache twitched. 'That sounds as if you have made up your mind that violence must be used against them.'

'Violence,' came the retort, 'is the last refuge of the incompetent. But I certainly don't intend to lay down the welcome mat and brush off the best furniture for their use.'

'I still don't like the way you put that,' insisted Fulham. 'It is a dangerous attitude; the more dangerous because we have noticed lately that a sizeable section of the populace seems to respond to all your suggestions just so. I might as well tell you, Mayor Hardin, that the Board is not quite blind to your recent activities.'

He paused and there was general agreement. Hardin shrugged.

Fulham went on: 'If you were to inflame the City into an act of violence, you would achieve elaborate suicide – and we don't intend to allow that. Our policy has but one cardinal principle, and that is the Encyclopedia. Whatever we decide to do or not to do will be so decided because it will be the measure required to keep that Encyclopedia safe.'

'Then,' said Hardin, 'you come to the conclusion that we must continue our intensive campaign of doing nothing.'

Pirenne said bitterly: 'You have yourself demonstrated that the Empire cannot help us; though how and why it can be so, I don't understand. If compromise is necessary—'

Hardin had the nightmarelike sensation of running at top

speed and getting nowhere. 'There *is* no compromise! Don't you realize that this bosh about military bases is a particularly inferior grade of drivel? Haut Rodric told us what Anacreon was after – outright annexion and imposition of its own feudal system of landed estates and peasant-aristocracy economy upon us. What is left of our bluff of atomic power may force them to move slowly, but they will move none the less.'

He had risen indignantly, and the rest rose with him – except for Jord Fara.

And then Jord Fara spoke. 'Everyone will please sit down. We've gone quite far enough, I think. Come, there's no use looking so furious, Mayor Hardin; none of us have been committing treason.'

'You'll have to convince me of that!'

Fara smiled gently. 'You know you don't mean that. Let me speak!'

His little shrewd eyes were half closed, and the perspiration gleamed on the smooth expanse of his chin. 'There seems no point in concealing that the Board has come to the decision that the real solution to the Anacreonian problem lies in what is to be revealed to us when the Vault opens in six days from now.'

'Is that your contribution to the matter?'

'Yes.'

'We are to do nothing, is that right, except to wait in quiet serenity and utter faith for the *deus ex machina* to pop out of the Vault?'

'Stripped of your emotional phraseology, that's the idea.'

'Such unsubtle escapism! Really, Dr Fara, such folly smacks of genius. A lesser mind would be incapable of it.'

Fara smiled indulgently. 'Your taste in epigrams is amusing, Hardin, but out of place. As a matter of fact, I think you remember my line of argument concerning the Vault about three weeks ago.'

'Yes, I remember it. I don't deny that it was anything but a stupid idea from the standpoint of deductive logic alone. You said – stop me when I make a mistake – that Hari Seldon was the greatest psychologist in the System; that, hence, he could foresee the right and uncomfortable spot we're in now; that, hence, he established the Vault as a method of telling us the way out.'

'You've got the essence of the idea.'

'Would it surprise you to hear that I've given considerable thought to the matter these last weeks?'

'Very flattering. With what result?'

'With the result that pure deduction is found wanting. Again what is needed is a little sprinkling of common sense.'

'For instance?'

'For instance, if he foresaw the Anacreonian mess, why not have placed us on some other planet nearer the Galactic centres? It's well known that Seldon manoeuvred the Commissioners on Trantor into ordering the Foundation established on Terminus. But why should he have done so? Why put us here at all if he could see in advance the break in communication lines, our isolation from the Galaxy, the threat of our neighbours – and our helplessness because of the lack of metals on Terminus? That above all! Or if he foresaw all this, why not have warned the original settlers in advance that they might have had time to prepare, rather than wait, as he is doing, until one foot is over the cliff, before doing so?

'And don't forget this. Even though he could foresee the problem *then*, we can see it equally well *now*. After all, Seldon was not a magician. There are no trick methods of escaping from a dilemma that he can see and we can't.'

'But, Hardin,' reminded Fara, 'we can't!'

'But you haven't *tried*. You haven't tried once. First, you refused to admit that there was a menace at all! Then you reposed an absolutely blind faith in the Emperor! Now you've shifted it to Hari Seldon. Throughout you have invariably relied on authority or on the past – never on yourselves.'

His fists balled spasmodically. 'It amounts to a diseased attitude – a conditional reflex that shunts aside the independence of your minds whenever it is a question of opposing authority. There seems no doubt ever in your minds that the Emperor is more powerful than you are, or Hari Seldon wiser. And that's wrong, don't you see?'

For some reason, no one cared to answer him.

Hardin continued: 'It isn't just you. It's the whole Galaxy. Pirenne heard Lord Dorwin's idea of scientific research. Lord Dorwin thought the way to be a good archaeologist was to read all the books on the subject – written by men who were dead for centuries. He thought that the way to solve archaeological puzzles was to weigh the opposing authorities. And Pirenne listened and made no objections. Don't you see that there's something wrong with that?'

Again the note of near-pleading in his voice. Again no answer.

He went on: 'And you men and half of Terminus as well are just as bad. We sit here, considering the Encyclopedia the all-in-all. We consider the greatest end of science is the classification of past data. It is important but is there no further work to be done? We're receding and forgetting, don't you see? Here in the Periphery they've lost atomic power. In Gamma Andromeda, a power plant has blown up because of poor repairs, and the Chancellor of the Empire complains that atomic technicians are scarce. And the solution? To train new ones? Never! Instead they're to restrict atomic power.'

And for the third time: 'Don't you see? It's Galaxy-wide. It's a worship of the past. It's a deterioration – a *stagnation!*'

He stared from one to the other and they gazed fixedly at him.

Fara was the first to recover. 'Well, mystical philosophy isn't going to help us here. Let us be concrete. Do you deny that Hari Seldon could easily have worked out historical trends of the future by simple psychological technique?'

'No, of course not,' cried Hardin. 'But we can't rely on him for a solution. At best, he might indicate the problem, but if ever there is to be a solution, we must work it out ourselves. He can't do it for us.'

Fulham spoke suddenly. 'What do you mean – "indicate the problem"? We *know* the problem.'

Hardin whirled on him. 'You think you do! You think Anacreon is all Hari Seldon is likely to be worried about. I disagree! I tell you, gentlemen, that as yet none of you has the faintest conception of what is really going on.'

'And you do?' questioned Pirenne, hostilely.

'I think so!' Hardin jumped up and pushed his chair away. His eyes were cold and hard. 'If there's one thing that's definite, it is that there's something smelly about the whole situation; something that is bigger than anything we've talked about yet. Just ask yourself this question: Why was it that among the original population of the Foundation not one first-class psychologist was included, except Bor Alurin? And *he* carefully refrained from training his pupils in more than the fundamentals.'

A short silence and Fara said: 'All right? Why?'

'Perhaps because a psychologist might have caught on to what this was all about – and too soon to suit Hari Seldon. As it is, we've been stumbling about, getting misty glimpses of the truth and no more. And that is what Hari Seldon wanted.'

He laughed harshly. 'Good day, gentlemen!'

He stalked out of the room.

6

Mayor Hardin chewed at the end of his cigar. It had gone out but he was past noticing that. He hadn't slept the night before and he had a good idea that he wouldn't sleep this coming night. His eyes showed it.

He said wearily, 'And that covers it?'

'I think so.' Yohan Lee put his hand to his chin. 'How does it sound?'

'Not too bad. It's got to be done, you understand, with impudence. That is, there is to be no hesitation; no time to allow them to grasp the situation. Once we are in a position to give orders, why, give them as though you were born to do so, and they'll obey out of habit. That's the essence of a *coup*.'

'If the Board remains irresolute for even—'

'The Board? Count them out. After tomorrow, their importance as a factor in Terminus affairs won't matter a rusty half-credit.'

Lee nodded slowly. 'Yet it is strange that they've done nothing to stop us so far. You say they weren't entirely in the dark.'

'Fara stumbled at the edges of the problem. Sometimes he makes me nervous. And Pirenne's been suspicious of me since I was elected. But, you see, they never had the capacity of really understanding what was up. Their whole training has been authoritarian. They are sure that the Emperor, just because he is the Emperor, is all-powerful. And they are sure that the Board of Trustees, simply because it is the Board of Trustees acting in the name of the Emperor, cannot be in a position where it does not give the orders. That incapacity to recognize the possibility of revolt is our best ally.'

He heaved out of his chair and went to the water cooler. 'They're not bad fellows, Lee, when they stick to their Encyclopedia – and we'll see that that's where they stick in the future. They're hopelessly incompetent when it comes to ruling Terminus. Go away now and start things rolling. I want to be alone.'

He sat down on the corner of his desk and stared at the cup of water.

Space! If only he were as confident as he pretended! The Anacreonians were landing in two days and what had he to go on but a set of notions and half-guesses as to what Hari Seldon had been driving at these past fifty years? He wasn't even a real, honest-to-goodness psychologist – just a fumbler with a little training trying to outguess the greatest mind of the age.

If Fara were right; if Anacreon were all the problems Hari Seldon had foreseen; if the Encyclopedia was all he was interested in preserving – then what price *coup d'état*?

He shrugged and drank his water.

7

The Vault was furnished with considerably more than six chairs, as though a larger company had been expected. Hardin noted that thoughtfully and seated himself wearily in a corner just as far from the other five as possible.

The Board members did not seem to object to that arrangement. They spoke among themselves in whispers, which fell off into sibilant monosyllables, and then into nothing at all. Of them all, only Jord Fara seemed even reasonably calm. He had produced a watch and was staring at it sombrely.

Hardin glanced at his own watch and then at the glass cubicle – absolutely empty – that dominated half the room. It was the only unusual feature of the room, for aside from that there was no indication that somewhere a speck of radium was wasting away toward that precise moment when a tumbler would fall, a connection be made and—

The lights went dim!

They didn't go out, but merely yellowed and sank with a suddenness that made Hardin jump. He had lifted his eyes to the ceiling lights in startled fashion, and when he brought them down the glass cubicle was no longer empty.

A figure occupied it – a figure in a wheel-chair!

It said nothing for a few moments, but it closed the book upon its lap and fingered it idly. And then it smiled, and the face seemed all alive.

It said, 'I am Hari Seldon.' The voice was old and soft.

Hardin almost rose to acknowledge the introduction and stopped himself in the act.

The voice continued conversationally: 'As you see, I am confined to this chair and cannot rise to greet you. Your grandparents left for Terminus a few months back in my time and since then I have suffered a rather inconvenient paralysis. I can't see you, you know, so I can't greet you properly. I don't even know how many of you there are, so all this must be conducted informally. If any of you are standing, please sit down; and if you care to smoke, I wouldn't mind.' There was a light chuckle. 'Why should I? I'm not really here.'

Hardin fumbled for a cigar almost automatically, but thought better of it.

Hari Seldon put away his book – as if laying it upon a desk at his side – and when his fingers let go, it disappeared.

He said: 'It is fifty years now since this Foundation was established – fifty years in which the members of the Foundation have been ignorant of what it was they were working toward. It was necesary that they be ignorant, but now the necessity is gone.

'The Encyclopedia Foundation, to begin with, is a fraud, and always has been!'

There was a sound of a scramble behind Hardin and one or two muffled exclamations, but he did not turn around.

Hari Seldon was, of course, undisturbed. He went on: 'It is a fraud in the sense that neither I nor my colleagues care at all whether a single volume of the Encyclopedia is ever published. It has served its purpose, since by it we extracted an imperial charter from the Emperor, by it we attracted the hundred thousand humans necessary for our scheme, and by it we managed to keep them preoccupied while events shaped themselves, until it was too late for any of them to draw back.

'In the fifty years that you have worked on this fraudulent project – there is no use in softening phrases – your retreat has been cut off, and you have now no choice but to proceed on the infinitely more important project that was, and is, our real plan.

'To that end we have placed you on such a planet and at such a time that in fifty years you were manoeuvred to the point where you no longer have freedom of action. From now on, and into the centuries, the path you must take is inevitable. You will be faced with a series of crises, as you are now faced with the first, and in each case your freedom of action will become similarly circumscribed so that you will be forced along one, and only one, path.

'It is that path which our psychology has worked out – and for a reason.

'For centuries Galactic civilization has stagnated and declined, though only a few ever realized that. But now, at last, the Periphery is breaking away and the political unity of the Empire is shattered. Somewhere in the fifty years just past is where the historians of the future will place an arbitrary line and say: "This marks the Fall of the Galactic Empire."

'And they will be right, though scarcely any will recognize that Fall for additional centuries.

'And after the Fall will come inevitable barbarism, a period which, our psychohistory tells us, should, under ordinary circumstances, last for thirty thousand years. We cannot stop the Fall. We do not wish to; for Empire culture has lost whatever virility and worth it once had. But we can shorten the period of Barbarism that must follow – down to a single thousand of years.

'The ins and outs of that shortening, we cannot tell you; just as we could not tell you the truth about the Foundation fifty years ago. Were you to discover those ins and outs, our plan might fail; as it would have, had you penetrated the fraud of the Encyclopedia earlier; for then, by knowledge, your freedom of action would be expanded and the number of additional variables introduced would become greater than our psychology could handle.

'But you won't, for there are no psychologists on Terminus, and never were, but for Alurin – and he was one of us.

'But this I can tell you: Terminus and its companion Foundation at the other end of the Galaxy are the seeds of the

Renascence and the future founders of the Second Galactic Empire. And it is the present crisis that is starting Terminus off to that climax.

'This, by the way, is a rather straightforward crisis, much simpler than many of those that are ahead. To reduce it to its fundamentals, it is this: you are a planet suddenly cut off from the still-civilized centres of the Galaxy, and threatened by your stronger neighbours. You are a small world of scientists surrounded by a vast and rapidly expanding reaches of barbarism. You are an island of atomic power in a growing ocean of more primitive energy; but are helpless despite that, because of your lack of metals.

'You see, then, that you are faced by hard necessity, and that action is forced on you. The nature of that action – that is, the solution to your dilemma – is, of course, obvious!'

The image of Hari Seldon reached into open air and the book once more appeared in his hand. He opened it and said:

'But whatever devious course your future history may take, impress it always upon your descendants that the path has been marked out, and that at its end is new and greater Empire!'

And as his eyes bent to his book, he flicked into nothingness, and the lights brightened once more.

Hardin looked up to see Pirenne facing him, eyes tragic and lips trembling.

The chairman's voice was firm but toneless. 'You were right, it seems. If you will see us tonight at six, the Board will consult with you as to the next move.'

They shook his hand, each one, and left; and Hardin smiled to himself. They were fundamentally sound at that; for they were scientists enough to admit that they were wrong – but for them, it was too late.

He looked at his watch. By this time, it was all over. Lee's men were in control and the Board was giving orders no longer.

The Anacreonians were landing their first space-ships tomorrow, but that was all right, too. In six months, *they* would be giving orders no longer.

In fact, as Hari Seldon had said, and as Salvor Hardin had

guessed since the day that Anselm haut Rodric had first revealed to him Anacreon's lack of atomic power – the solution to this crisis was obvious.

Obvious as hell!

Part III

THE MAYORS

1

THE FOUR KINGDOMS *The name given to those portions of the Province of Anacreon which broke away from the First Empire in the early years of the Foundational Era to form independent and short-lived kingdoms. The largest and most powerful of these was Anacreon itself which in area . . .*

. . . Undoubtedly the most interesting aspect of the history of the Four Kingdoms involves the strange society forced temporarily upon it during the administration of Salvor Hardin. . .

ENCYCLOPEDIA GALACTICA

A deputation!

That Salvor Hardin had seen it coming made it none the more pleasant. On the contrary, he found anticipation distinctly annoying.

Yohan Lee advocated extreme measures. 'I don't see, Hardin,' he said, 'that we need waste any time. They can't do anything till next election – legally, anyway – and that gives us a year. Give them a brush-off.'

Hardin pursed his lips. 'Lee, you'll never learn. In the forty years I've known you, you've never once learned the gentle art of sneaking up from behind.'

'It's not my way of fighting,' grumbled Lee.

'Yes, I know that. I suppose that's why you're the one man I trust.' He paused and reached for a cigar. 'We've come a long way, Lee, since we engineered our *coup* against the Encyclopedists way back. I'm getting old. Sixty-two. Do you ever think how fast those thirty years went?'

Lee snorted. '*I* don't feel old, and I'm sixty-six.'

'Yes, but I haven't your digestion.' Hardin sucked lazily at his cigar. He had long since stopped wishing for the mild Vegan tobacco of his youth. Those days when the planet, Terminus, had trafficked with every part of the Galactic Empire belonged in the limbo to which all Good Old Days go. Toward the same limbo where the Galactic Empire was heading. He wondered who the new emperor was – or if there was a new emperor at all – or any Empire. Space! For thirty years now, since the break-up of communications here at the edge of the Galaxy, the whole universe of Terminus had consisted of itself and the four surrounding kingdoms.

How the mighty had fallen! *Kingdoms!* They were prefects in the old days, all part of the same province, which in turn had been part of a sector, which in turn had been part of a quadrant, which in turn had been part of the all-embracing Galactic Empire. And now that the Empire had lost control over the farther reaches of the Galaxy, these little splinter groups of planets became kingdoms – with comic-opera kings and nobles, and petty, meaningless wars, and a life that went on pathetically among the ruins.

A civilization falling. Atomic power forgotten. Science fading to mythology – until the Foundation had stepped in. The Foundation that Hari Seldon had established for just that purpose here on Terminus.

Lee was at the window and his voice broke in on Hardin's reverie. 'They've come,' he said, 'in a last-model ground car, the young pups.' He took a few uncertain steps toward the door and then looked at Hardin.

Hardin smiled, and waved him back. 'I've given orders to have them brought up here.'

'Here! What for? You're making them too important.'

'Why go through all the ceremonies of an official mayor's audience? I'm getting too old for red tape. Besides which, flattery is useful when dealing with youngsters – particularly when it doesn't commit you to anything.' He winked. 'Sit down, Lee, and give me your moral backing. I'll need it with this young Sermak.'

'That fellow, Sermak,' said Lee, heavily, 'is dangerous. He's got a following, Hardin, so don't underestimate him.'

'Have I ever underestimated anybody?'

'Well, then, arrest him. You can accuse him of something or other afterward.'

Hardin ignored that last bit of advice. 'There they are, Lee.' In response to the signal, he stepped on the pedal beneath his desk, and the door slid aside.

They filed in, the four that composed the deputation, and Hardin waved them gently to the arm-chairs that faced his desk in a semicircle. They bowed and waited for the mayor to speak first.

Hardin flicked open the curiously carved silver lid of the cigar-box that had once belonged to Jord Fara of the old Board of Trustees in the long-dead days of the Encyclopedists. It was a genuine Empire product from Santanni, though the cigars it now contained were home-grown. One by one, with grave solemnity, the four of the deputation accepted cigars and lit up in ritualistic fashion.

Sef Sermak was second from the right, the youngest of the young group – and the most interesting with his bristly yellow moustache trimmed precisely, and his sunken eyes of uncertain colour. The other three Hardin dismissed almost immediately; they were rank and file on the face of them. It was on Sermak that he concentrated, the Sermak who had already, in his first term in the City Council, turned that sedate body topsy-turvy more than once, and it was to Sermak that he said:

'I've been particularly anxious to see you, Councilman, ever since your very excellent speech last month. Your attack on the foreign policy of this government was a most capable one.'

Sermak's eyes smouldered. 'Your interest honours me. The attack may or may not have been capable, but it was certainly justified.'

'Perhaps! Your opinions are yours, of course. Still you are rather young.'

Dryly. 'It is a fault that most people are guilty of at some period of their life. You became mayor of the City when you were two years younger than I am now.'

Hardin smiled to himself. The yearling was a cool customer. He said, 'I take it now that you have come to see me concerning this same foreign policy that annoys you so greatly in the Council Chamber. Are you speaking for your three colleagues, or must I listen to each of you separately?'

There were quick mutual glances among the four young men, a slight flickering of eyelids.

Sermak said grimly, 'I speak for the people of Terminus – a people who are not truly represented in the rubber-stamp body they call the Council.'

'I see. Go ahead, then!'

'It comes to this, Mr Mayor. We are dissatisfied—'

'By "we" you mean "the people", don't you?'

Sermak stared hostilely, sensing a trap, and replied coldly, 'I believe that my views reflect those of the majority of the voters of Terminus. Does that suit you?'

'Well, a statement like that is all the better for proof, but go on, anyway. You are dissatisfied.'

'Yes, dissatisfied with the policy which for thirty years has been stripping Terminus defenceless against the inevitable attack from outside.'

'I see. And therefore? Go on, go on.'

'It's nice of you to anticipate. And therefore we are forming a new political party; one that will stand for the immediate needs of Terminus and not for a mystic "manifest destiny" of future Empire. We are going to throw you and your lick-spittle clique of appeasers out of City Hall – and that soon.'

'Unless? There's always an "unless", you know.'

'Not much of one in this case: unless you resign now. I'm not asking you to change your policies – I wouldn't trust you that far. Your promises are worth nothing. An outright resignation is all we'll take.'

'I see.' Hardin crossed his legs and teetered his chair back on two legs. 'That's your ultimatum. Nice of you to give me warning. But, you see, I rather think I'll ignore it.'

'Don't think it was a warning, Mr Mayor. It was an announcement of principles and of action. The new party has already been formed, and it will begin its official activities tomorrow. There is neither room nor desire for compromise, and, frankly, it was only our recognition of your services to the City that induced us to offer the easy way out. I didn't think you'd take it, but my conscience is clear. The next election will be a more forcible and quite irresistible reminder that resignation is necessary.'

He rose and motioned the rest up.

Hardin lifted his arm. 'Hold on! Sit down!'

Sef Sermak seated himself once more with just a shade too much alacrity and Hardin smiled behind a straight face. In spite of his words, he was waiting for an offer - an offer.

Hardin said, 'In exactly what way do you want our foreign policy changed? Do you want us to attack the Four Kingdoms, now, at once, and all four simultaneously?'

'I make no such suggestion, Mr Mayor. It is our simple proposition that all appeasement cease immediately. Throughout your administration, you have carried out a policy of scientific aid to the Kingdoms. You have given them atomic power. You have helped rebuild power plants on their territories. You have established medical clinics, chemical laboratories and factories.'

'Well? And your objection?'

'You have done this in order to keep them from attacking us. With these as bribes, you have been playing the fool in a colossal game of blackmail, in which you have allowed Terminus to be sucked dry - with the result that now we are at the mercy of these barbarians.'

'In what way?'

'Because you have given them power, given them weapons, actually serviced the ships of their navies; they are infinitely stronger than they were three decades ago. Their demands are increasing, and with their new weapons, they will eventually satisfy all their demands at once by violent annexation of

Terminus. Isn't that the way blackmail usually ends?'

'And your remedy?'

'Stop the bribes immediately and while you can. Spend your effort in strengthening Terminus itself – and attack first!'

Hardin watched the young fellow's little blond moustache with an almost morbid interest. Sermak felt sure of himself or he wouldn't talk so much. There was no doubt that his remarks were the reflection of a pretty huge segment of the population, pretty huge.

His voice did not betray the slightly perturbed current of his thoughts. It was almost negligent. 'Are you finished?'

'For the moment.'

'Well, then, do you notice the framed statement I have on the wall behind me? Read it, if you will!'

Sermak's lips twitched. 'It says: "Violence is the last refuge of the incompetent." That's an old man's doctrine, Mr Mayor.'

'I applied it as a young man, Mr Councilman – and successfully. You were busily being born when it happened, but perhaps you may have read something of it in school.'

He eyed Sermak closely and continued in measured tones, 'When Hari Seldon established the Foundation here, it was for the ostensible purpose of producing a great Encyclopedia, and for fifty years we followed that will-of-the-wisp, before discovering what he was really after. By that time, it was almost too late. When communications with the central regions of the old Empire broke down, we found ourselves a world of scientists concentrated in a single city, possessing no industries and surrounded by newly created kingdoms, hostile and largely barbarous. We were a tiny island of atomic power in this ocean of barbarism, and an infinitely valuable prize.

'Anacreon then as now, the most powerful of the Four Kingdoms, demanded and actually established a military base upon Terminus, and the then rulers of the City, the Encyclopedists, knew very well that this was only a preliminary to taking over the entire planet. That is how matters stood when I . . . uh . . . assumed actual government. What would you have done?'

Sermak shrugged his shoulders. 'That's an academic question. Of course, I know what *you* did.'

'I'll repeat it, anyway. Perhaps you don't get the point. The temptation was great to muster what force we could and put up a fight. It's the easiest way out, and the most satisfactory to self-respect - but, nearly invariably, the stupidest. *You* would have done it; you and your talk of "attack first". What I did, instead, was to visit the three other kingdoms, one by one; point out to each that to allow the secret of atomic power to fall into the hands of Anacreon was the quickest way of cutting their own throats; and suggest gently that they do the obvious thing. That was all. One month after the Anacreonian force had landed on Terminus, their king received a joint ultimatum from his three neighbours. In seven days, the last Anacreonian was off Terminus.

'Now tell me, where was the need for violence?'

The young councilman regarded his cigar stub thoughtfully and tossed it into the incinerator chute. 'I fail to see the analogy. Insulin will bring a diabetic to normal without the faintest need of a knife, but appendicitis needs an operation. You can't help that. When other courses have failed, what is left but, as you put it, the last refuge? It's your fault that we're driven to it.'

'I? Oh, yes, again my policy of appeasement. You still seem to lack grasp of the fundamental necessities of our position. Our problem wasn't over with the departure of the Anacreonians. They had just begun. The Four Kingdoms were more our enemies than ever, for each wanted atomic power - and each was kept off our throats only for fear of the other three. We are balanced on the point of a very sharp sword, and the slightest sway in any direction— If, for instance, one kingdom becomes too strong; or if two form a coalition— You understand?'

'Certainly. That was the time to begin all-out preparations for war.'

'On the contrary. That was the time to begin all-out prevention of war. I played them one against the other. I helped each in turn. I offered them science, trade, education, scientific medicine. I made Terminus of more value to them as a flourishing world than as a military prize. It worked for thirty years.'

'Yes, but you were forced to surround these scientific gifts with the most outrageous mummery. You've made half religion, half balderdash out of it. You've erected a hierarchy of priests and complicated, meaningless ritual.'

Hardin frowned. 'What of that? I don't see that it has anything to do with the argument at all. I started that way at first because the barbarians looked upon our science as a sort of magical sorcery, and it was easier to get them to accept it on that basis. The priesthood built itself and if we help it along we are only following the line of least resistance. It is a minor matter.'

'But these priests are in charge of the power plants. That is *not* a minor matter.'

'True, but *we* have trained them. Their knowledge of their tools is purely empirical; and they have a firm belief in the mummery that surrounds them.'

'And if one pierces through the mummery, and has the genius to brush aside empiricism, what is to prevent him from learning actual techniques, and selling out to the most satisfactory bidder? What price our value to the kingdoms, then?'

'Little chance of that, Sermak. You are being superficial. The best men on the planets of the kingdoms are sent here to the Foundation each year and educated into the priesthood. And the best of these remain here as research students. If you think that those who are left, with practically no knowledge of the elementals of science, or worse still, with the distorted knowledge the priests receive, can penetrate at a bound to atomic power, to electronics, to the theory of the hyperwarp – you have a very romantic and very foolish idea of science. It takes lifetimes of training and an excellent brain to get that far.'

Yohan Lee had risen abruptly during the foregoing speech and left the room. He had returned now and when Hardin finished speaking, he bent to his superior's ear. A whisper was exchanged and then a leaden cylinder. Then, with one short hostile look at the deputation, Lee resumed his chair.

Hardin turned the cylinder end for end in his hands, watching the deputation through his lashes. And then he opened it with a hard, sudden twist and only Sermak had the sense not to throw a rapid look at the rolled paper that fell out.

'In short, gentlemen,' he said, 'the Government is of the opinion that it knows what it is doing.'

He read as he spoke. There were the lines of intricate, meaningless code that covered the page and the three pencilled words scrawled in one corner that carried the message. He took it in at a glance and tossed it casually into the incinerator shaft.

'That,' Hardin then said, 'ends the interview, I'm afraid. Glad to have met you all. Thank you for coming.' He shook hands with each in perfunctory fashion, and they filed out.

Hardin had almost gotten out of the habit of laughing, but after Sermak and his three silent partners were well out of earshot, he indulged in a dry chuckle and bent an amused look on Lee.

'How did you like that battle of bluffs, Lee?'

Lee snorted grumpily. 'I'm not sure that *he* was bluffing. Treat him with kid gloves and he's quite liable to win the next election, just as he says.'

'Oh, quite likely, quite likely – if nothing happens first.'

'Make sure they don't happen in the wrong direction this time, Hardin. I tell you this Sermak has a following. What if he doesn't wait till the next election? There was a time when you and I put things through violently, in spite of your slogan about what violence is.'

Hardin cocked an eyebrow. 'You *are* pessimistic today, Lee. And singularly contrary, too, or you wouldn't speak of violence. Our own little putsch was carried through without loss of life, you remember. It was a necessary measure put through at the proper moment, and went over smoothly, painlessly, and all but effortlessly. As for Sermak, he's up against a different proposition. You and I, Lee, aren't the

Encyclopedists. *We* stand prepared. Stick your men on to these youngsters in a nice way, old fellow. Don't let them know they're being watched – but eyes open, you understand.'

Lee laughed in sour amusement. 'I'd be a fine one to wait for your orders, wouldn't I, Hardin? Sermak and his men have been under surveillance for a month now.'

The mayor chuckled. 'Got in first, did you? All right. By the way,' he observed, and added softly, 'Ambassador Verisof is returning to Terminus. Temporarily, I hope.'

There was a short silence, faintly horrified, and then Lee said, 'Was that the message? Are things breaking already?'

'Don't know. I can't tell till I hear what Verisof has to say. They may be, though. After all, they *have* to before election. But what are you looking so dead about?'

'Because I don't know how it's going to turn out. You're too deep, Hardin, and you're playing the game too close to your chest.'

'Thou, too, Brutus,' murmured Hardin. And aloud, 'Does that mean you're going to join Sermak's new party?'

Lee smiled against his will. 'All right. You win. How about lunch now?'

2

There are many epigrams attributed to Hardin – a confirmed epigrammatist – a good many of which are probably apocryphal. Nevertheless, it is reported that on a certain occasion, he said:

'It pays to be obvious, especially if you have a reputation for subtlety.'

Poly Verisof had had occasion to act on that advice more than once for he was now in the fourteenth year of his double status on Anacreon – a double status the upkeep of which reminded him often and unpleasantly of a dance performed barefoot on hot metal.

To the people of Anacreon he was high priest, representative of that Foundation which, to those 'barbarians', was the acme of mystery and the physical centre of this religion they had created – with Hardin's help – in the last three decades. As such, he received a homage that had become horribly wearying, for from his soul he despised the ritual of which he was the centre.

But to the King of Anacreon – the old one that had been, and the young grandson that was now on the throne – he was simply the ambassador of a power at once feared and coveted.

On the whole, it was an uncomfortable job, and his first trip to the Foundation in three years, despite the disturbing incident that had made it necessary, was something in the nature of a holiday.

And since it was not the first time he had had to travel in absolute secrecy, he again made use of Hardin's epigram on the uses of the obvious.

He changed into his civilian clothes – a holiday in itself – and boarded a passenger liner to the Foundation, second class. Once at Terminus, he threaded his way through the crowd at the space-port and called up City Hall at a public visiphone.

He said, 'My name is Jan Smite. I have an appointment with the mayor this afternoon.'

The dead-voiced but efficient young lady at the other end made a second connection and exchanged a few rapid words, then said to Verisof in dry, mechanical tone, 'Mayor Hardin will see you in half an hour, sir,' and the screen went blank.

Whereupon the ambassador to Anacreon bought the latest edition of the Terminus City *Journal*, sauntered casually to City Hall Park and, sitting down on the first empty bench he came to, read the editorial page, sport section and comic sheet while waiting. At the end of half an hour, he tucked the paper under his arm, entered City Hall and presented himself in the anteroom.

In doing all this he remained safely and thoroughly unrecognized, for since he was so entirely obvious, no one gave him a second look.

Hardin looked up at him and grinned. 'Have a cigar! How was the trip?'

Verisof helped himself. 'Interesting. There was a priest in the next cabin on his way here to take a special course in the preparation of radioactive synthetics – for the treatment of cancer, you know—'

'Surely, he didn't call it radioactive synthetics, now?'

'I guess *not*! It was the Holy Food to him.'

The mayor smiled. 'Go on.'

'He inveigled me into a theological discussion and did his level best to elevate me out of sordid materialism.'

'And never recognized his own high priest?'

'Without my crimson robe? Besides, he was a Smyrnian. It was an interesting experience, though. It *is* remarkable, Hardin, how the religion of science has grabbed hold. I've written an essay on the subject – entirely for my own amusement; it wouldn't do to have it published. Treating the problem sociologically, it would seem that when the old Empire began to rot at the fringes, it could be considered that science, as science, had failed the outer worlds. To be reaccepted it would have to present in itself another guise – and it has done just that. It works out beautifully when you use symbolic logic to help out.'

'Interesting!' The mayor placed his arms behind his neck and said suddenly, 'Start talking about the situation at Anacreon!'

The ambassador frowned and withdrew the cigar from his mouth. He looked at it distastefully and put it down. 'Well, it's pretty bad.'

'You wouldn't be here, otherwise.'

'Scarcely. Here's the position. The key man at Anacreon is the Prince Regent, Wienis. He's King Lepold's uncle.'

'I know. But Lepold is coming of age next year, isn't he? I

believe he'll be sixteen in February.'

'Yes.' Pause, and then a wry addition. '*If* he lives. The king's father died under suspicious circumstances. A needle bullet through the chest during a hunt. It was called an accident.'

'Hmph. I seem to remember Wienis the time I was on Anacreon, when we kicked them off Terminus. It was before your time. Let's see now. If I remember, he was a dark young fellow, black hair and a squint in his right eye. He had a funny hook in his nose.'

'Same fellow. The hook and the squint are still there, but his hair's grey now. He plays the game dirty. Luckily, he's the most egregious fool on the planet. Fancies himself as a shrewd devil, too, which makes his folly the more transparent.'

'That's usually the way.'

'His notion of cracking an egg is to shoot an atomic blast at it. Witness the tax on Temple property he tried to impose just after the old king died two years ago. Remember?'

Hardin nodded thoughtfully, then smiled. 'The priests raised a howl.'

'They raised one you could hear way out to Lucreza. He's shown more caution in dealing with the priesthood since, but he still manages to do things the hard way. In a way, it's unfortunate for us; he has unlimited self-confidence.'

'Probably an over-compensated inferiority complex. Younger sons of royalty get that way, you know.'

'But it amounts to the same thing. He's foaming at the mouth with eagerness to attack the Foundation. He scarcely troubles to conceal it. And he's in a position to do it, too, from the standpoint of armament. The old king built up a magnificent navy, and Wienis hasn't been sleeping the last two years. In fact the tax on Temple property was originally intended for further armament and when that fell through he increased the income tax twice.'

'Any grumbling at that?'

'None of serious importance. Obedience to appointed authority was the text of every sermon in the kingdom for weeks. Not that Wienis showed any gratitude.'

'All right. I've got the background. Now what's happened?'

'Two weeks ago an Anacreonian merchant ship came across a derelict battle cruiser of the old Imperial navy. It must have been drifting in space for at least three centuries.'

Interest flickered in Hardin's eyes. He sat up. 'Yes, I've heard of that. The Board of Navigation has sent me a petition asking me to obtain the ship for purposes of study. It is in good condition, I understand.'

'In entirely too good condition,' responded Verisof, dryly. 'When Wienis received your suggestion last week that he turn the ship over to the Foundation, he almost had convulsions.'

'He hasn't answered yet.'

'He won't – except with guns, or so he thinks. You see, he came to me on the day I left Anacreon and requested that the Foundation put this battle cruiser into fighting order and turn it over to the Anacreonian navy. He had the infernal gall to say that your note of last week indicated a plan of the Foundation's to attack Anacreon. He said that refusal to repair the battle cruiser would confirm his suspicions; and indicated that measures for the self-defence of Anacreon would be forced upon him. Those are his words. Forced upon him! And that's why I'm here.'

Hardin laughed gently.

Verisof smiled and continued, 'Of course, he expects a refusal, and it would be a perfect excuse – in his eyes – for immediate attack.'

'I see that, Verisof. Well, we have at least six months to spare, so have the ship fixed up and present it with my compliments. Have it renamed the Wienis as a mark of our esteem and affection.'

He laughed again.

And again Verisof responded with the faintest trace of a smile, 'I suppose it's the logical step, Hardin – but I'm worried.'

'What about?'

'It's a *ship*! They could *build* in those days. Its cubic capacity is half again that of the entire Anacreonian navy. It's got atomic blasts capable of blowing up a planet, and a shield that could take a Q-beam without working up radiation. Too much of a good thing, Hardin—'

'Superficial, Verisof, superficial. You and I both know that the armament he now has could defeat Terminus handily, long before we could repair the cruiser for our own use. What does it matter, then, if we give him the cruiser as well? You know it won't ever come to actual war.'

'I suppose so. Yes.' The ambassador looked up. 'But, Hardin—'

'Well? Why do you stop? Go ahead.'

'Look. This isn't my province. But I've been reading the paper.' He placed the *Journal* on the desk and indicated the front page. 'What's this all about?'

Hardin dropped a casual glance, '"A group of Councilmen are forming a new political party."'

'That's what it says.' Verisof fidgeted. 'I know you're in better touch with internal matters than I am, but they're attacking you with everything short of physical violence. How strong are they?'

'Damned strong. They'll probably control the Council after next election.'

'Not before?' Verisof looked at the mayor obliquely. 'There are ways of gaining control besides elections.'

'Do you take me for Wienis?'

'No. But repairing the ship will take months and an attack after that is certain. Our yielding will be taken as a sign of appalling weakness and the addition of the Imperial cruiser will just about double the strength of Wienis' navy. He'll attack as sure as I'm a high priest. Why take chances? Do one of two things. Either reveal the plan of campaign to the Council, or force the issue with Anacreon now!'

Hardin frowned. 'Force the issue now? Before the crisis comes? It's the one thing I mustn't do. There's Hari Seldon and the Plan, you know.'

Verisof hesitated, then muttered, 'You're absolutely sure, then, that there is a Plan?'

'There can scarcely be any doubt,' came the stiff reply. 'I was present at the opening of the Time Vault and Seldon's recording revealed it then.'

'I didn't mean that, Hardin. I just don't see how it could be possible to chart history for a thousand years ahead. Maybe Seldon overestimated himself.' He shrivelled a bit at Hardin's ironical smile, and added, 'Well, I'm no psychologist.'

'Exactly. None of us are. But I did receive some elementary training in my youth – enough to know what psychology is capable of, even if I can't exploit its capabilities myself. There's no doubt but that Seldon did exactly what he claims to have done. The Foundation, as he says, was established as a scientific refuge – the means by which the science and culture of the dying Empire was to be preserved through the centuries of barbarism that have begun, to be rekindled in the end into a second Empire.'

Verisof nodded, a trifle doubtfully. 'Everyone knows that's the way things are *supposed* to go. But can we afford to take chances? Can we risk the present for the sake of a nebulous future?'

'We must – because the future isn't nebulous. It's been calculated out by Seldon and charted. Each successive crisis in our history is mapped and each depends in a measure on the successful conclusion of the ones previous. This is only the second crisis and Space knows what effect even a trifling deviation would have in the end.'

'That's rather empty speculation.'

'*No*! Hari Seldon said in the Time Vault, that at each crisis our freedom of action would become circumscribed to the point where only one course of action was possible.'

'So as to keep us on the straight and narrow?'

'So as to keep us from deviating, yes. But, conversely, as long as *more* than one course of action is possible, the crisis has not been reached. We *must* let things drift so long as we possibly can, and by Space, that's what I intend doing.'

Verisof didn't answer. He chewed his lower lip in a grudging silence. It had only been the year before that Hardin had first discussed the problem with him – the real problem; the problem of countering Anacreon's hostile preparations. And then only because he, Verisof, had balked at further appeasement.

Hardin seemed to follow his ambassador's thoughts. 'I would much rather never have told you anything about this.'

'What makes you say that?' cried Verisof, in surprise.

'Because there are six people now – you and I, the other three ambassadors and Yohan Lee – who have a fair notion of what's ahead; and I'm damned afraid that it was Seldon's idea to have no one know.'

'Why so?'

'Because even Seldon's advanced psychology was limited. It could not handle too many independent variables. He couldn't work with individuals over any length of time; any more than you could apply the kinetic theory of gases to single molecules. He worked with mobs, populations of whole planets, and only *blind* mobs who do not possess foreknowledge of the results of their own actions.'

'That's not plain.'

'I can't help it. I'm not psychologist enough to explain it scientifically. But this you know. There are no trained psychologists on Terminus and no mathematical texts on the science. It is plain that he wanted no one on Terminus capable of working out the future in advance. Seldon wanted us to proceed blindly – and therefore correctly – according to the law of mob psychology. As I once told you, I never knew where we were heading when I first drove out the Anacreonians. My idea had been to maintain balance of power, no more than that. It was only afterward that I thought I saw a pattern in events; but

I've done my level best not to act on that knowledge. Interference due to foresight would have knocked the Plan out of kilter.'

Verisof nodded thoughtfully. 'I've heard arguments almost as complicated in the Temples back on Anacreon. How do you expect to spot the right moment of action?'

'It's spotted already. You admit that once we repair the battle cruiser nothing will stop Wienis from attacking us. There will no longer be any alternative in that respect.'

'Yes.'

'All right. That accounts for the external aspect. Meanwhile, you'll further admit that the next election will see a new and hostile Council that will force action against Anacreon. There is no alternative there.'

'Yes.'

'And as soon as all the alternatives disappear, the crisis has come. Just the same – I get worried.'

He paused, and Verisof waited. Slowly, almost reluctantly. Hardin continued: 'I've got the idea – just a notion – that the external and internal pressures were planned to come to a head simultaneously. As it is, there's a few months difference, Wienis will probably attack before spring, and elections are still a year off.'

'That doesn't sound important.'

'I don't know. It may be due merely to unavoidable errors of calculation, or it might be due to the fact that I knew too much. I tried never to let my foresight influence my action, but how can I tell? And what effect will the discrepancy have? Anyway,' he looked up, 'there's one thing I've decided.'

'And what's that?'

'When the crisis does begin to break, I'm going to Anacreon. I want to be on the spot ... Oh, that's enough, Verisof. It's getting late. Let's go out and make a night of it. I want some relaxation.'

'Then get it right here,' said Verisof. 'I don't want to be recognized, or you know what this new party your precious

Councilmen are forming would you say. Call for the brandy.'

And Hardin did – but not for too much.

3

In the ancient days when the Galactic Empire had embraced the Galaxy, and Anacreon had been the richest of the prefects of the Periphery, more than one emperor had visited the Viceregal Palace in state. And not one had left without at least one effort to pit his skill with air speedster and needle gun against the feathered flying fortress they call the Nyakbird.

The fame of Anacreon had withered to nothing with the decay of the times. The Viceregal Palace was a drafty mass of ruins except for the wing that Foundation workmen had restored. And no Emperor had been seen in Anacreon for two hundred years.

But Nyak hunting was still the royal sport and a good eye with the needle gun still the first requirements of Anacreon's kings.

Lepold I, King of Anacreon and – as was invariably, but untruthfully added – Lord of the Outer Dominions, though not yet sixteen, had already proved his skill many times over. He had brought down his first Nyak when scarcely thirteen; had brought down his tenth the week after his accession to the throne; and was returning now from his forty-sixth.

'Fifty before I come of age,' he had exulted. 'Who'll take the wager?'

But courtiers don't take wagers against the king's skill. There is the deadly danger of winning. So no one did, and the king left to change his clothes in high spirits.

'Lepold!'

The king stopped mid-step at the one voice that could cause him to do so. He turned sulkily.

Wienis stood upon the threshold of his chambers and beetled at his young nephew.

'Send them away,' he motioned impatiently. 'Get rid of them.'

The king nodded curtly and the two chamberlains bowed and backed down the stairs. Lepold entered his uncle's room.

Wienis stared at the king's hunting suit morosely. 'You'll have more important things to tend to than Nyak hunting soon enough.'

He turned his back and stumped to his desk. Since he had grown too old for the rush of air, the perilous dive within wingbeat of the Nyak, the roll and climb of the speedster at the motion of a foot, he had soured upon the whole sport.

Lepold appreciated his uncle's sour-grapes attitude and it was not without malice that he began enthusiastically, 'But you should have been with us today, uncle. We flushed one in the wilds of Samia that was a monster. And game as they come. We had it out for two hours over at least seventy square miles of ground. And then I got to Sunwards' – he was motioning graphically, as though he were once more in his speedster – 'and dived torque-wise. Caught him on the rise just under the left wing at quarters. It maddened him and he canted athwart. I took his dare and veered a-left, waiting for the plummet. Sure enough, down he came. He was within wing-beat before I moved and then—'

'Lepold!'

'Well! – I got him.'

'I'm sure you did. Now *will* you attend?'

The king shrugged and gravitated to the end table where he nibbled at a Lera nut in quite an unregal sulk. He did not dare to meet his uncle's eyes.

Wienis said, by way of preamble, 'I've been to the ship today.'

'What ship?'

'There is only one ship. *The* ship. The one the Foundation is repairing for the navy. The old Imperial cruiser. Do I make myself sufficiently plain?'

'That one? You see, I told you the Foundation would repair it if we asked them to. It's all poppycock, you know, that story of yours about their wanting to attack us. Because if they did, why would they fix the ship? It doesn't make sense, you know.'

'Lepold, you're a fool!'

The king, who had just discarded the shell of the Lera nut and was lifting another to his lips, flushed.

'Well now, look here,' he said, with anger that scarcely rose above peevishness, 'I don't think you ought to call me that. You forget yourself. I'll be of age in two months, you know.'

'Yes, and you're in a fine position to assume regal responsibilities. If you spent half the time on public affairs that you do on Nyak hunting, I'd resign the regency directly with a clear conscience.'

'I don't care. That has nothing to do with the case, you know. The fact is that even if you are the regent and my uncle, I'm still king and you're still my subject. You oughtn't to call me a fool and you oughtn't to sit in my presence, anyway. You haven't asked my permission. I think you ought to be careful, or I might do something about it – pretty soon.'

Wienis' gaze was cold. 'May I refer to you as "your majesty"?'

'Yes.'

'Very well! You are a fool, your majesty!'

His dark eyes blazed from beneath his grizzled brows and the young king sat down slowly. For a moment, there was sardonic satisfaction in the regent's face, but it faded quickly. His thick lips parted in a smile and one hand fell upon the king's shoulder.

'Never mind, Lepold. I should not have spoken harshly to you. It is difficult sometimes to behave with true propriety when the pressure of such events is such as— You understand?' But if the words were conciliatory, there was something in his eyes that had not softened.

Lepold said uncertainly, 'Yes. Affairs of State are deuced difficult, you know.' He wondered, not without apprehension, whether he were not in for a dull siege of meaningless details on the year's trade with Smyrno and the long, wrangling dispute over the sparsely settled worlds on the Red Corridor.

Wienis was speaking again. 'My boy, I had thought to speak of this to you earlier, and perhaps I should have, but I know that your youthful spirits are impatient of the dry detail of statecraft.'

Lepold nodded. 'Well, that's all right—'

His uncle broke in firmly and continued: 'However, you will come of age in two months. Moreover, in the difficult times that are coming, you will have to take a full and active part. You will be *king* henceforward, Lepold.'

Again Lepold nodded, but his expression was quite blank.

'There will be war, Lepold.'

'War! But there's been truce with Smyrno—'

'Not Smyrno. The Foundation itself.'

'But, uncle, they've agreed to repair the ship. You said—'

His voice choked off at the twist of his uncle's lip.

'Lepold' – some of the friendliness had gone – 'we are to talk man to man. There is to be war with the Foundation, whether the ship is repaired or not; all the sooner, in fact, since it is being repaired. The Foundation is the source of power and might. All the greatness of Anacreon; all its ships and its cities and its people and its commerce depend on the dribbles and leavings of power that the Foundation have given us grudgingly. I remember the time – I, myself – when the cities of Anacreon were warmed by the burning of coal and oil. But never mind that; you would have no conception of it.'

'It seems,' suggested the king, timidly, 'that we ought to be grateful—'

'Grateful?' roared Wienis. 'Grateful that they begrudge us the mearest dregs, while keeping Space knows what for themselves – and keeping it with what purpose in mind? Why, only that they may some day rule the Galaxy.'

His hand came down on his nephew's knee, and his eyes narrowed. 'Lepold, you are king of Anacreon. Your children and your children's children may be kings of the universe – if you have the power that the Foundation is keeping from us!'

'There's something in that.' Lepold's eyes gained a sparkle and his back straightened. 'After all, what right have they to keep it to themselves? Not fair, you know. Anacreon counts for something, too.'

'You see, you're beginning to understand. And now, my boy, what if Smyrno decides to attack the Foundation for its own part and thus gains all that power? How long do you suppose we could escape becoming a vassal power? How long would you hold your throne?'

Lepold grew excited. 'Space, yes. You're absolutely right, you know. We must strike first. It's simply self-defence.'

Wienis' smile broadened slightly. 'Furthermore, once, at the very beginning of the reign of your grandfather, Anacreon actually established a military base on the Foundation's planet, Terminus – a base vitally needed for national defence. We were forced to abandon that base as a result of the machinations of the leader of that Foundation, a sly cur, a scholar, with not a drop of noble blood in his veins. You understand, Lepold? Your grandfather was humiliated by this commoner. I remember him! He was scarcely older than myself, when he came to Anacreon with his devil's smile and devil's brain – and the power of the other three kingdoms behind him, combined in cowardly union against the greatness of Anacreon.'

Lepold flushed and the sparkle in his eyes blazed. 'By Seldon, if I had been my grandfather, I would have fought even so.'

'No, Lepold. We decided to wait – to wipe out the insult at a fitter time. It had been your father's hope, before his untimely death, that he might be the one to— Well, well!' Wienis turned away for a moment. Then, as if stifling emotion, 'He was my brother. And yet, if his son were—'

'Yes, uncle, I'll not fail him. I have decided. It seems only proper that Anacreon wipe out this nest of trouble-makers, and that immediately.'

'No, not immediately. First, we must wait for the repairs of the battle cruiser to be completed. The mere fact that they are willing to undertake these repairs proves that they fear us. The fools attempt to placate us, but we are not to be turned from our path, are we?'

And Lepold's fist slammed against his cupped palm. 'Not while *I* am king of Anacreon.'

Wienis' lip twitched sardonically. 'Besides which we must wait for Salvor Hardin to arrive.'

'Salvor Hardin!' The king grew suddenly round-eyed, and the youthful contour of his beardless face lost the almost hard lines into which they had been compressed.

'Yes, Lepold, the leader of the Foundation himself is coming to Anacreon on your birthday – probably to soothe us with buttered words. But it won't help him.'

'Salvor Hardin!' It was the merest murmur.

Wienis frowned. 'Are you afraid of the name? It is the same Salvor Hardin, who on his previous visit, ground our noses into the dust. You're not forgetting that deadly insult to the royal house? And from a commoner. The dregs of the gutter.'

'No. I guess not. No, I won't. I won't! We'll pay him back – but ... but – I'm afraid – a little.'

The regent rose. 'Afraid? Of what? Of what, you young—' He choked off.

'It would be ... uh ... sort of blasphemous, you know, to attack the Foundation. I mean—' He paused.

'Go on.'

Lepold said confusedly: 'I mean, if there were *really* a Galactic Spirit, he ... uh ... it mightn't like it. Don't you think?'

'No, I don't,' was the hard answer. Wienis sat down again and his lips twisted in a queer smile. 'And so you really bother your head a great deal over the Galactic Spirit, do you? That's what comes of letting you run wild. You've been listening to Verisof quite a bit, I take it.'

'He's explained a great deal—'

'About the Galactic Spirit?'

'Yes.'

'Why, you unweaned cub, he believes in that mummery a good deal less than I do, and I don't believe in it at all. How many times have you been told that all this talk is nonsense?'

'Well, I know that. But Verisof says—'

'Damnation to Verisof. It's nonsense.'

There was a short, rebellious silence, and then Lepold said: 'Everyone believes it just the same. I mean all this talk about the Prophet Hari Seldon and how he appointed the Foundation to carry on his commandments that there might some day be a return to the Earthly Paradise: and how anyone who disobeys his commandments will be destroyed for eternity. They believe it. I've presided at festivals, and I'm sure they do.'

'Yes, *they* do; but we don't. And you may be thankful it's so, for according to this foolishness, you are king by divine right – and are semi-divine yourself. Very handy. It eliminates all possibilities of revolts and ensures absolute obedience in everything. And that is why, Lepold, you must take an active part in ordering the war against the Foundation. I am only regent, and quite human. You are king, and more than half a god – to them.'

'But I suppose I'm not really,' said the king, reflectively.

'No, not really,' came the ironic response, 'but you are to everyone but the people of the Foundation. Get that? To everyone but those of the Foundation. Once they are removed there will be no one to deny you the godhead. Think of that!'

'And after that we will ourselves be able to operate the power boxes of the temples and the ships that fly without men and the holy food that cures cancer and all the rest? Verisof said only those blessed with the Galactic Spirit could—'

'Yes, Verisof said! Verisof, next to Salvor Hardin, is your greatest enemy. Stay with me, Lepold, and don't worry about them. Together we will recreate an empire – not just the kingdoms of Anacreon – but one comprising every one of the billions of suns of the Galaxy. Is that better than a wordy

"Earthly Paradise"?'

'Ye-s.'

'Can Verisof promise more?'

'No.'

'Very well.' His voice became peremptory. 'I suppose we may consider the matter settled.' He waited for no answer. 'Get along. I'll be down later. And just one thing, Lepold.'

The young kind turned on the threshold.

Wienis was smiling with all but his eyes. 'Be careful on these Nyak hunts, my boy. Since the unfortunate accident to your father, I have had the strangest presentiments concerning you, at times. In the confusion, with needle guns thickening the air with darts, one can never tell. You *will* be careful, I hope. And you'll do as I say about the Foundation, won't you?'

Lepold's eyes widened and dropped away from those of his uncle. 'Yes – certainly.'

'Good!' He stared after his departing nephew, expressionlessly, and returned to his desk.

And Lepold's thoughts as he left were sombre and not unfearful. Perhaps it *would* be best to defeat the Foundation and gain the power Wienis spoke of. But afterward, when the war was over and he was secure on his throne— He became acutely conscious of the fact that Wienis and his two arrogant sons were at present next in line to the throne.

But he was king. And kings could order people shot.

Even uncles and cousins.

4

Next to Sermak himself, Lewis Bort was most active in rallying those dissident elements which had fused into the now-vociferous Action Party. Ye he had not been one of the deputation that had called on Salvor Hardin almost half a year previously. That this was so was not due to any lack of recognition of his efforts; quite the contrary. He was absent for the very good reason that he was on Anacreon's capital world at the time.

He visited it as a private citizen. He saw no official and he did nothing of importance. He merely watched the obscure corners of the busy planet and poked his stubby nose into dusty crannies.

He arrived home toward the end of a short winter day that had started with clouds and was finishing with snow, and within an hour was seated at the octagonal table in Sermak's home.

His first words were not calculated to improve the atmosphere of a gathering already considerably depressed by the deepening snow-filled twilight outside.

'I'm afraid,' he said, 'that our position is what is usually termed, in melodramatic phraseology, a "Lost Cause".'

'You think so?' said Sermak, gloomily.

'It's gone past thought, Sermak. There's no room for any other opinion.'

'Armaments –' began Dokor Walto, somewhat officiously, but Bort broke in at once.

'Forget that. That's an old story.' His eyes travelled round the circle. 'I'm referring to the people. I admit that it was my idea originally that we attempt to foster a palace rebellion of some sort to install as king someone more favourable to the Foundation. It was a good idea. It still is. The only trifling flaw about it is that it is impossible. The great Salvor Hardin saw to that.'

Sermak said sourly, 'If you'd give us the details, Bort—'

'Details! There aren't any! It isn't as simple as that. It's the whole damned situation on Anacreon. It's this religion the Foundation has established. It works!'

'Well!'

'You've got to *see* it work to appreciate it. All you see here is that we have a large school devoted to the training of priests, and that occasionally a special show is put on in some obscure corner of the city for the benefit of pilgrims – and that's all. The whole business hardly affects us as a general thing. But on Anacreon—'

Lem Tarki smoothed his prim little Vandyke with one finger, and cleared his throat. 'What kind of a religion is it? Hardin's always said that it was just a fluffy flummery to get them to accept our science without question. You remember, Sermak, he told us that day—'

'Hardin's explanations,' reminded Sermak, 'don't often mean much at face value. But what kind of a religion is it, Bort?'

Bort considered. 'Ethically, it's fine. It scarcely varies from the various philosophies of the old Empire. High moral standards and all that. There's nothing to complain about it from that viewpoint. Religion is one of the great civilizing influences of history and in that respect it's fulfilling—'

'We know that,' interrupted Sermak, impatiently. 'Get to the point.'

'Here it is.' Bort was a trifle disconcerted, but didn't show it. 'The religion – which the Foundation has fostered and encouraged, mind you – is built on strictly authoritarian lines. The priesthood has sole control of the instruments of science we have given Anacreon, but they've learned to handle these tools only empirically. They believe in this religion entirely, and in the ... uh ... spiritual value of the power they handle. For instance, two months ago some fool tampered with the power plant in the Thessalekian Temple – one of the large ones. He blew up five city blocks, of course. It was considered divine vengeance by everyone, including the priests.'

'I remember. The papers had some garbled version of the story at the time. I don't see what you're driving at.'

'Then, listen,' said Bort, stiffly. 'The priesthood forms a hierarchy at the apex of which is the king, who is regarded as a sort of minor god. He's an absolute monarch by divine right, and the people believe it, thoroughly, and the priests, too. You can't overthrow a king like that. *Now* do you get the point?'

'Hold on,' said Walto, at this point. 'What did you mean when you said Hardin's done all this? How does he come in?'

Bort glanced at his questioner bitterly. 'The Foundation has fostered this delusion assiduously. We've put all our scientific backing behind the hoax. There isn't a festival at which the king does not preside surrounded by a radioactive aura shining forth all over his body and raising itself like a coronet above his head. Anyone touching him is severely burned. He can move from place to place through the air at crucial moments, supposedly by inspiration of divine spirit. He fills the temple with a pearly, internal light at a gesture. There is no end to these quite simple tricks that we perform for his benefit; but even the priests believe them, while working them personally.'

'Bad!' said Sermak, biting his lip.

'I could cry – like the fountain in City Hall Park,' said Bort, earnestly, 'when I think of the chance we muffed. Take the situation thirty years ago, when Hardin saved the Foundation from Anacreon. At that time, the Anacreonian people had no real conception of the fact that the Empire was running down. They had been more or less running their own affairs since the Zeonian revolt, but even after communications broke down and the Lepold's pirate of a grandfather made himself king, they never quite realized that the Empire had gone *kaput*.

'If the Emperor had had the nerve to try, he could have taken over again with two cruisers and with the help of the internal revolt that would have certainly sprung to life. And we, *we* could have done the same; but no, Hardin established monarch worship. Personally, I don't understand it. Why? Why? Why?'

'What,' demanded Jaim Orsy, suddenly, 'does Verisof do? There was a day when he was an advanced Actionist. What's he doing there? Is he blind, too?'

'I don't know,' said Bort, curtly. 'He's high priest to them. As far as I know, he does nothing but act as adviser to the priesthood on technical details. Figurehead, blast him, figurehead!'

There was silence all around and all eyes turned to Sermak.

The younger party leader was biting a fingernail nervously, and then said loudly, 'No good. It's fishy!'

He looked around him, and added more energetically. 'Is Hardin then such a fool?'

'Seems to be,' shrugged Bort.

'Never! There's something wrong. To cut our own throats so thoroughly and so hopelessly would require colossal stupidity. More than Hardin could possibly have even if he were a fool, which I deny. On the other hand, to establish a religion that would wipe out all chance of internal troubles. On the other hand, to arm Anacreon with all weapons of warfare. I don't see it.'

'The matter *is* a little obscure, I admit,' said Bort, 'but the facts are there. What else can we think?'

Waldo said, jerkily, 'Outright treason. He's in their pay.'

But Sermak shook his head impatiently. 'I don't see that, either. The whole affair is as insane and meaningless— Tell me, Bort, have you heard anything about a battle cruiser that the Foundation is supposed to have put into shape for use in the Anacreon navy?'

'Battle cruiser?'

'An old Imperial cruiser—'

'No, I haven't. But that doesn't mean much. The navy yards are religious sanctuaries completely inviolate on the part of the lay public. No one ever hears anything about the fleet.'

'Well, rumours have leaked out. Some of the Party have brought the matter up in Council. Hardin never denied it, you know. His spokesman denounced rumour-mongers and let it go at that. I might have significance.'

'It's of a piece with the rest,' said Bort. 'If true, it's absolutely crazy. But it wouldn't be worse than the rest.'

'I suppose,' said Orsy, 'Hardin hasn't any secret weapon waiting. That might—'

'Yes,' said Sermak, viciously, 'a huge Jack-in-the-box that will jump out at the psychological moment and scare old Wienis into fits. The Foundation may as well blow itself out of existence and save itself the agony of suspense if it has to depend on any secret weapon.'

'Well,' said Orsy, changing the subject hurriedly, 'the question comes down to this: How much time have we left? Eh, Bort?'

'All right. It is the question. But don't look at me; I don't know. The Anacreonian press never mentions the Foundation at all. Right now, it's full of the approaching celebrations and nothing else. Lepold is coming of age next week, you know.'

'We have months then.' Walto smiled for the first time that evening. 'That gives us time—'

'That gives us time, my foot,' ground out Bort, impatiently. 'The king's a god, I tell you. Do you suppose he has to carry on a campaign of propaganda to get his people into fighting spirit? Do you suppose he has to accuse us of aggression and pull out all stops on cheap emotionalism? When the time comes to strike, Lepold gives the order and the people fight. Just like that. That's the damnedness of the system. You don't question a god. He may give the order tomorrow for all I know; and you can wrap tobacco round that and smoke it.'

Everyone tried at once and Sermak was slamming the table for silence, when the front door opened and Levi Norast stamped in. He bounded up the stairs, overcoat on, trailing snow.

'Look at that!' he cried, tossing a cold, snow-speckled newspaper on the table. 'The visicasters are full of it, too.'

The newspaper was unfolded and five heads bent over it.

Sermak said, in a hushed voice, 'Great Space, he's going to Anacreon! *Going to Anacreon!*'

'It *is* treason,' squeaked Tarki, in sudden excitement. 'I'll be damned if Walto isn't right. He's sold us out and now he's going there to collect his wage.'

Sermak had risen. 'We've no choice now. I'm going to ask the Council tomorrow that Hardin be impeached. And if *that* fails—'

5

The snow had ceased, but it caked the ground deeply now and the sleek ground car advanced through the deserted streets with lumbering effort. The murky grey light of incipient dawn was cold not only in the poetical sense but also in a very literal way – and even in the then turbulent state of the Foundation's politics, no one, whether Actionist or pro-Hardin found his spirits sufficiently ardent to begin street activity that early.

Yohan Lee did not like that and his grumblings grew audible. 'It's going to look bad, Hardin. They're going to say you sneaked away.'

'Let them say it if they wish. I've got to get to Anacreon and I want to do it without trouble. Now that's enough, Lee.'

Hardin leaned back into the cushioned seat and shivered slightly. It wasn't cold inside the well-heated car, but there was something frigid about a snow-covered world, even through glass, that annoyed him.

He said, reflectively, 'Some day when we get around to it we ought to weather-condition Terminus. It could be done.'

'I,' replied Lee, 'would like to see a few other things done first. For instance, what about weather-conditioning Sermak? A nice, dry cell fitted for twenty-five centigrade all year round would be just right.'

'And then I'd really *need* bodyguards,' said Hardin, 'and not just those two.' He indicated two of Lee's bully-boys sitting up front with the driver, hard eyes on the empty streets, ready hands at their atom blasts. 'You evidently want to stir up civil war.'

'*I* do? There are other sticks in the fire and it won't require much stirring, I can tell you.' He counted off on blunt fingers, 'One: Sermak raised hell yesterday in the City Council and called for an impeachment.'

'He had a perfect right to do so,' responded Hardin, coolly. 'Besides which, his motion was defeated 206 to 184.'

'Certainly. A majority of twenty-two when we had counted on sixty as a minimum. Don't deny it; you know you did.'

'It was close,' admitted Hardin.

'All right. And two: After the vote, the fifty-nine members of the Actionist Party reared upon their hind legs and stamped out of the council Chambers.'

Hardin was silent, and Lee continued, 'And three: Before leaving, Sermak howled that you were a traitor, that you were going to Anacreon to collect your thirty pieces of silver, that the Chamber majority in refusing to vote impeachment had participated in the treason, and that the name of their party was not 'Actionist' for nothing. What does *that* sound like?'

'Trouble, I suppose.'

'And now you're chasing off at daybreak, like a criminal. You ought to face them, Hardin - and if you have to, declare martial law, by space!'

'Violence is the last refuge—'

'- of the incompetent. Nuts!'

'All right. We'll see. Now listen to me carefully, Lee. Thirty years ago, the Time Vault opened, and on the fiftieth anniversary of the beginning of the Foundation, there appeared a Hari Seldon recording to give us our first idea of what was really going on.'

'I remember,' Lee nodded reminiscently, with a half smile. 'It was the day we took over the government.'

'That's right. It was the first of our first major crisis. This is our second - and three weeks from date will be the eightieth anniversary of the beginning of the Foundation. Does that strike you as in any way significant?'

'You mean he's coming again?'

'I'm not finished. Seldon never said anything about returning, you understand, but that's of a piece with his whole plan. He's always done his best to keep all foreknowledge from us. Nor is there any way of telling whether the radium lock is set for further openings short of dismantling the Vault - and it's probably set to destroy itself if we were to try that. I've been there every anniversary since the first appearance, just on the chance. He's never shown up, but this is the first time since then that there's really been a crisis.'

'Then he'll come.'

'Maybe. I don't know. However, this is the point. At today's session of the Council, just after you announce that I have left for Anacreon, you will further announce, officially, that on March 14th next, there will be another Hari Seldon recording, containing a message of the utmost importance regarding the recent successfully concluded crisis. That's very important, Lee. Don't add anything more no matter how many questions are asked.'

Lee stared. 'Will they believe it?'

'That doesn't matter. It will confuse them, which is all I want. Between wondering whether it is true and what I mean by it if it isn't – they'll decide to postpone action till after March 14th. I'll be back considerably before then.'

Lee looked uncertain. 'But that 'successfully concluded'. That's bull!'

'Highly confusing bull. Here's the airport!'

The waiting space-ship bulked sombrely in the dimness. Hardin stamped through the snow toward it and at the open air lock turned about with outstretched hand.

'Good-bye, Lee. I hate to leave you in the frying-pan like this, but there's not another I can trust. Now please keep out of the fire.'

'Don't worry. The frying-pan is hot enough. I'll follow orders.' He stepped back, and the air lock closed.

6

Salvor Hardin did not travel to the planet Anacreon – from which planet the kingdom derived its name – immediately. It was only on the day before the coronation that he arrived, after having made flying visits to eight of the larger stellar systems of the kingdom, stopping only long enough to confer with the local representatives of the Foundation.

The trip left him with an oppressive realization of the vastness of the kingdom. It was a little splinter, an insignificant fly speck compared to the inconceivable reaches of the Galactic Empire of which it had once formed so distinguished a part; but to one whose habits of thought had been built around a single planet, and a sparsely settled one at that, Anacreon's size in area and population was staggering.

Following closely the boundaries of the old Prefect of Anacreon, it embraced twenty-five stellar systems, six of which included more than one habitable world. The population of nineteen billion, though still far less than it had been in the Empire's heyday, was rising rapidly with the increasing scientific development fostered by the Foundation.

And it was only now that Hardin found himself floored by the magnitude of *that* task. Even in thirty years, only the capital world had been powered. The outer provinces still possessed immense stretches where atomic power had not yet been re-introduced. Even the progress that had been made might have been impossible had it not been for the still workable relics left over by the ebbing tide of Empire.

When Hardin did arrive at the capital world, it was to find all normal business at an absolute standstill. In the outer provinces there had been and still were celebrations; but here on the planet Anacreon, not a person but took feverish part in the hectic religious pageantry that heralded the coming-of-age of their god-king, Lepold.

Hardin had been able to snatch only half an hour from a haggard and harried Verisof before his ambassador was forced to rush off to supervise still another temple festival. But the half-hour was a most profitable one, and Hardin prepared himself for the night's fireworks well satisfied.

In all, he acted as an observer, for he had no stomach for the religious tasks he would undoubtedly have had to undertake if his identity became known. So, when the palace's ballroom filled itself with a glittering horde of the kingdom's very highest and most exalted nobility, he found himself hugging the wall, little noticed or totally ignored.

He had been introduced to Lepold as one of a long line of introducees, and from a safe distance, for the king stood apart in lonely and impressive grandeur, surrounded by his deadly blaze of radioactive aura. And in less than an hour this same king would take his seat upon the massive throne of rhodiumriridium alloy with jewel-set gold chasings, and then, throne and all would rise majestically into the air, skim the ground slowly to hover before the great window from which the great crowds of common folk could see their king and shout themselves into near apoplexy. The throne would not have been so massive, of course, if it had not had an atomic motor built into it.

It was past eleven. Hardin fidgeted and stood on his toes to better his view. He resisted an impulse to stand on a chair. And then he saw Wienis threading through the crowd toward him and he relaxed.

Wienis' progress was slow. At almost every step, he had to pass a kindly sentence with some revered noble whose grandfather had helped Lepold's grandfather brigandize the kingdom and had received a dukedom therefore.

And then he disentangled himself from the last uniformed peer and reached Hardin. His smile crooked itself into a smirk and his black eyes peered from under grizzled brows with glints of satisfactio ı in them.

'My dear Hardin,' he said, in a low voice, 'you must expect to be bored, when you refuse to announce your identity.'

'I am not bored, your highness. This is all extremely interesting. We have no comparable spectacles on Terminus, you know.'

'No doubt. But would you care to step into my private chambers, where we can speak at greater length and with considerably more privacy?'

'Certainly.'

With arms linked, the two ascended the staircase, and more than one dowager duchess raised her lorgnette in surprise and wonder at the identity of this insignificantly dressed and uninteresting-looking stranger on whom such signal honour was being conferred by the prince regent.

In Wienis' chambers, Hardin relaxed in perfect comfort and accepted with a murmur of gratitude the glass of liquor that had been poured out by the regent's own hand.

'Locris wine, Hardin,' said Wienis, 'from the royal cellars. The real thing – two centuries in age. It was laid down ten years before the Zeonian Rebellion.'

'A really royal drink,' agreed Hardin, politely. 'To Lepold I, King of Anacreon.'

They drank, and Wienis added blandly, at the pause, 'And soon to be Emperor of the Periphery, and further, who knows? The Galaxy may be some day reunited.'

'Undoubtedly. By Anacreon?'

'Why not? With the help of the Foundation, our scientific superiority over the rest of the Periphery would be indisputable.'

Hardin set his empty glass down and said, 'Well, yes, except that, of course, the Foundation is bound to help any nation that requests scientific aid to it. Due to the high idealism of our government and the great moral purpose of our founder, Hari Seldon, we are unable to play favourites. That can't be helped, your highness.'

Wienis' smile broadened. 'The Galactic Spirit, to use the

popular cant, helps those who helps themselves. I quite understand that, left to itself, the Foundation would never co-operate.'

'I wouldn't say that. We repaired the Imperial cruiser for you, though my board of navigation wished it for themselves for research purposes.'

The regent repeated the last words ironically. 'Research purposes! Yes! Yet you would not have repaired it, had I not threatened war.'

Hardin made a deprecatory gesture. 'I don't know.'

'*I* do. And that threat always stood.'

'And still stands now?'

'Now it is rather too late to speak of threats.' Wienis had cast a rapid glance at the clock on his desk. 'Look here, Hardin, you were on Anacreon once before. You were young then; we were both young. But even then we had entirely different ways of looking at things. You're what they call a man of peace, aren't you?'

'I suppose I am. At least, I consider violence an uneconomical way of attaining an end. There are always better substitutes, though they may sometimes be a little less direct.'

'Yes. I've heard of your famous remark: "Violence is the last refuge of the incompetent." And yet' – the regent scratched one ear gently in affected abstraction— 'I wouldn't call myself exactly incompetent.'

Hardin nodded politely and said nothing.

'And in spite of that,' Wienis continued, 'I have always believed in direct action. I have believed in carving a straight path to my objective and following that path. I have accomplished much that way, and fully expect to accomplish still more.'

'I know,' interrupted Hardin. 'I believe you are carving a path such as you describe for yourself and your children that leads directly to the throne, considering the late unfortunate death of the king's father – your elder brother – and the king's own precarious state of health. He *is* in a precarious state of health, is he not?'

Wienis frowned at the shot, and his voice grew harder. 'You might find it advisable, Hardin, to avoid certain subjects. You may consider yourself privileged as mayor of Terminus to make ... uh ... injudicious remarks, but if you do, please disabuse yourself of the notion. I am not one to be frightened at words. It has been my philosophy of life that difficulties vanish when faced boldy, and I have never turned my back upon one yet.'

'I don't doubt that. What particular difficulty are you refusing to turn your back upon at the present moment?'

'The difficulty, Hardin, of persuading the Foundation to co-operate. Your policy of peace, you see, has led you into making several very serious mistakes, simply because you underestimated the boldness of your adversary. Not everyone is as afraid of direct action as you are.'

'For instance?' suggested Hardin.

'For instance, you came to Anacreon alone and accompanied me to my chambers alone.'

Hardin looked about him. 'And what is wrong with that?'

'Nothing,' said the regent, 'except that outside this room are five police guards, well armed and ready to shoot. I don't think you can leave, Hardin.'

The mayor's eyebrows lifted. 'I have no immediate desire to leave. Do you then fear me so much?'

'I don't fear you at all. But this may serve to impress you with my determination. Shall we call it a gesture?'

'Call it what you please,' said Hardin, indifferently. 'I shall not discommode myself over the incident, whatever you choose to call it.'

'I'm sure that attitude will change with time. But you have made another error, Hardin, a more serious one. It seems that the planet Terminus is almost wholly undefended.'

'Naturally. What have we to fear? We threaten no one's interest and serve all alike.'

'And while remaining helpless,' Wienis went on, 'you kindly helped us to arm ourselves, aiding us particularly in the development of a navy of our own, a great navy. In fact, a navy which, since your donation of the Imperial cruiser, is quite irresistible.'

'Your highness, you are wasting time.' Hardin made as if to rise from his seat. 'If you mean to declare war, and are informing me of the fact, you will allow me to communicate with my government at once.'

'Sit down, Hardin. I am not declaring war, and you are not communicating with your government at all. When the war is fought – not declared, Hardin, *fought* – the Foundation will be informed of it in due time by the atom blasts of the Anacreonian navy under the lead of my own son upon the flagship *Wienis*, once a cruiser of the Imperial navy.'

Hardin frowned. 'When will all this happen?'

'If you're really interested, the ships of the fleet left Anacreaon exactly fifty minutes ago, at eleven, and the first shot will be fired as soon as they sight Terminus, which should be at noon tomorrow. You may consider yourself a prisoner of war.'

'That's exactly what I do consider myself, your highness,' said Hardin, still frowning. 'But I'm disappointed.'

Wienis chuckled contemptuously. 'Is that all?'

'Yes. I had thought that the moment of coronation – midnight, you know – would be the logical time to set the fleet in motion. Evidently, you wanted to start the war while you were still regent. It would have been more dramatic the other way.'

The regent stared. 'What in Space are you talking about?'

'Don't you understand?' said Hardin, softly. 'I had set my counterstroke for midnight.'

Wienis started from his chair. 'You are not bluffing me. There is no counterstroke. If you are counting on the support of the other kingdoms, forget it. Their navies, combined, are no match for ours.'

'I know that. I don't intend firing a shot. It is simply that the word went out a week ago that at midnight tonight, the planet Anacreon goes under the interdict.'

'The interdict?'

'Yes. If you don't understand, I might explain that every priest in Anacreon is going on strike, unless I countermand the order. But I can't while I'm being held incommunicado; nor do I wish to even if I weren't!' He leaned forward and added, with sudden animation, 'Do you realize, your highness, that an attack on the Foundation is nothing short of sacrilege of the highest order?'

Wienis was groping visibly for self-control. 'Give me none of that, Hardin. Save it for the mob.'

'My dear Wienis, whoever do you think I *am* saving it for? I imagine that for the last half-hour every temple on Anacreon has been the centre of a mob listening to a priest exhorting them upon that very subject. There's not a man or woman on Anacreon that doesn't know that their government has launched a vicious, unprovoked attack upon the centre of their religion. But it lacks only four minutes of midnight now. You'd better go down to the ballroom to watch events. I'll be safe here with five guards outside the door.' He leaned back in his chair, helped himself to another glass of Locris wine, and gazed at the ceiling with perfect indifference.

Wienis blistered the air with a muffled oath and rushed out of the room.

A hush had fallen over the *élite* in the ballroom, as a broad path was cleared for the throne. Lepold sat on it now, hands solidly on its arms, head high, face frozen. The huge chandeliers had dimmed and in the diffused multicoloured light from the tiny Atomo bulbs that bespangled the vaulted ceiling, the royal aura shone out bravely, lifting high above his head to form a blazing coronet.

Wienis paused on the stairway. No one saw him; all eyes were on the throne. He clenched his fists and remained where he was; Hardin would *not* bluff him into silly action.

And then the throne stirred. Noiselessly, it lifted upward – and drifted. Off the dais, slowly down the steps, and then horizontally, six inches off the floor, it worked itself toward the huge, open window.

At the sound of the deep-toned bell that signified midnight, it stopped before the window – and the king's aura died.

For a frozen second, the king did not move, face twisted in surprise, without an aura, merely human; and then the throne wobbled and fell six inches to the floor with a crashing thump, just as every light in the palace went out.

Through the shrieking din and confusion, Wienis' bull voice sounded. 'Get the flares! Get the flares!'

He buffeted right and left through the crowd and forced his way to the door. From without, palace guards had streamed into the darkness.

Somehow the flares were brought back to the ballroom; flares that were to have been used in the gigantic torchlight procession through the streets of the city after the coronation.

Back to the ballroom guardsmen swarmed with torches – blue, green, and red; where the strange light lit up frightened, confused faces.

'There is no harm done,' shouted Wienis. 'Keep your places. Power will return in a moment.'

He turned to the captain of the guard who stood stiffly at attention. 'What is it, Captain?'

'Your highness,' was the instant response, 'the palace is surrounded by the people of the city.'

'What do they want?' snarled Weinis.

'A priest is at the head. He has been identified as High Priest Poly Verisof. He demands the immediate release of Mayor Salvor Hardin and cessation of the war against the Foundation.' The report was made in the expressionless tones of an officer, but his eyes shifted uneasily.

Wienis cried, 'If any of the rabble attempt to pass the palace gates, blast them out of existence. For the moment, nothing more. Let them howl! There will be an accounting tomorrow.'

The torches had been distributed now, and the ballroom was again alight. Wienis rushed to the throne, still standing by the window, and dragged the stricken, wax-faced Lepold to his feet.

'Come with me.' He cast one look out of the window. The

city was pitch-black. From below there were the hoarse confused cries of the mob. Only toward the right, where the Argolid Temple stood, was there illumination. He swore angrily and dragged the king away.

Wienis burst into his chambers, the five guardsmen at his heels. Lepold followed, wide-eyed, scared speechless.

'Hardin,' said Wienis, huskily, 'you are playing with forces too great for you.'

The mayor ignored the speaker. In the pearly light of the pocket Atomo bulb at his side, he remained seated, a slightly ironic smile on his face.

'Good morning, your majesty,' he said to Lepold. 'I congratulate you on your coronation.'

'Hardin,' cried Wienis again, 'order your priests back to their jobs.'

Hardin looked up coolly. 'Order them yourself, Wienis, and see who is playing with forces too great for whom. Right now, there's not a wheel turning in Anacreon. There's not a light burning, except in the temples. There's not a drop of water running, except in the temples. On the wintry half of the planet, there's not a calorie of heat, except in the temples. The hospitals are taking in no more patients. The power plants have shut down. All ships are grounded. If you don't like it, Wienis, *you* can order the priests back to their jobs. *I* don't wish to.'

'By Space, Hardin, I will. If it's to be a showdown, so be it. We'll see if your priests can withstand the army. Tonight, every temple on the planet will be put under army supervision.'

'Very good, but how are you going to give the orders? Every line of communication on the planet is shut down. You'll find that radio won't work and the televisors won't work and the ultrawave won't work. In fact, the only communicator of the planet that will work – outside of the temples, of course – is the televisor right here in this room, and I've fitted it only for reception.'

Wienis struggled vainly for breath, and Hardin continued, 'If you wish you can order your army into the Argolid Temple just outside the palace and then use the ultrawave sets there to contact other portions of the planet. But if you do that, I'm afraid the army contingent will be cut to pieces by the mob, and then what will protect your palace, Wienis? And your *lives*, Wienis?'

Wienis said thickly, 'We can hold out, devil. We'll last the day. Let the mob howl and let the power die, but we'll hold out. And when the news comes back that the Foundation has been taken, your precious mob will find what vacuum their religion has been built, and they'll desert your priests and turn against them. I give you until noon tomorrow, Hardin, because you can stop the power on Anacreon but *you can't stop my fleet.*' His voice croaked exultantly. 'They're on their way, Hardin, with the great cruiser you yourself ordered repaired, at the head.'

Hardin replied lightly. 'Yes, the cruiser I myself ordered repaired – but in my own way. Tell me, Wienis, have you ever heard of an ultrawave relay? No, I see you haven't. Well, in about two minutes you'll find out what one can do.'

The televisor flashed to life as he spoke, and he amended, 'No, in two seconds. Sit down, Wienis, and listen.'

7

Theo Aporat was one of the very highest ranking priests of Anacreon. From the standpoint of precedence alone, he deserved his appointment as head priest – attendant upon the flagship *Wienis*.

But it was not only rank or precedence. He knew the ship. He had worked directly under the holy men from the Foundation itself in repairing the ship. He had gone over the motors under their orders. He had rewired the 'visors; revamped the communications system; replated the punctured hull; reinforced the beams. He had even been permitted to help while the wise men of the Foundation had installed a device so holy it had never been placed in any previous ship, but had been reserved only for this magnificent colossus of a vessel – the ultrawave relay.

It was no wonder that he felt heartsick over the purposes to which the glorious ship was perverted. He had never wanted to believe what Verisof had told him – that the ship was to be used for appalling wickedness; that its guns were to be turned on the great Foundation. Turned on that Foundation, where he had been trained as a youth, from which all blessedness was derived.

Yet he could not doubt now, after what the admiral had told him.

How could the kind, divinely blessed, allow this abominable act? Or was it the king? Was it not, perhaps, an action of the accursed regent, Wienis, without the knowledge of the king at all? And it was the son of this same Wienis that was the admiral who five minutes before had told him:

'Attend to your souls and your blessings, priest. *I* will attend to my ship.'

Aporat smiled crookedly. He would attend to his souls and his blessings – and also to his cursings; and Prince Lefkin would whine soon enough.

He had entered the general communications room now. His acolyte preceded him and the two officers in charge made no move to interfere. The head priest-attendant had the right of free entry anywhere on the ship.

'Close the door,' Aporat ordered, and looked at the chronometer. It lacked five minutes of twelve. He had timed it well.

With quick practised motions, he moved the little levers that opened all communications, so that every part of the two-mile-long ship was within reach of his voice and his image.

'Soldiers of the royal flagship *Wienis*, attend! It is your priest-attendant that speaks!' The sound of his voice reverberated, he knew, from the stern atom blast in the extreme rear to the navigation tables in the prow.

'Your ship,' he cried, 'is engaged in sacrilege. Without your knowledge, it is performing such an act as will doom the soul of every man among you to the eternal frigidity of space! Listen! It is the intention of your commander to take this ship to the Foundation and there to bombard that source of all blessings into submission to his sinful will. And since that is his intention, I, in the name of the Galactic Spirit, remove him from his command, for there is no command where the blessing of the Galactic Spirit has been withdrawn. The divine king himself may not maintain his kingship without the consent of the Spirit.'

His voice took on a deeper tone, while the acolyte listened with veneration and the two soldiers with mounting fear. 'And because this ship is upon such a devil's errand, the blessing of the Spirit is removed from it as well.'

He lifted his arms solemnly, and before a thousand televisors throughout the ship, soldiers cowered, as the stately image of their priest-attendant spoke:

'In the name of the Galactic Spirit and of his prophet, Hari Seldon, and of his interpreters, the holy men of the Foundation, I curse this ship. Let the televisors of this ship, which are its eyes, become blind. Let its grapples, which are its arms, be paralysed. Let the atom blasts, which are its fists, lose their function. Let the motors, which are its heart, cease to beat. Let the communications, which are its voice, become dumb. Let its ventilations, which are its breath, fade. Let its lights, which are its soul, shrivel into nothing. In the name of the Galactic Spirit, I so curse this ship.'

And with his last word, at the stroke of midnight, a hand light-years distant in the Argolid Temple, opened an ultrawave relay, which at the instantaneous speed of the ultrawave, opened another on the flagship *Wienis*.

And the ship died!

For it is the chief characteristic of the religion of science, that it works, and that such curses as that of Aporat's are really deadly.

Aporat saw the darkness close down on the ship and heard the sudden ceasing of the soft, distant purring of the hyperatomic motors. He exulted and from the pocket of his long robe withdrew a self-powered Atomo bulb that filled the room with pearly light.

He looked down at the two soldiers, who, brave men though they undoubtedly were, writhed on their knees in the last extremity of mortal terror. 'Save our souls, your reverence. We are poor men, ignorant of the crimes of our leaders,' one whimpered.

'Follow,' said Aporat, sternly. 'Your soul is not yet lost.'

The ship was a turmoil of darkness in which fear was so thick and palpable, it was all but a miasmic smell. Soldiers crowded close wherever Aporat and his circle of light passed, striving to touch the hem of his robe, pleading for the tiniest scrap of mercy.

And always his answer was, 'Follow me!'

He found Prince Lefkin, groping his way through the officers' quarters, cursing loudly for lights. The admiral stared at the priest-attendant with hating eyes.

'There you are!' Lefkin inherited his blue eyes from his mother, but there was that about the hook in his nose and the squint in his eye that marked him as the son of Wienis. 'What is the meaning of your treasonable actions? Return the power to the ship. I am commander here.'

'No longer,' said Aporat, sombrely.

Lefkin looked about wildly. 'Seize that man. Arrest him, or by Space, I will send every man within reach of my voice out the air lock in the nude.' He paused, and then shrieked, 'It is your admiral that orders. Arrest him.'

Then, as he lost his head entirely, 'Are you allowing yourselves to be fooled by this mountebank, this harlequin? Do you cringe before a religion compounded of clouds and moonbeams? This man is an imposter and the Galactic Spirit he speaks of a fraud of the imagination devised to—'

Aporat interrupted furiously. 'Seize the blasphemer. You listen to him at the peril of your souls.'

And promptly, the noble admiral went down under the clutching hands of a score of soldiers.

'Take him with you and follow me.'

Aporat turned, and with Lefkin dragged along after him, and the corridors behind black with soldiery, he returned to the communications room. There, he ordered the ex-commander before the one televisor that worked.

'Order the rest of the fleet to cease course and to prepare for the return to Anacreon.'

The dishevelled Lefkin, bleeding, beaten, and half stunned, did so.

'And now,' continued Aporat, grimly, 'we are in contact with Anacreon on the ultrawave beam. Speak as I order you.'

Lefkin made a gesture of negation, and the mob in the room and the others crowding the corridor beyond, growled fearfully.

'Speak!' said Aporat. 'Begin: The Anacreonian navy—'

Lefkin began.

8

There was absolute silence in Wienis' chambers when the image of Prince Lefkin appeared at the televisor. There had been one startled gasp from the regent at the haggard face and shredded uniform of his son, and then he collapsed into a chair, face contorted with surprise and apprehension.

Hardin listened stolidly, hands clasped lightly in his lap, while the just-crowned King Lepold sat shrivelled in the most shadowy corner, biting spasmodically at his gold-braided sleeve. Even the soldiers had lost the emotionless stare that is the prerogative of the military, and from where they lined up against the door, atom blasts ready, peered furtively at the figure upon the televisor.

Lefkin spoke, reluctantly, with a tired voice that paused at intervals as though he were being prompted – and not gently:

'The Anacreonian navy ... aware of the nature of its mission ... and refusing to be a party ... to abominable sacrilege ... is returning to Anacreon ... with the following ultimatum issued ... to those blaspheming sinners ... who would dare to use profane force ... against the Foundation ... source of all blessings ... and against the Galactic Spirit. Cease at once all war against ... the true faith ... and guarantee in a manner suiting us of the navy ... as represented by our ... priest-attendant, Theo Aporat ... that such war will never in the future ... be resumed, and that' – here a long pause, and then continuing— 'and that the one-time prince regent, Wienis ... be imprisoned ... and tried before an ecclesiastical court ... for his crimes. Otherwise the royal navy ... upon returning to Anacreon ... will blast the palace to the ground ... and take whatever other measures ... are necessary ... to destroy the nest of sinners ... and the den of destroyers ... of men's souls that now prevail.'

The voice ended with half a sob and the screen went blank.

Hardin's fingers passed rapidly over the Atomo bulb and its light faded until in the dimness, the hitherto regent, the king, and the soldiers were hazy, edged shadows; and for the first time it could be seen that an aura encompassed Hardin.

It was not the blazing light that was the prerogative of kings, but one less spectacular, less impressive, and yet one more effective in its own way, and more useful.

Hardin's voice was softly ironic, as he addressed the same Wienis who had one hour earlier declared him a prisoner of war and Terminus on the point of destruction, and who now was a huddled shadow, broken and silent.

'There is an old fable,' said Hardin, 'as old perhaps as humanity, for the oldest records containing it are merely copies of other records still older, that might interest you. It runs as follows:

'A horse having a wolf as a powerful and dangerous enemy

lived in constant fear of his life. Being driven to desperation, it occurred to him to seek a strong ally. Whereupon he approached a man, and offered an alliance, pointing out that the wolf was likewise an enemy of the man. The man accepted the partnership at once and offered to kill the wolf immediately, if his new partner would only co-operate by placing his greater speed at the man's disposal. The horse was willing, and allowed the man to place bridle and saddle upon him. The man mounted, hunted down the wolf, and killed him.

'The horse, joyful and relieved, thanked the man, and said: "Now that our enemy is dead, remove your bridle and saddle and restore my freedom."

'Whereupon the man laughed loudly and replied, "The hell you say. Giddy-ap, Dobbin," and applied the spurs with a will.'

Silence still. The shadow that was Wienis did not stir.

Hardin continued quietly, 'You see the analogy, I hope. In their anxiety to cement for ever total domination over their own people, the kings of the Four Kingdoms accepted the religion of science that made them divine; and that same religion of science was their bridle and saddle, for it placed the life blood of atomic power in the hands of the priesthood – who took their orders from us, be it noted, and not from you. You killed the wolf, but could not get rid of them—'

Wienis sprang to his feet, and in the shadows his eyes were maddened hollows. His voice was thick, incoherent. 'And yet I'll get you. You won't escape. You'll rot! Let them blow us up. Let them blow everything up. You'll rot! I'll get you!

'Soldiers!' he thundered, hysterically. 'Shoot me down that devil. Blast him! Blast him!'

Hardin turned about in his chair to face the soldiers and smiled. One aimed his atom blast and then lowered it. The others never budged. Salvor Hardin, mayor of Terminus, surrounded by that soft aura, smiling so confidently, and before whom all the power of Anacreon had crumbled to powder was too much for them, despite the orders of the shrieking maniac just beyond.

Wienis screamed a curse and staggered to the nearest soldier. Wildly, he wrested the atom blast from the man's hand – aimed it at Hardin, who didn't stir, shoved the lever and held it contacted.

The pale continuous beam impinged upon the force-field that surrounded the mayor of Terminus and was sucked harmlessly to neutralization. Wienis pressed harder and laughed tearingly.

Hardin still smiled and his force-field aura scarcely brightened as it absorbed the energies of the atom blast. From his corner Lepold covered his eyes and moaned.

And, with a yell of despair, Wienis changed his aim and shot again – and toppled to the floor with his head blown into nothingness.

Hardin winced at the sight and muttered, 'A man of "direct action" to the end. The last refuge!'

9

The Time Vault was filled; filled far beyond the available seating capacity, and men lined the back of the room, three deep.

Salvor Hardin compared this large company with the few men attending the first appearance of Hari Seldon, thirty years earlier. There had only been six, then; the five old Encyclopedists – all dead now – and himself, the young figurehead of a mayor. It had been on that day, that he, with Yohan Lee's assistance, had removed the 'figurehead' stigma from his office.

It was quite different now; different in every respect. Every man of the City Council was awaiting Seldon's appearance. He, himself, was still mayor, but all-powerful now; and since the utter rout of Anacreon, all-popular. When he had returned from Anacreon with the news of the death of Wienis, and the new treaty signed with the trembling Lepold, he was greeted with a vote of confidence of shrieking unanimity. When this was followed in rapid order, by similar treaties signed with each of the other three kingdoms - treaties that gave the Foundation powers such as would for ever prevent any attempts at attack similar to that of Anacreon's - torchlight processions had been held in every city street of Terminus. Not even Hari Seldon's name had been more loudly cheered.

Hardin's lips twitched. Such popularity had been his after the first crisis also.

Across the room, Sef Sermak and Lewis Bort were engaged in animated discussion, and recent events seemed to have put them out not at all. They had joined in the vote of confidence; made speeches in which they publicly admitted that they had been in the wrong, apologized handsomely for the use of certain phrases in earlier debates, excused themselves delicately by declaring they had merely followed the dictates of their judgement and their conscience - and immediately launched a new Actionist campaign.

Yohan Lee touched Hardin's sleeve and pointed significantly to his watch.

Hardin looked up. 'Hello there, Lee. Are you still sour? What's wrong now?'

'He's due in five minutes, isn't he?'

'I presume so. He appeared at noon last time.'

'What if he doesn't?'

'Are you going to wear me down with your worries all your life? If he doesn't, he won't.'

Lee frowned and shook his head slowly. 'If this thing flops, we're in another mess. Without Seldon's backing for what we've done, Sermak will be free to start all over. He wants outright annexation of the Four Kingdoms, and immediate expansion of the Foundation - by force, if necessary. He's begun his campaign , already.'

'I know. A fire-eater must eat fire even if he has to kindle it himself. And you, Lee, have got to worry even if you must kill yourself to invent something to worry about.'

Lee would have answered, but he lost his breath at just that moment – as the lights yellowed and went dim. He raised his arm to point to the glass cubicle that dominated half the room and then collapsed into a chair with a windy sigh.

Hardin himself straightened at the sight of the figure that now filled the cubicle – a figure in a wheel-chair! He alone of all those present could remember the day, decades ago, when that figure had appeared first. He had been young then, and the figure old. Since then, the figure had not aged a day, but he himself had in turn grown old.

The figure stared straight ahead, hands fingering a book in its lap.

It said, 'I am Hari Seldon!' The voice was old and soft.

There was a breathless silence in the room and Hari Seldon continued conversationally, 'This is the second time I've been here. Of course, I don't know if any of you were here the first time. In fact, I have no way of telling, by sense perception, that there is anyone here at all, but that doesn't matter. If the second crisis has been overcome safely, you are bound to be here; there is no way out. If you are not here, then the second crisis has been too much for you.'

He smiled engagingly. 'I doubt *that*, however, for my figures show a 98.4 per cent probability there is to be no significant deviation from the Plan in the first eighty years.

'According to our calculations, you have now reached domination of the barbarian kingdoms immediately surrounding the Foundation. Just as in the first crisis you held them off by the use of the Balance of Power, so in the second, you gained mastery by the Spiritual Power as against the Temporal.

'However, I might warn you here against overconfidence. It is not my way to grant you any foreknowledge in these recordings, but it would be safe to indicate that what you have now achieved is merely a new balance – though one in which your position is considerably better. The Spiritual Power, while sufficient to ward off attacks of the Temporal is *not* sufficient to attack in turn. Because of the invariable growth of the counteracting force known as Regionalism, or Nationalism, the Spiritual Power cannot prevail. I am telling you nothing new, I'm sure.

'You must pardon me, by the way, for speaking to you in this vague way. The terms I use are at best mere approximations, but none of you is qualified to understand the true symbology of psychohistory, and so I must do the best I can.

'In this case, the Foundation is only at the start of the path that leads to New Empire. The neighbouring kingdoms, in manpower and resources are still overwhelmingly powerful as compared to yourselves. Outside them lies the vast tangled jungle of barbarism that extends around the entire breadth of the Galaxy. Within that rim there is still what is left of the Galactic Empire – and that, weakened and decaying though it is, is still incomparably mighty.'

At this point, Hari Seldon lifted his book and opened it. His face grew solemn. 'And never forget there was *another* Foundation established eighty years ago; a Foundation at the other end of the Galaxy, at Star's End. They will always be there for consideration. Gentlemen, nine hundred and twenty years of the Plan stretch ahead of you. The problem is yours! Go to it!'

He dropped his eyes to his book and flicked out of existence, while the lights brightened to fullness. In the babble that followed, Lee leaned over to Hardin's ear. 'He didn't say when he'd be back.'

Hardin replied, 'I know – but I trust that he won't return until you and I are safely and cosily dead!'

Part IV

THE TRADERS

1

TRADERS ... *and constantly in advance of the political hegemony of the Foundation were the Traders, reaching out tenuous fingerholds through the tremendous distances of the Periphery. Months or years might pass between landings on Terminus; their ships were often nothing more than patch-quilts of home-made repairs and improvisations; their honesty was none of the highest; their daring ...*

Through it all they forged an empire more enduring than the pseudo-religious despotism of the Four Kingdoms ...

Tales without end are told of these massive, lonely figures who bore half-seriously, half-mockingly a motto adopted from one of Salvor Hardin's epigrams, 'Never let your sense of morals prevent you from doing what is right!' It is difficult now to tell which tales are real and which apocryphal. There are none probably that have not suffered some exaggerations ...

ENCYCLOPEDIA GALACTICA

Limmar Ponyets was completely a-lather when the call reached his receiver – which proves that the old bromide about telemessages and the bathtub holds true even in the dark, hard space of the Galactic Periphery.

Luckily that part of a free-lance trade ship which is not given over to miscellaneous merchandise is extremely snug. So much so, that the shower, hot water included, is located in a two-by-four cubby, ten feet from the control panels. Ponyets heard the staccato rattle of the receiver quite plainly.

Dripping suds and a curse, he stepped out to adjust the vocal, and three hours later a second trade ship was alongside, and a grinning youngster entered through the air tube between the ships.

Ponyets rattled his best chair forward and perched himself on the pilot-swivel.

'What've you been doing, Gorm?' he asked, darkly. 'Chasing me all the way from the Foundation?'

Les Gorm broke out a cigarette, and shook his head definitely. 'Me? Not a chance. I'm just the sucker who happened to land on Glyptal IV the day after the mail. So they sent me out after you with this.'

The tiny, gleaming sphere changed hands, and Gorm added, 'It's confidential. Super-secret. Can't be trusted to the sub-ether and all that. Or so I gather. At least, it's a Personal Capsule, and won't open for anyone but you.'

Ponyets regarded the capsule distastefully. 'I can see that. And I never knew one of these to hold good news, either.'

It opened in his hand and the thin, transparent tape unrolled stiffly. His eyes swept the message quickly, for when the last of the tape had emerged, the first was already brown and crinkled. In a minute and a half it had turned black and, molecule by molecule, fallen apart.

Ponyets grunted hollowly, 'Oh *Galaxy*!'

Les Gorm said quietly, 'Can I help somehow? Or is it too secret?'

'It will bear telling, since you're of the Guild. I've got to go to Askone.'

'That place? How come?'

'They've imprisoned a trader. But keep it to yourself.'

Gorm's expression jolted into anger. 'Imprisoned! That's against the Convention.'

'So is interference with local politics.'

'Oh! Is that what he did?' Gorm meditated. 'Who's the trader? Anyone I know?'

'No!' said Ponyets sharply, and Gorm accepted the implication and asked no further questions.

Ponyets was up and staring darkly out of the visiplate. He mumbled strong expressions at that part of the misty lens-form that was the body of the Galaxy, then said loudly, 'Damnedest mess! I'm way behind quota.'

Light broke on Gorm's intellect. 'Hey, friend, Askone is a closed area.'

'That's right. You can't sell as much as a penknife on Askone. They won't buy atomic gadgets of *any* sort. With my quota dead on its feet, it's murder to go there.'

'Can't get out of it?'

Ponyets shook his head absently. 'I know the fellow involved. Can't walk out on a friend. What of it? I am in the nads of the Galactic Spirit and walk cheerfully in the way he points out.'

Gorm said blankly, 'Huh?'

Ponyets looked at him, and laughed shortly. 'I forgot. You never read the *Book of the Spirit*, did you?'

'Never heard of it,' said Gorm, curtly.

'Well, you would if *you'd* had a religious training.'

'Religious training? For the *priesthood*?' Gorm was profoundly shocked.

'Afraid so. It's my dark shame and secret. I was too much for the Revered Fathers, though. They expelled me, for reasons sufficient to promote me to a secular education under the Foundation. Well, look, I'd better push off. How's your quota this year?'

Gorm crushed out his cigarette and adjusted his cap, 'I've got my last cargo going now. I'll make it.'

'Lucky fellow,' gloomed Ponyets, and for many minutes after Les Gorm left, he sat in motionless reverie.

So Eskel Gorov was on Askone – and in prison as well!

That was bad! In fact, considerably worse than it might appear. It was one thing to tell a curious youngster a diluted version of the business to throw him off and send him about his own. It was a thing of a different sort to face the truth.

For Limmar Ponyets was one of the few people who happened to know that Master Trader Eskel Gorov was not a trader at all; but that entirely different thing, an agent of the Foundation!

2

Two weeks gone! Two weeks wasted.

One week to reach Askone, at the extreme borders of which the vigilant warships speared out to meet him in converging numbers. Whatever their detection system was, it worked – and well.

They sidled him in slowly, without a signal, maintaining their cold distance, and pointing him harshly toward the central sun of Askone.

Ponyets could have handled them at a pinch. Those ships were holdovers from the dead-and-gone Galactic Empire – but they were sports cruisers, not warships; and without atomic weapons, they were so many picturesque and impotent ellipsoids. But Eskel Gorov was a prisoner in their hands, and Gorov was not a hostage to lose. The Askonians must know that.

And then another week – a week to wind a weary way through the clouds of minor officials that formed the buffer between the Grand Master and the outer world. Each little sub-secretary required soothing and concilation. Each required careful and nauseating milking for the flourishing signature that was the pathway to the next official one higher up.
careful and nauseating milking for the flourishing signature that was the pathway to the next official one higher up.

For the first time, Ponyets found his trader's identification papers useless.

Now, at last, the Grand Master was on the other side of the Guard-flanked gilded door – and two weeks had gone.

Gorov was still a prisoner and Ponyet's cargo rotted useless in the holds of his ship.

The Grand Master was a small man; a small man with a balding head and very wrinkled face, whose body seemed weighed down to motionlessness by the huge, glossy fur collar about his neck.

His fingers moved on either side, and the line of armed men backed away to form a passage, along which Ponyets strode to the foot of the Chair of State.

'Don't speak,' snapped the Grand Master, and Ponyets' opening lips closed tightly.

'That's right' – the Askonian ruler relaxed visibly – 'I can't endure useless chatter. You cannot threaten and I won't abide flattery. Nor is there room for injured complaints. I have lost count of the times you wanderers have been warned that your devil's machines are not wanted anywhere in Askone.'

'Sir,' said Ponyets, quietly, 'there is no attempt to justify the trader in question. It is not the policy of traders to intrude where they are not wanted. But the Galaxy is great, and it has happened before that a boundary has been trespassed unwittingly. It was a deplorable mistake.'

'Deplorable, certainly,' squeaked the Grand Master. 'But mistake? Your people on Glyptal IV have been bombarding me with pleas for negotiation since two hours after the sacrilegious wretch was seized. I have been warned by them of your own coming many times over. It seems a well-organized rescue campaign. Much seems to have been anticipated – a little too much for mistakes, deplorable or otherwise.'

The Askonian's black eyes were scornful. He raced on. 'And are you traders, flitting from world to world like mad little butterflies, so mad in your own right that you can land on Askone's largest world, in the centre of its system, and consider it an unwitting boundary mix-up? Come, surely not.'

Ponyets winced without showing it. He said, doggedly, 'If the attempt to trade was deliberate, your Veneration, it was most injudicious and contrary to the strictest regulations of our Guild.'

'Injudicious, yes,' said the Askonian, curtly. 'So much so,

that your comrade is likely to lose life in payment.'

Ponyets' stomach knotted. There was no irresolution there. He said, 'Death, your Veneration, is so absolute and irrevocable a phenomenon that certainly there must be some alternative.'

There was a pause before the guarded answer came, 'I have heard that the Foundation is rich.'

'Rich? Certainly. But our riches are that which you refuse to take. Our atomic goods are worth—'

'Your goods are worthless in that they lack the ancestral blessing. Your goods are wicked and accursed in that they lie under the ancestral interdict.' The sentences were intoned; the recitation of a formula.

The Grand Master's eyelids dropped, and he said with meaning, 'You have nothing else of value?'

The meaning was lost on the trader. 'I don't understand. What is it you want?'

The Askonian's hands spread apart. 'You ask me to trade places with you, and make known to you *my* wants. I think not. Your colleague, it seems, must suffer the punishment set for sacrilege by the Askonian code. Death by gas. We are just people. The poorest peasant, in like case, would suffer no more. I, myself, would suffer no less.'

Ponyets mumbled hopelessly, 'Your Veneration, would it be permitted that I speak to the prisoner?'

'Askonian law,' said the Grand Master coldly, 'allows no communication with a condemned man.'

Mentally, Ponyets held his breath, 'Your Veneration, I ask you to be merciful toward a man's soul, in the hour when his body stands forfeit. He has been separated from spiritual consolation in all the time that his life has been in danger. Even now, he faces the prospect of going unprepared to the bosom of the Spirit that rules all.'

The Grand Master said slowly and suspiciously, 'You are a Tender of the Soul?'

Ponyets dropped a humble head, 'I have been so trained. In

the empty expanse of space, the wandering traders need men like myself to care for the spiritual side of a life so given over to commerce and worldly pursuits.'

The Askonian ruler sucked thoughtfully at his lower lip. 'Every man should prepare his soul for his journey to his ancestral spirits. Yet I had never thought you traders to be believers.'

3

Eskel Gorov stirred on his couch and opened one eye as Limmar Ponyets entered the heavily reinforced door. It boomed shut behind him. Gorov sputtered and came to his feet.

Ponyets! They sent you?'

'Pure chance,' said Ponyets, bitterly, 'or the work of my own personal malevolent demon. Item one, you get into a mess on Askone. Item two, my sales route, as known to the Board of Trade, carries me within fifty parsecs of the system at just the time of item one. Item three, we've worked together before and the Board knows it. Isn't that a sweet, inevitable set-up? The answer just pops out of a slot.'

'Be careful,' said Gorov, tautly. 'There'll be someone listening. Are you wearing a Field Distorter?'

Ponyets indicated the ornamented bracelet that hugged his wrist and Gorov relaxed.

Ponyets looked about him. The cell was bare, but large. It was well-lit and it lacked offensive odours. He said, 'Not bad. They're treating you with kid gloves.'

Gorov brushed the remark aside, 'Listen, how did you get down here? I've been in strict solitary for almost two weeks.'

'Ever since I came, huh? Well, it seems the old bird who's

boss here has his weak points. He leans toward pious speeches, so I took a chance that worked. I'm here in the capacity of your spiritual adviser. There's something about a pious man such as he. He will cheefully cut your throat if it suits him, but he will hesitate to endanger the welfare of your immaterial and problematical soul. It's just a piece of empirical psychology. A trader has to know a little of everything.'

Gorov's smile was sardonic. 'And you've been to theological school as well. You're all right, Ponyets. I'm glad they sent you. But the Grand Master doesn't love my soul exclusively. Has he mentioned a ransom?'

The trader's eyes narrowed. 'He hinted – barely. And he also threated death by gas. I played safe, and dodged; it might easily have been a trap. So it's extortion, is it? What is it he wants?'

'Gold.'

'Gold!' Ponyets frowned. 'The metal itself? What for?'

'It's their medium of exchange.'

'Is it? And where do I get gold from?'

'Wherever you can. Listen to me; this is important. Nothing will happen to me as long as the Grand Master has the scent of gold in his nose. Promise it to him; as much as he asks for. Then go back to the Foundation, if necessary to get it. When I'm free, we'll be escorted out of the system, and then we part company.'

Ponyets stared disapprovingly, 'And then you'll come back and try again.'

'It's my assignment to sell atomics to Askone.'

'They'll get you before you've gone a parsec in space. You know that, I suppose?'

'I don't,' said Gorov. 'And if I did, it wouldn't affect things.'

'They'll kill you the second time.'

Gorov shrugged.

Ponyets said quietly, 'If I'm going to negotiate with the Grand Master again, I want to know the whole story. So far, I've been working it too blind. As it was, the few wild remarks I did make almost threw his Veneration into fits.'

'It's simple enough,' said Gorov. 'The only way we can

increase the security of the Foundation here in the Periphery is to form a religion-controlled commercial empire. We're still too weak to be able to force political control. It's all we can do to hold the Four Kingdoms.'

Ponyets was nodding, 'This I realize. And any system that doesn't accept atomic gadgets can never be placed under our religious control—'

'And can therefore become a focal point for independence and hostility. Yes.'

'All right, then,' said Ponyets, 'so much for theory. Now what exactly prevents the sale? Religion? The Grand Master implied as much.'

'It's a form of ancestor worship. Their traditions tell of an evil past from which they were saved by the simple and virtuous heroes of the past generations. It amounts to a distortion of the anarchic period a century ago, when the imperial troops were driven out and an independent government was set up. Advanced science and atomic power in particular became identified with the old imperial regime they remember with horror.'

'That so? But they have nice little ships which spotted me very handily two parsecs away. That smells of atomics to me.'

Gorov shrugged. 'Those ships are holdovers of the Empire, no doubt. Probably with atomic drive. What they have, they keep. The point is that they will not innovate and their internal economy is entirely non-atomic. That is what we must change.'

'How were you going to do it?'

'By breaking the resistance at one point. To put it simply, if I could sell a penknife with a force-field blade to a nobleman, it would be to his interest to force laws that would allow him to use it. Put that baldly, it sounds silly, but it is sound psychologically. To make strategic sales, at strategic points, would be to create a pro-atomics faction at court.'

'And they send *you* for that purpose, while I'm only here to ransom you and leave, while you keep on trying? Isn't that sort of tail-backward?'

'In what way?' said Gorov, guardedly.

'Listen,' Ponyets was suddenly exasperated, 'you're a diplomat, not a trader, and calling you a trader won't make you one. This case is for one who's made a business of selling – and I'm here with a full cargo stinking into uselessness, and a quota that won't be met, it looks like.'

'You mean you're going to risk your life on something that isn't your business?' Gorov smiled thinly.

Ponyets said, 'You mean that this is a matter of patriotism and traders aren't patriotic?'

'Notoriously not. Pioneers never are.'

'All right. I'll grant that. I don't scoot about space to save the Foundation or anything like that. But I'm out to make money, and this is my chance. If it helps the Foundation at the same time, all the better. And I've risked my life on slimmer chances.'

Ponyets rose, and Gorov rose with him, 'What are you going to do?'

The trader smiled. 'Gorov, I don't know – not yet. But if the crux of the matter is to make a sale, then I'm your man. I'm not a boaster as a general thing, but there's one thing I'll always back up. I've never *ended up* below quota yet.'

The door to the cell opened almost instantly when he knocked, and two guards fell in on either side.

4

'A show!' said the Grand Master, grimly. He settled himself well into his furs, and one thin hand grasped the iron cudgel he used as a cane.

'And gold, your Veneration.'

'*And* gold,' agreed the Grand Master, carelessly.

Ponyets set the box down and opened it with as fine an

appearance of confidence as he could manage. He felt alone in the face of universal hostility; the way he had felt out in space his first year. The semicircle of bearded councillors who faced him down, stared unpleasantly. Among them was Pherl, the thin-faced favourite who sat next to the Grand Master in stiff hostility. Ponyets had met him once already and marked him immediately as prime enemy, and, as a consequence, prime victim.

Outside the hall, a small army awaited events. Ponyets was effectively isolated from his ship; he lacked any weapon, but his attempted bribe; and Gorov was still a hostage.

He made the final adjustments on the clumsy monstrosity that had cost him a week of ingenuity, and prayed once again that the lead-lined quartz would stand the strain.

'What is it?' asked the Grand Master.

'This,' said Ponyets, stepping back, 'is a small device I have constructed myself.'

'That is obvious, but it is not the information I want. It is one of the black-magic abominations of your world?'

'It is atomic nature,' admitted Ponyets, gravely, 'but none of you need touch it, or have anything to do with it. It is for myself alone, and if it contains abominations, I take the foulness of it upon myself.'

The Grand Master had raised his iron cane at the machine in a threatening gesture and his lips moved rapidly and silently in a purifying invocation. The thin-faced councillor at his right leaned towards him and his straggled red moustache approached the Grand Master's ear. The ancient Askonian petulantly shrugged himself free.

'And what is the connection of your intruments of evil and the gold that may save your countryman's life?'

'With this machine,' began Ponyets, as his hand dropped softly on to the central chamber and caressed its hard, round flanks, 'I can turn the iron you discard into gold of the finest quality. It is the only device known to man that will take iron – the ugly iron, your Veneration, that props up the chair you sit in and the walls of this building – and change it to shining, heavy, yellow gold.'

Ponyets felt himself botching it. His usual sales talk was smooth, facile and plausible; but this limped like a shot-up space wagon. But it was the content, not the form, that interested the Grand Master.

'So? Transmutation? There have been fools who have claimed the ability. They have paid for their prying sacrilege.'

'Had they succeeded?'

'No.' The Grand Master seemed coldly amused. 'Success at producing gold would have been a crime that carried its own antidote. It is the attempt plus the failure that is fatal. Here, what can you do with my staff?' He pounded the floor with it.

'Your Veneration will excuse me. My device is a small model, prepared by myself, and your staff is too long.'

The Grand Master's small shining eye wandered and stopped. 'Randel, your buckles. Come, man, they shall be replaced double if need be.'

The buckles passed down the line, hand to hand. The Grand Master weighed them thoughtfully.

'Here,' he said, and threw them to the floor.

Ponyets picked them up. He tugged hard before the cylinder opened, and his eyes blinked and squinted with effort as he centred the buckles carefully on the anode screen. Later, it would be easier but there must be no failures the first time.

The home-made transmuter crackled malevolently for ten minutes while the odour of ozone became faintly present. The Askonians backed away, muttering, and again Pherl whispered urgently into his ruler's ear. The Grand Master's expression was stony. He did not budge.

And the buckles were gold.

Ponyets held them out to the Grand Master with a murmured, 'Your Veneration!' but the old man hesitated, then gestured them away. His stare lingered upon the transmuter.

Ponyets said rapidly, 'Gentlemen, this is gold. Gold through and through. You may subject it every known physical and chemical test, if you wish to prove the point. It cannot be identified from naturally-occurring gold in any way. Any iron can be so treated. Rust will not interfere, nor will a moderate amount of alloying metals—'

But Ponyets spoke only to fill a vacuum. He let the buckles remain in his outstretched hand, and it was the gold that argued for him.

The Grand Master stretched out a slow hand at last, and the thin-faced Pherl was roused to open speech. 'Your Veneration, the gold is from a poisoned source.'

And Ponyets counted. 'A rose can grow from the mud, your Veneration. In your dealings with your neighbours, you buy material of all imaginable variety, without inquiring as to where they get it, whether from an orthodox machine blessed by your benign ancestors or from some space-spawned outrage. Come, I don't offer the machine. I offer the gold.'

'Your Veneration,' said Pherl, 'you are not responsible for the sins of foreigners who work neither with your consent nor knowledge. But to accept this strange pseudo-gold made sinfully from iron in your presence and with your consent is an affront to the living spirits of our holy ancestors.'

'Yet gold is gold,' said the Grand Master, doubtfully, 'and is but an exchange for the heathen person of a convicted felon. Pherl, you are too critical.' But he withdrew his hand.

Ponyets said, 'You are wisdom, itself, your Veneration. Consider – to give up a heathen is to lose nothing for your ancestors, whereas with the gold you get in exchange you can ornament the shrines of their holy spirits. And surely, were gold evil in itself, if such a thing could be, the evil would depart of necessity once the metal were put to such pious use.'

'Now by the bones of my grandfather,' said the Grand Master with surprising vehemence. His lips separated in a shrill laugh. 'Pherl, what do you say of this young man? The statement is valid. It is as valid as the words of my ancestors.'

Pherl said gloomily, 'So it would seem. Grant that the validity does not turn out to be a device of the Malignant Spirit.'

'I'll make it even better,' said Ponyets, suddenly. 'Hold the gold in hostage. Place it on the altars of your ancestors as an offering and hold me for thirty days. If at the end of that time there is no evidence of displeasure – if no disasters occur – surely, it would be proof that the offering was accepted. What more can be offered?'

And when the Grand Master rose to his feet to search out disapproval, not a man in the council failed to signal his agreement. Even Pherl chewed the ragged end of his moustache and nodded curtly.

Ponyets smiled and meditated on the uses of a religious education.

5

Another week rubbed away before the meeting with Pherl was arranged. Ponyets felt the tension, but he was used to the feeling of physical helplessness now. He had left city limits under guard. He was in Pherl's suburban villa under guard. There was nothing to do but accept it without even looking over his shoulder.

Pherl was taller and younger outside the circle of Elders. In nonformal costume, he seemed no Elder at all.

He said abruptly, 'You're a peculiar man.' His close-set eyes seemed to quiver. 'You've done nothing this last week, and particularly these last two hours, but imply that I need gold. It seems useless labour, for who does not? Why not advance one step?'

'It is not simply gold,' said Ponyets, discreetly. 'Not *simply* gold. Not merely a coin or two. It is rather all that lies behind gold.'

'Now what can lie behind gold?' prodded Pherl, with a down-curved smile. 'Certainly this is not the preliminary of another clumsy demonstration.'

'Clumsy?' Ponyets frowned slightly.

'Oh, definitely.' Pherl folded his hands and nudged them gently with his chin. 'I don't criticize you. The clumsiness was on purpose, I am sure. I might have warned this Veneration of *that*, had I been certain of the motive. Now had I been you, I would have produced the gold upon my ship, and offered it alone. The show you offered us and the antagonism you aroused would have been dispensed with.'

'True,' Ponyets admitted, 'but since I was myself, I accepted the antagonism for the sake of attracting your attention.'

'Is that it? Simply that?' Pherl made no effort to hide his contemptuous amusement. 'And I imagine you suggested the thirty-day purification period that you might assure yourself time to turn the attraction into something a bit more substantial. But what if the gold turns out to be impure?'

Ponyets allowed himself a dark humour in return. 'When the judgement of that impurity depends upon those who are most interested in finding it pure?'

Pherl lifted his eyes and stared narrowly at the trader. He seemed at once surprised and satisfied.

'A sensible point. Now tell me why you wished to attract me.'

'This I will do. In the short time I have been here, I have observed useful facts that concern you and interest me. For instance, you are young – very young for a member of the council, and even of a relatively young family.'

'You criticize my family?'

'Not at all. Your ancestors are great and holy; all will admit that. But there are those that say you are not a member of one of the Five Tribes.'

Pherl leaned back. 'With all respect to those involved,' and he did not hide his venom, 'the Five Tribes have impoverished loins and thin blood. Not fifty members of the Tribes are alive.'

'Yet there are those who say the nation would not be willing to see any man outside the Tribes as Grand Master. And so young and newly-advanced a favourite of the Grand Master is bound to make powerful enemies among the great ones of the State – it is said. His Veneration is ageing and his protection will not last past his death, when it is an enemy of yours who will undoubtedly be the one to interpret the words of his Spirit.'

Pherl scowled. 'For a foreigner you hear much. Such ears are made for cropping.'

'That may be decided later.'

'Let me anticipate.' Pherl stirred impatiently in his seat. 'You're going to offer me wealth and power in terms of those evil little machines you carry in your ship. Well?'

'Suppose it so. What would be your objection? Simply your standard of good and evil?'

Pherl shook his head. 'Not at all. Look, my Outlander, your opinion of us in your heathen agnosticism is what it is – but I am not the entire slave of our mythology, though I may appear so. I am an educated man, sir, and, I hope, an enlightened one. The full depth of our religious customs, in the ritualistic rather than the ethical sense, is for the masses.'

'Your objection, then?' pressed Ponyets, gently.

'Just that. The masses. *I* might be willing to deal with you, but your little machines must be used to be useful. How might riches come to me, if I had to use – what is it you sell? – well, a razor, for instance, only in the strictest, trembling secrecy. Even if my chin were more simply and more cleanly shaven, how would I become rich? And how would I avoid death by gas chamber or mob frightfulness if I were ever once caught using it?'

Ponyets shrugged, 'You are correct. I might point out that the remedy would be to educate your own people into the use of atomics for their convenience and your own substantial profit. It would be a gigantic piece of work; I don't deny it; but the returns would be still more gigantic. Still that is your concern, and, at the moment, not mine at all. For I offer neither razor, knife, nor mechanical garbage disposer.'

'What do you offer?'

'Gold itself. Directly. You may have the machine I demonstrated last week.'

And now Pherl stiffened and the skin on his forehead moved jerkily. 'The transmuter?'

'Exactly. Your supply of gold will equal your supply of iron. That, I imagine, is sufficient for all needs. Sufficient for the Grand Mastership itself, despite youth and enemies. And it is safe.'

'In what way?'

'In that secrecy is the essence of its use; that same secrecy you described as the only safety with regard to atomics. You may bury the transmuter in the deepest dungeon of the strongest fortress on your farthest estate, and it will bring you instant wealth. It is the *gold* you buy, not the machine, and that gold bears no trace of its manufacture, for it cannot be told from the natural creation.'

'And who is to operate the machine?'

'Yourself. Five minutes teaching is all you will require. I'll set it up for you wherever you wish.'

'And in return?'

'Well.' Ponyets grew cautious. 'I ask a price and a handsome one. It is my living. Let us say – for it is a valuable machine – the equivalent of a cubic foot of gold in wrought iron.'

Pherl laughed, and Ponyets grew red. 'I point out, sir,' he added, stiffly, 'that you can get your price back in two hours.'

'True, and in one hour, you might be gone, and my machine might suddenly turn out to be useless. I'll need a guarantee.'

'You have my word.'

'A very good one,' Pherl bowed sardonically, 'but your presence would be an even better assurance. I'll give you *my* word to pay you one week after delivery in working order.'

'Impossible.'

'Impossible? When you've already incurred the death penalty very handily by even offering to sell me anything. The only alternative is my word that you'll get the gas chamber tomorrow otherwise.'

Ponyet's face was expressionless, but his eyes might have flickered. He said, 'It is an unfair advantage. You will at least put your promise in writing?'

'And also become liable for execution? No, sir!' Pherl smiled a broad satisfaction. 'No, sir! Only one of us is a fool.'

The trader said in a small voice, 'It is agreed, then.'

6

Gorov was released on the thirtieth day, and five hundred pounds of the yellowest gold took place. And with him was released the guaranteed and untouched abomination that was his ship.

Then, as on the journey into the Askonian system, so on the journey out, the cylinder of sleek little ships ushered them on their way.

Ponyets watched the dimly sun-lit speck that was Gorov's ship while Gorov's voice pierced through to him, clear and thin on the tight, distortion-bounded ether-beam.

He was saying, 'But it isn't what's wanted, Ponyets. A transmuter won't do. Where did you get one, anyway?'

'I didn't.' Ponyets' answer was patient. 'I juiced it up out of a food irradiation chamber. It isn't any good, really. The power consumption is prohibitive on any large scale or the Foundation would use transmutation instead of chasing all over the Galaxy for heavy metals. It's one of the standard tricks every trader uses, except that I never saw an iron-to-gold one before. But it's impressive, and it works – very temporarily.'

'All right. But that particular trick is no good.'

'It got you out of a nasty spot.'

'That is very far from the point. Especially since I've got to go back, once we shake our solicitious escort.'

'Why?'

'You yourself explained it to this politician of yours.' Gorov's voice was on edge. 'Your entire sales-point rested on the fact that the transmuter was a means to an end, but of no value in itself; that he was buying the gold, not the machine. It was good psychology, since it worked, but—'

'But?' Ponyets urged blandly and obtusely.

The voice from the receiver grew shriller. 'But we want to sell them a machine of value in itself; something they would want to use openly; something that would tend to force them out in favour of atomic techniques as a matter of self-interest.'

'I understand all that,' said Ponyets, gently. 'You once explained it. But look at what follows from my sale, will you? As long as that transmuter lasts, Pherl will coin gold; and it will last long enough to buy him the next election. The present Grand Master won't last long.'

'You count on gratitude?' asked Gorov, coldly.

'No – on intelligent self-interest. The transmuter gets him an election; other mechanisms—'

'No! No! Your premise is twisted. It's not the transmuter he'll credit – it'll be the good, old-fashioned gold. That's what I'm trying to tell you.'

Ponyets grinned and shifted into a more comfortable position. All right. He'd baited the poor fellow sufficiently. Gorov was beginning to sound wild.

The trader said, 'Not so fast, Gorov. I haven't finished. There are other gadgets already involved.'

There was a short silence. Then Gorov's voice sounded cautiously, 'What other gadgets?'

Ponyets gestured automatically and uselessly. 'You see that escort?'

'I do,' said Gorov shortly. 'Tell me about those gadgets.'

'I will – if you'll listen. That's Pherl's private navy escorting us; a special honour to him from the Grand Master. He managed to squeeze that out.'

'So?'

'And where do you think he's taking us? To his mining estates on the outskirts of Askone, that's where. Listen!' Ponyets was suddenly fiery. 'I told you I was in this to make money, not to save worlds. All right. I sold that transmuter for nothing. Nothing except the risk of the gas chamber and that doesn't count toward the quota.'

'Get back to the mining estates, Ponyets. Where do they come in?'

'With the profits. We're stacking up on tin, Gorov. Tin to fill every last cubic foot this old scow can scrape up, and then some more for yours. I'm going down with Pherl to collect, old man, and you're going to cover me from upstairs with every gun you've got – just in case Pherl isn't as sporting about the matter as he lets on to be. That tin's my profit.'

'For the transmuter?'

'*For my entire cargo of atomics*. At double price, plus a bonus.' He shrugged, almost apologetically. 'I admit I gouged him, but I've got to make quota, don't I?'

Gorov was evidently lost. He said, weakly, 'Do you mind explaining?'

'What's there to explain? It's obvious, Gorov. Look, the clever dog thought he had me in a foolproof trap, because his word was worth more than mine to the Grand Master. He took the transmuter. That was a capital crime in Askone. But at any time he could say that he had lured me on into a trap with the purest of patriotic motives, and denounce me as a seller of forbidden things.'

'*That* was obvious.'

'Sure, but word against simple word wasn't all there was to it. You see, Pherl had never heard nor conceived of a microfilm-recorder.'

Gorov laughed suddenly.

'That's right,' said Ponyets. 'He had the upper hand. I was properly chastened. But when I set up the transmuter for him in my whipped-dog fashion, I incorporated the recorder into the device and removed it in the next day's overhaul. I had a perfect record of his sanctum sanctorum, his holy-of-holies, with himself, poor Pherl, operating the transmuter for all the ergs it had and crowing over his first piece of gold as if it were an egg he had just laid.'

'You showed him the results?'

'Two days later. The poor sap had never seen three-dimensional colour-sound images in his life. He claims he isn't superstitious, but if I ever saw an adult look as scared as he did then, call me rookie. When I told him I had a recorder planted in the city square, set to go off at midday with a million fanatical Askonians to watch, and to tear him to pieces subsequently, he was gibbering at my knees in half a second. He was ready to make any deal I wanted.'

'Did you?' Gorov's voice was suppressing laughter. 'I mean, have one planted in the city square.'

'No, but that didn't matter. He made the deal. He bought every gadget I had, and every one you had for as much tin as we could carry. At that moment, he believed me capable of anything. The agreement is in writing and you'll have a copy before I go down with him, just as another precaution.'

'But you've damaged his ego,' said Gorov. 'Will he use the gadgets?'

'Why not? It's his only way of recouping his losses, and if he makes money out of it, he'll salve his pride. And he *will* be the next Grand Master – and the best man we could have in our favour.'

'Yes,' said Gorov, 'it was a good sale. Yet you've certainly got an uncomfortable sales technique. No wonder you were kicked out of a seminary. Have you no sense of morals?'

'What are the odds?' said Ponyets, indifferently. 'You know what Salvor Hardin said about a sense of morals.'

Part V

THE MERCHANT PRINCES

1

TRADERS ... *With psychohistoric inevitability, economic control of the Foundation grew. The traders grew rich; and with riches came power ...*

It is sometimes forgotten that Hober Mallow began life as an ordinary trader. It is never forgotten that he ended it as the first of the Merchant Princes ...

ENCYCLOPEDIA GALACTICA

Jorane Sutt put the tips of carefully-manicured fingers together and said, 'It's something of a puzzle. In fact – and this is in the strictest confidence – it may be another one of Hari Seldon's crises.'

The man opposite felt in the pocket of his short Smyrnian jacket for a cigarette. 'Don't know about that, Sutt. As a general rule, politicians start shouting 'Seldon crisis' at every mayoralty campaign.'

Sutt smiled very faintly, 'I'm not campaigning, Mallow. We're facing atomic weapons, and we don't know where they're coming from.'

Hober Mallow of Smyrno, master Trader, smoked quietly, almost indifferently. 'Go on. If you have more to say, get it out.' Mallow never made the mistake of being overpolite to a Foundation man. He might be an Outlander, but a man's a man for a' that.

Sutt indicated the trimensional star-map on the table. He adjusted the controls and a cluster of some half-dozen stellar systems blazed red.

'That,' he said quietly, 'is the Korellian Republic.'

The trader nodded, 'I've been there. Stinking rathole! I suppose you can call it a republic but it's always someone out of the Argo family that gets elected Commdor each time. And if you ever don't like it - *things* happen to you.' He twisted his lip and repeated, 'I've been there.'

'But you've come back, which hasn't always happened. Three trade ships, inviolate under the Conventions, have disappeared within the territory of the Republic in the last year. And those ships were armed with all the usual nuclear explosives and forcefield defences.'

'What was the last word heard from the ships?'

'Routine reports. Nothing else.'

'What did Korell say?'

Sutt's eyes gleamed sardonically, 'There was no way of asking. The Foundation's greatest asset throughout the Periphery is its reputation of power. Do you think we can lose three ships and *ask* for them?'

'Well, then, suppose you tell me what you want with *me*.'

Jorane Sutt did not waste his time in the luxury of annoyance. As secretary to the mayor, he had held off opposition councilmen, jobseekers, reformers, and crackpots who claimed to have solved in its entirety the course of future history as worked out by Hari Seldon. With training like that, it took a good deal to disturb him.

He said methodically, 'In a moment. You see, three ships lost in the same sector in the same year can't be accident, and atomic power can be conquered only by more atomic power. The question automatically arises: if Korell has atomic weapons, where is it getting them?'

'And where does it?'

'Two alternatives. Either the Korellians have constructed them themselves—'

'Far-fetched!'

'Very! But the other possibility is that we are being afflicted with a case of treason.'

'You think so?' Mallow's voice was cold.

The secretary said calmly, 'There's nothing miraculous about the possibility. Since the Four Kingdoms accepted the

Foundation Convention, we have had to deal with considerable groups of dissident populations in each nation. Each former kingdom has its pretenders and its former noblemen, who can't very well pretend to love the Foundation. Some of them are becoming active, perhaps.'

Mallow was a dull red. 'I see. Is there anything you want to say to *me*? I'm a Smyrnian.'

'I know. You're a Smyrnian – born in Smyrno, one of the former Four Kingdoms. You're a Foundation man by education only. By birth, you're an Outlander and a foreigner. No doubt your grandfather was a baron at the time of the wars with Anacreon and Loris, and no doubt your family estates were taken away when Sef Sermak redistributed the land.'

'No, by Black Space, no! My grandfather was a blood-poor son-of-a-spacer who died heaving coal at starving wages before the Foundation. I owe nothing to the old regime. But I was born in Smyrno, and I'm not ashamed of either Smyrno or Smyrnians, by the Galaxy. Your sly little hints of treason aren't going to panic me into licking Foundation spittle. And now you can either give your orders or make your accusations, I don't care which.'

'My good Master Trader, I don't care an electron whether your grandfather was King of Smyrno or the greatest pauper on the planet. I recited that rigmarole about your birth and ancestry to show you that I'm not interested in them. Evidently you missed the point. Let's go back now. You're a Smyrnian. You know the Outlanders. Also, you're a trader and one of the best. You've been to Korell and you know the Korellians. That's where you've got to go.'

Mallow breathed deeply, 'As a spy?'

'Not at all. As a trader – but with your eyes open. If you can find out where the power is coming from – I might remind you, since you're a Smyrnian, that two of those lost trade ships had Smyrnian crews.'

'When do I start?'

'When will your ship be ready?'

'In six days.'

'Then that's when you start. You'll have all the details at the Admiralty.'

'Right!' The trader rose, shook hands roughly, and strode out.

Sutt waited, spreading his fingers gingerly and rubbing out the pressure; then shrugged his shoulders and stepped into the mayor's office.

The mayor deadened the visiplate and leaned back. 'What do *you* make of it, Sutt?'

'He could be a good actor,' said Sutt, and stared thoughtfully ahead.

2

It was evening of the same day, and in Jorane Sutt's bachelor apartment on the twenty-first floor of the Hardin Building Publis Manlio was sipping wine slowly.

It was Publis Manlio in whose slight, ageing body were fulfilled two great offices of the Foundation. He was Foreign Secretary in the mayor's cabinet, and to all the outer suns, barring only the Foundation itself, he was, in addition, Primate of the Church, Purveyor of the Holy Food, Master of the Temples, and so forth almost indefinitely in confusing but sonorous syllables.

He was saying, 'But he agreed to let you send out that trader. It is a point.'

'But such a small one,' said Sutt. 'It gets us nothing immediately. The whole business is the crudest sort of stratagem, since we have no way of foreseeing it to the end. It is a mere paying out of rope on the chance that somewhere along the length of it will be a noose.'

'True. And this Mallow is a capable man. What if he is not an easy prey to dupery?'

'That is a chance that must be run. If there is treachery, it is the capable men that are implicated. If not, we need a capable man to detect the truth. And Mallow will be guarded. Your glass is empty.'

'No, thanks. I've had enough.'

Sutt filled his own glass and patiently endured the other's uneasy reverie.

Of whatever the reverie consisted, it ended indecisively, for the primate said suddenly, almost explosively, 'Sutt, what's on your mind?'

'I'll tell you, Manlio.' His thin lips parted. 'We're in the middle of a Seldon crisis.'

Manlio stared, then said softly, 'How do you know? Has Seldon appeared in the Time Vault again?'

'That much, my friend, is not necessary. Look, reason it out. Since the Galactic Empire abandoned the Periphery, and threw us on our own, we have never had an opponent who possessed atomic power. Now, for the first time, we have one. That seems significant even if it stood by itself. And it doesn't. For the first time in over seventy years, we are facing a major domestic political crisis. I should think the synchronization of the two crisis, inner and outer, puts it beyond all doubt.'

Manilo's eyes narrowed, 'If that's all, it's not enough. There have been two Seldon crises so far, and both times the Foundation was in danger of extermination. Nothing can be a third crisis till that danger returns.'

Sutt never showed impatience. 'That danger is coming. Any fool can tell a crisis when it arrives. The real service to the State is to detect it in embryo. Look, Manilo, we're proceeding along a planned history. We *know* that Hari Seldon worked out the historical probabilities of the future. We *know* that some day we're to rebuild the Galactic Empire. We *know* that it will take a thousand years or thereabouts. And we *know* that in that interval we will face certain definite crises.

'Now the first crisis came fifty years after the establishment of the Foundation, and the second, thirty years later than that. Almost seventy-five years have gone since. It's time, Manlio, it's time.'

Manlio rubbed his nose uncertaintly. 'And you've made your plans to meet this crisis?'

Sutt nodded.

'And I,' continued Manlio, 'am to play a part in it?'

Sutt nodded again, 'Before we can meet the foreign threat of atomic power, you've got to put your own house in order. These traders—'

'Ah!' The primate stiffened, and his eyes grew sharp.

'That's right. These traders. They are useful, but they are too strong – and too uncontrolled. They are Outlanders, educated apart from religion. On the one hand, we put knowledge into their hands, and on the other, we remove our strongest hold upon them.'

'If we can prove treachery?'

'If we could, direct action would be simple and sufficient. But that doesn't signify in the least. Even if treason among them did not exist, they would form an uncertain element in our society. They wouldn't be bound to us by patriotism or common descent, or even by religious awe. Under their secular leadership, the outer provinces, which, since Hardin's time, look to us as the Holy Planet, might break away.'

'I see all that, but the cure—'

'The cure must come quickly, before the Seldon Crisis becomes acute. If atomic weapons are without and disaffection within, the odds might be too great.' Sutt put down the empty glass he had been fingering. 'This is obviously your job.'

'Mine?'

'*I* can't do it. My office is appointive and has no legislative standing.'

'The mayor—'

'Impossible. His personality is entirely negative. He i

energetic only in evading responsibility. But if an independent party arose that might endanger re-election, he might allow himself to be led.'

'But, Sutt, I lack the aptitude for practical politics.'

'Leave that to me. Who knows, Manlio? Since Salvor Hardin's time, the primacy and the mayoralty have never been combined in a single person. But it might happen now – if your job were well done.'

3

And at the other end of town, in homelier surroundings, Hober Mallow kept a second appointment. He had listened long, and now he said cautiously, 'Yes, I've heard of your campaigns to get direct trader representation in the council. But why *me*, Twer?'

Jaim Twer, who would remind you any time, asked or unasked, that he was in the first group of Outlanders to receive a lay education at the Foundation, beamed.

'I know what I'm doing,' he said. 'Remember when I met you first, last year.'

'At the Traders' Convention.'

'Right. You ran that meeting. You had those red-necked oxen planted in their seats, then put them in your shirt-pocket and walked off with them. And you're all right with the Foundation masses, too. You've got *glamour* – or, at any rate, solid adventure-publicity, which is the same thing.'

'Very good,' said Mallow, dryly. 'But why now?'

'Because now's our chance. Do you know that the Secretary of Education has handed in his resignation? It's not out in the open yet, but it will be.'

'How do *you* know?'

'That – never mind—' He waved a disgusted hand. 'It's so.

The Actionist party is splitting wide open, and we can murder it right now on a straight question of equal rights for traders or, rather, democracy, pro and anti.'

Mallow lounged back in his chair and stared at his thick fingers. 'Uh-uh. Sorry, Twer. I'm leaving next week on business. You'll have to get someone else.'

Twer stared, 'Business? What kind of business?'

'Very super-secret. Triple-A priority. All that, you know. Had a talk with the mayor's own secretary.'

'Snake Sutt?' Jaim Twer grew excited. 'A trick. The son-of-a-spacer is getting rid of you. Mallow—'

'Hold on!' Mallow's hand fell on the other's balled fist. 'Don't go into a blaze. If it's a trick, I'll be back some day for the reckoning. If it isn't, your snake, Sutt, *is* playing into our hands. Listen, there's a Seldon crisis coming up.'

Mallow waited for a reaction but it never came. Twer merely stared. 'What's a Seldon crisis?'

'Galaxy!' Mallow exploded angrily at the anticlimax. 'What the blue blazes did you do when you went to school? What do you mean anyway by a fool question like that?'

The older man frowned. 'If you'll explain—'

There was a long pause, then, 'I'll explain.' Mallow's eyebrows lowered, and he spoke slowly. 'When the Galactic Empire began to die at the edges, and when the ends of the Galaxy reverted to barbarism and dropped away, Hari Seldon and his band of psychologists planted a colony, the Foundation, out here in the middle of the mess, so that we could incubate art, science, and technology, and form the nucleus of the Second Empire.'

'Oh, yes, yes—'

'I'm not finished,' said the trader, coldly. 'The future course of the Foundation was plotted according to the science of psychohistory, then highly developed, and conditions arranged so as to bring about a series of crises that will force us most rapidly along the route to future Empire. Each crisis, each *Seldon* crisis, marks an epoch in our history. We' approaching one now – our third.'

'Of course!' Twer shrugged, 'I should have remembered. But I've been out of school a long time – longer than you.'

'I suppose so. Forget it. What matters is that I'm being sent out into the middle of the development of this crisis. There's no telling what I'll have when I come back, and there is a council election every year.'

Twer looked up, 'Are you on the track of anything?'

'No.'

'You have definite plans?'

'Not the faintest inkling of one.'

'Well—'

'Well, nothing. Hardin once said: "To succeed, planning alone is insufficient. One must improvise as well." I'll improvise.'

Twer shook his head uncertainly, and they stood, looking at each other.

Mallow said, quite suddenly, but quite matter-of-factly, 'I tell you what, how about coming with me? Don't stare, man. You've been a trader before you decided there was more excitement in politics. Or so I've heard.'

'Where are you going? Tell me that.'

'Towards the Whassallian Rift. I can't be more specific till we're out in space. What do you say?'

'Suppose Sutt decides he wants me where he can see me.'

'Not likely. If he's anxious to get rid of me, why not of you as well? Besides which, no trader would hit space if he couldn't pick his own crew. I take whom I please.'

There was a queer glint in the older man's eyes, 'All right. I'll go.' He held out his hand, 'It'll be my first trip in three years.'

Mallow grasped and shook the other's hand, 'Good! All fired good! And now I've got to round up the boys. You know where the *Far Star* docks, don't you? Then show up tomorrow. Goodbye.'

4

Korell is that frequent phenomenon in history: the republic whose ruler has every attribute of the absolute monarch but the name. It therefore enjoyed the usual despotism unrestrained even by those two moderating influences in the legitimate monarchies: regal 'honour' and court etiquette.

Materially, its prosperity was low. The day of the Galactic Empire had departed, with nothing but silent memorials and broken structures to testify to it. The day of the Foundation has not yet come – and in the fierce determination of its ruler, the Commdor Asper Argo, with his strict regulation of the traders and his stricter prohibition of the missionaries, it was never coming.

The space-port itself was decrepit and decayed, and the crew of the *Far Star* were drearily aware of that. The mouldering hangers made for a mouldering atmosphere and Jaim Twer itched and fretted over a game of solitaire.

Hober Mallow said thoughtfully, 'Good trading material here.' He was staring quietly out the viewport. So far, there was little else to be said about Korell. The trip here was uneventful. The squadron of Korellian ships that had shot out to intercept the *Far Star* had been tiny, limping relics of ancient glory or battered, clumsy hulks. They had maintained their distance fearfully, and still maintained it, and for a week now, Mallow's requests for an audience with the local government had been unanswered.

Mallow repeated, 'Good trading here. You might call this virgin territory.'

Jaim Twer looked up impatiently, and threw his cards aside. 'What the devil do you intend doing, Mallow?' The crew's grumbling, the officers are worried, and I'm wondering—'

'Wondering? About what?'

'About the situation. And about you. What are we doing?'

'Waiting.'

The old trader snorted and grew red. He growled, 'You're going it blind, Mallow. There's a guard around the field and there are ships overhead. Suppose they're getting ready to blow us into a hole in the ground.'

'They've had a week.'

'Maybe they're waiting for reinforcements.' Twer's eyes were sharp and hard.

Mallow sat down abruptly. 'Yes, I'd thought of that. You see, it poses a pretty problem. First, we got here without trouble. That may mean nothing, however, for only three ships out of better than three hundred went a-glimmer last year. The percentage is low. But that may mean also that the number of their ships equipped with atomic power is small, and that they dare not expose them needlessly, until that number grows.

'But it could mean, on the other hand, that they haven't atomic power after all. Or maybe they have and are keeping under cover, for fear we know something. It's one thing, after all, to piratize blundering, light-armed merchant ships. It's another to fool around with an accredited envoy of the Foundation when the mere fact of his presence may mean the Foundation is growing suspicious.

'Combine this—'

'Hold on, Mallow, hold on.' Twer raised his hands. 'You're just about drowning me with talk. What're you getting at? Never mind the in-betweens.'

'You've *got* to have the in-betweens, or you won't understand, Twer. We're both waiting. They don't know what I'm doing here and I don't know what they've got here. But I'm in the weaker position because I'm one and they're an entire world – maybe with atomic power. I can't afford to be the one to weaken. Sure it's dangerous. Sure there may be a hole in the ground waiting for us. But we knew that from the start. What else is there to do?'

'I don't— Who's that, now?'

Mallow looked up patiently, and tuned the receiver. The visiplate glowed into the craggy face of the watch sergeant.

'Speak, sergeant.'

The sergeant said, 'Pardon, sir. The men have given entry to a Foundation missionary.'

'A *what*?' Mallow's face grew livid.

'A missionary, sir.He's in need of hospitalization sir—'

'There'll be more than one in need of that, sergeant, for this piece of work. Order the men to battle stations.'

Crew's lounge was almost empty. Five minutes after the order, even the men on the off-shift were at their guns. It was speed that was the great virtue in the anarchic regions of the interstellar space of the Periphery, and it was in speed above all that a crew of a master trade excelled.

Mallow entered slowly, and stared the missionary up and down and around. His eye slid to Lieutenant Tinter, who shifted uneasily to one side and to Watch-Sergeant Demen, whose blank face and stolid figure flanked the other.

The Master Trader turned to Twer and paused thoughtfully, 'Well, then, Twer, get the officers here quietly, except for the co-ordinators and the trajectorian. The men are to remain at stations till further orders.'

There was a five-minute hiatus, in which Mallow kicked open the doors to the lavatories, looked behind the bar, pulled the draperies across the thick windows. For half a minute he left the room altogether, and when he returned he was humming abstractedly.

Men filed in. Twer followed, and closed the door silently.

Mallow said quietly, 'First, who let this man in without orders from me?'

The watch sergeant stepped forward. Every eye shifted. 'Pardon, sir. It was no definite person. It was a sort of mutual agreement. He was one of us, you might say, and these foreigners here—'

Mallow cut him short, 'I sympathize with your feelings, sergeant, and understand them. These men, were they under your command?'

'Yes, sir.'

'When this is over, they're to be confined to individual quarters for a week. You yourself are relieved of all supervisory duties for a similar period. Understood?'

The sergeant's face never changed, but there was the slightest droop in his shoulders. He said, crisply, 'Yes, sir.'

'You may leave. Get to your gun station.'

The door closed behind him and the babble rose.

Twer broke in, 'Why the punishment, Mallow? You know that these Korellians kill captured missionaries.'

'An action against my orders is bad in itself whatever other reasons there may be in its favour. No one was to leave or enter the ship without permission.'

Lieutenant Tinter murmured rebelliously: 'Seven days without action. You can't maintain discipline that way.'

Mallow said icily, '*I* can. There's no merit in discipline under ideal circumstances. I'll have it in the face of death, or it's useless. Where's this missionary? Get him here in front of me.'

The trader sat down, while the scarlet-cloaked figure was carefully brought forward.

'What's your name, reverend?'

'Eh?' The scarlet-robed figure wheeled toward Mallow, the whole body turning as a unit. His eyes were blankly open and there was a bruise on one temple. He had not spoken, nor, as far as Mallow could tell, moved during all the previous interval.

'Your name, revered one?'

The missionary started to sudden feverish life. His arms went out in an embracing gesture. 'My son – my children. May you always be in the protecting arms of the Galactic Spirit.'

Twer stepped forward, eyes troubled, voice husky, 'The man's sick. Take him to bed, somebody. Order him to bed, Mallow, and have him seen to. He's badly hurt.'

Mallow's great arm shoved him back. 'Don't interfere, Twer, or I'll have you out of the room. Your name, revered one?'

The missionary's hands clasped in sudden supplication, 'As you are enlightened men, save me from the heathen.' The words tumbled out. 'Save me from these brutes and darkened ones who raven after me and would afflict the Galactic Spirit with their crimes. I am Jord Parma, of the Anacreonian worlds. Educated at the Foundation; the Foundation itself, my children. I am a Priest of the Spirit educated into all the mysteries, who have come here where the inner voice called me.' He was gasping. 'I have suffered at the hands of the unenlightened. As you are Children of the Spirit; and in the name of that Spirit, protect me from them.'

A voice broke in upon them, as the emergency alarm box clamoured metallically:

'Enemy units in sight! Instruction desired!'

Every eye shot mechanically upward to the speaker.

Mallow swore violently. He clicked open the reverse and yelled, 'Maintain vigil! That is all!' and turned it off.

He made his way to the thick drapes that rustled aside at a touch and stared grimly out.

Enemy units! Several thousands of them in the persons of the individual members of a Korellian mob. The rolling rabble encompassed the port from extreme end to extreme end, and in the cold hard light of magnesium flares the foremost straggled closer.

'Tinter!' The trader never turned, but the back of his neck was red. 'Get the outer speaker working and find out what they want. Ask if they have a representative of the law with them. Make no promises and no threats, or I'll kill you.'

Tinter turned and left.

Mallow felt a rough hand on his shoulder and he struck it aside. It was Twer. His voice was an angry hiss in his ear, 'Mallow, you're bound to hold on to this man. There's no way of maintaining decency and honour otherwise. He's of the

Foundation and, after all, he – *is* a priest. These savages outside – Do you hear me?'

'I hear you, Twer.' Mallow's voice was incisive. 'I've got more to do here than guard missionaries. I'll do, sir, what I please, and, by Seldon and all the Galaxy, if you try to stop me, I'll tear out your stinking windpipe. Don't get in my way, Twer, or it will be the last of you.'

He turned and strode past. 'You! Revered Parma! Did you know that, by covention, no Foundation missionary may enter the Korellian territory?'

The missionary was trembling. 'I can but go where the Spirit leads, my son. If the darkened ones refuse enlightenment, is it not the greater sign of their need for it?'

'That's outside the question, revered one. You are here against the law of both Korell and the Foundation. I cannot in law protect you.'

The missionary's hands were raised again. His earlier bewilderment was gone. There was the raucous clamour of the ship's outer communication system in action, and the faint, undulating gabble of the angry horde in response. The sound made his eyes wild.

'You hear them? Why do you talk of law to me, of a law made by men? There are higher laws. Was it not the Galactic Spirit that said: Thou shalt not stand idly by to the hurt of thy fellow man. And has he not said: Even as thou dealest with the humble and defenceless, thus shalt thou be dealt with.

'Have you not guns? Have you not a ship? And behind you is there not the Foundation? And above and all about you is there not the Spirit that rules the universe?' He paused for breath.

And then the great outer voice of the *Far Star* ceased and Lieutenant Tinter was back, troubled.

'Speak!' said Mallow, shortly.

'Sir, they demand the person of Jord Parma.'

'If not?'

'There are various threats, sir. It is difficult to make much out. There are so many – and they seem quite mad. There is someone who says he governs the district and has police powers, but he is quite evidently not his own master.'

'Master or not,' shrugged Mallow, 'he is the law. Tell them that if this governor, or policeman, or whatever he is, approaches the ship alone, he can have the Revered Jord Parma.'

And there was suddenly a gun in his hand. He added, 'I don't know what insurbordination is. I have never had any experience with it. But if there's anyone here who thinks he can teach me, I'd like to teach him my antidote in return.'

The gun swivelled slowly, and rested on Twer. With an effort, the old trader's face untwisted and his hands unclenched and lowered. His breath was a harsh rasp in his nostrils.

Tinter left, and in five minute a puny figure detached itself from the crowd. It approched slowly and hesitantly, plainly drenched in fear and apprehension. Twice it turned back, and twice the patently obvious threats of the many-headed monster urged him on.

'All right,' Mallow gestured with the hand-blaster, which remained unsheathed. 'Grun and Upshur, take him out.'

The missionary screeched. He raised his arms and rigid fingers speared upward as the voluminous sleeve fell away to reveal the thin, veined arms. There was a momentary, tiny flash of light that came and went in a breath. Mallow blinked and gestured again, contemptuously.

The missionary's voice poured out as he struggled in the two-fold grasp. 'Cursed be the traitor who abandons his fellow man to evil and to death. Deafened be the ears that are deaf to the pleadings of the helpless. Blind be the eyes that are blind to innocence. Blackened for ever be the soul that consorts with blackness—'

Twer clamped his hands tightly over his ears.

Mallow flipped his blaster and put it away. 'Disperse,' he said, evenly, 'to respective stations. Maintain full vigil for six hours after dispersion of crowd. Double stations for forty-eight hours thereafter. Further instructions at that time. Twer, come with me.'

They were alone in Mallow's private quarters. Mallow indicated a chair and Twer sat down. His stocky figure looked shrunken.

Mallow stared him down, sardonically. 'Twer,' he said, 'I'm disappointed. Your three years in politics seem to have gotten you out of trader habits. Remember, I may be a democrat back at the Foundation, but there's nothing short of tyranny that can run my ship the way I want it run. I never had to pull a blaster on my men before, and I wouldn't have had to now, if you hadn't gone out of line.

'Twer, you have no official position, but you're here on my invitation, and I'll extend to you every courtesy – in private. However, from now on, in the presence of my officers or men, I'm "sir", and "Mallow". And when I give an order, you'll jump faster than a third-class recruit just for luck, or I'll have you ironed in the sub-level even faster. Understand?'

The party-leader swallowed dryly. He said, reluctantly, 'My apologies.'

'Accepted! Will you shake?'

Twer's fingers were swallowed in Mallow's huge palm. Twer said, 'My motives were good. It's difficult to send a man out to be lynched. That wobbly-kneed governor or whatever-he-was can't save him. It's murder.'

'I can't help that. Frankly, the incident smelled too bad. Didn't you notice?'

'Notice what?'

'This space-port is deep in the middle of a sleepy far section. Suddenly a missionary escapes. Where from? He comes here. Coincidence? A huge crowd gathers. From where? The nearest city of any size must be at least a hundred miles away. But they arrive in half an hour. How?'

'How?' echoed Twer.

'Well, what if the missionary were brought here and released as bait. Our friend, Revered Parma, was considerably

confused. He seemed at no time to be in complete possession o
his wits.'

'Hard usage—' murmured Twer bitterly.

'Maybe! And maybe the idea was to have us go all chivalrou
and gallant, into a stupid defence of the man. He was her
against the laws of Korell and the Foundation. If I withhol
him, it is an act of war against Korell, and the Foundatio
would have no legal right to defend *us*.'

'That – that's pretty far-fetched.'

The speaker blared and forestalled Mallow's answer: 'Sir
official communication received.'

'Submit immediately!'

The gleaming cylinder arrived in its slot with a click. Mallo
opened it and shook out the silver-impregnated sheet it held
He rubbed it appreciatively between thumb and finger an
said, 'Teleported direct from the capital. Commdor's ow
stationery.'

He read it in a glance and laughed shortly. 'So my idea wa
far-fetched, was it?'

He tossed it to Twer, and added, 'Half an hour after we han
back the missionary, we finally get a very polite invitation to th
Commdor's august presence – after seven days of previou
waiting. *I* think we passed a test.'

5

Commdor Asper was a man of the people, by self-acclamatio
His remaining back-fringe of grey hair drooped limply to h
shoulders, his shirt needed laundering, and he spoke with
snuffle.

'There is no ostentation here, Trader Mallow,' he said. 'N
false show. In me, you see merely the first citizen of the Stat
That's what Commdor means, and that's the only title I have

He seemed inordinately pleased with it all: 'In fact, I consider that fact one of the strongest bonds between Korell and your nation. I understand you people enjoy the republican blessings we do.'

'Exactly, Commdor,' said Mallow gravely, taking mental exception to the comparison, 'an argument which I consider strongly in favour of continued peace and friendship between our governments.'

'Peace! Ah!' The Commdor's sparse grey beard twitched to the sentimental grimaces of his face. 'I don't think there is anyone in the Periphery who has so next to his heart the ideal of Peace, as I have. I can truthfully say that since I succeeded my illustrious father to the leadership of the State, the reign of Peace has never been broken. Perhaps I shouldn't say it' – he coughed gently – 'but I *have* been told that my people, my fellow-citizens rather, know me as Asper, the Well-Beloved.'

Mallow's eyes wandered over the well-kept garden. Perhaps the tall men and the strangely-designed but openly-vicious weapons they carried just happened to be lurking in odd corners as a precaution against himself. That would be understandable. But the lofty, steel-girdered walls that circled the place had quite obviously been recently strengthened – an unfitting occupation for such a Well-Beloved Asper.

He said, 'It is fortunate that I have you to deal with then, Commdor. The despots and monarchs of surrounding worlds, which haven't the benefit of enlightened administration, often lack the qualities that would make a ruler well-beloved.'

'Such as?' There was a cautious note in the Commdor's voice.

'Such as their concern for the best interests of their people. You, on the other hand, would understand.'

The Commdor kept his eyes on the gravel path as they walked leisurely. His hands caressed each other behind his back.

Mallow went on smoothly, 'Up to now, trade between our two nations has suffered because of the restrictions placed upon our traders by your government. Surely, it has long been evident to you that unlimited trade—'

'Free Trade!' mumbled the Commdor.

'Free Trade, then. You must see that it would be of benefit to both of us. There are things you have that we want, and things we have that you want. It asks only an exchange to bring increased prosperity. An enlightened ruler such as yourself, a friend of the people – I might say, a *member* of the people – needs no elaboration on that theme. I won't insult your intelligence by offering any.'

'True! I have see this. But what would you?' His voice was a plaintive whine. 'Your people have always been so unreasonable. I am in favour of all the trade our economy can support, but not on your terms. I am not sole master here.' His voice rose, 'I am only the servant of public opinion. My people will not take commerce which sparked in crimson and gold.'

Mallow drew himself up. 'A compulsory religion?'

'So it has always been in effect. Surely you remember the case of Askone twenty years ago. First they were sold some of your goods and then your people asked for complete freedom of missionary effort in order that the goods might be run properly; that Temples of Health be set up. There was then the establishment of religious schools; autonomous rights for all officers of the religion and with what result? Askone is now an integral member of the Foundation's system and the Grand Master cannot call his underwear his own. Oh, no! Oh, no! The dignity of an independent people could never suffer it.'

'None of what you speak is at all what I suggest,' interposed Mallow.

'No?'

'No. I'm a Master-Trader. Money is *my* religion. All thi mysticism and hocus-pocus of the missionaries annoy me, and I'm glad you refuse to countenance it. It makes you more m type of man.'

The Commdor's laugh was high-pitched and jerky. 'We said! The Foundation should have sent a man of your calibr before this.'

He laid a friendly hand upon the trader's bulking shoulder.

'But man, you have told me only half. You have told me what the catch is *not*. Now tell me what it *is*.'

'The only catch, Commdor, is that you're going to be burdened with an immense quantity of riches.'

'Indeed?' he snuffled. 'But what could I want with riches? The true wealth is the love of one's people. I have that.'

'You can have both, for it is possible to gather gold with one hand and love with the other.'

'Now that, my young man, would be an interesting phenomenon, if it were possible. How would you go about it?'

'Oh, in a number of ways. The difficulty is choosing among them. Let's see. Well, luxury items, for instance. This object here, now—'

Mallow drew gently out of an inner pocket a flat, linked chain of polished metal. 'This, for instance.'

'What is it?'

'That's got to be demonstrated. Can you get a girl? Any young female will do. *And* a mirror, full length.'

'Hm-m-m. Let's get indoors then.'

The Commodor referred to his dwelling-place as a house. The populace undoubtedly would call it a palace. To Mallow's straightforward eyes, it looked uncommonly like a fortress. It was built on an eminence that overlooked the capital. Its walls were thick and reinforced. Its approaches were guarded, and its architecture was shaped for defence. Just the type of dwelling, Mallow thought sourly, for Asper, the Well-Beloved.

A young girl was before them. She bent low to the Commdor, who said, 'This is one of the Commdora's girls. Will she do?'

'Perfectly!'

The Commdor watched carefully while Mallow snapped the chain about the girl's waist, and stepped back.

The Commdor snuffled, 'Well. Is that all?'

'Will you draw the curtain, Commdor. Young lady, there's a

little knob just near the snap. Will you move it upward, please? Go ahead, it won't hurt you.'

The girl did so, drew a sharp breath, looked at her hands and gasped, 'Oh!'

From her waist as a source she was drowned in a pale, streaming luminescence of shifting colour that drew itself over her head in a flashing coronet of liquid fire. It was as if someone had torn the aurora borealis out of the sky and moulded it into a cloak.

The girl stepped to the mirror and stared, fascinated.

'Here, take this.' Mallow handed her a necklace of dull pebbles. 'Put it around your neck.'

The girl did so, and each pebble, as it entered the luminescent field became an individual flame that leaped and sparkled in crimson and gold.

'What do you think of it?' Mallow asked her. The girl didn't answer but there was adoration in her eyes. The Commdor gestured and, reluctantly, she pushed the knob down, and the glory died. She left – with a memory.

'It's yours, Commdor,' said Mallow, 'for the Commdora. Consider it a small gift from the Foundation.'

'Hm-m-m.' The Commdor turned the belt and necklace over in his hand as though calculating the weight. 'How is it done?'

Mallow shrugged. 'That's a question for our technical experts. But it will work for you without – mark you, *without* – priestly help.'

'Well, it's only feminine frippery after all. What could you do with it? Where would the money come in?'

'You have balls, receptions, banquets – that sort of thing?'

'Oh, yes.'

'Do you realize what women will pay for that sort o jewellery? Ten thousand credits, at least.'

The Commdor seemed struck in a heap. 'Ah!'

'And since the power-unit of this particular item will not las longer than six months, there will be the necessity of frequen replacements. Now we can sell as many of these as you want fo the equivalent in wrought iron of one thousand credits. There's 900 per cent profit for you.'

The Commdor plucked at his beard and seemed engaged in awesome mental calculations. 'Galaxy, how the dowagers will fight for them. I'll keep the supply small and let them bid. Of course, it wouldn't do to let them know that I personally—'

Mallow said, 'We can explain the workings of dummy corporations, if you would like. Then, working further at random, take our complete line of household gadgets. We have collapsible stoves that will roast the toughest meats to the desired tenderness in two minutes. We've got knives that won't require sharpening. We've got the equivalent of a complete laundry that can be packed in a small closet and will work entirely automatically. Ditto dish-washers. Ditto-ditto floor-scrubbers, furniture polishers, dust-precipitators, lighting fixtures - oh, anything you like. Think of your increased popularity, *if* you make them available to the public. Think of your increased quantity of, uh, worldly goods, if they're available as a government monopoly at 900 per cent profit. It will be worth many times the money to them, and they needn't know what *you* pay for it. And, mind you, none of it will require priestly supervision. Everybody will be happy.'

'Except you, it seems. What do *you* get out of it?'

'Just what every trader gets by Foundation law. My men and I will collect half of whatever profits we take in. Just you buy all I want to sell you, and we'll both make out quite well. *Quite* well.'

The Commdor was enjoying his thoughts, 'What did you say you wanted to be paid with? Iron?'

'That, and coal, and bauxite. Also tobacco, pepper, magnesium, hardwood. Nothing you haven't got enough of.'

'It sounds well.'

'I think so. Oh, and still another item at random, Commdor. I could retool your factories.'

'Eh? How's that?'

'Well, take your steel foundries. I have handy little gadgets that could do tricks with steel that would cut production costs to one per cent of previous marks. You could cut prices by half, and still split extremely fat profits with the manufacturers. I tell you, I could show you exactly what I mean, if you allowed me a demonstration. Do you have a steel foundry in this city? It wouldn't take long.'

'It could be arranged, Trader Mallow. But tomorrow, tomorrow. Would you dine with us tonight?'

'My men—' began Mallow.

'Let them all come,' said the Commdor, expansively. 'A symbolic friendly union of our nations. It will give us a chance for further friendly discussion. But one thing.' his face lengthened and grew stern, 'none of your religion. Don't think that all this is an entering wedge for the missionaries.'

'Commdor,' said Mallow, dryly, 'I give you my word that religion would cut my profits.'

'Then that will do for now. You'll be escorted back to your ship.'

6

The Commdora was much younger than her husband. Her face was pale and coldly formed and her black hair was drawn smoothly and tightly back.

Her voice was tart. 'You are quite finished, my gracious and noble husband? Quite, *quite* finished? I suppose I may even enter the garden if I wish, now.'

'There is no need for dramatics, Licia, my dear,' said the Commdor, mildly. 'The young man will attend at dinner tonight, and you can speak with him all you wish and even amuse yourself by listening to all I say. Room will have to be arranged for his men somewhere about the place. The stars grant that they be few in number.'

'Most likely they'll be great hogs of eaters who will eat meat by the quarter-animal and wine by the hogshead. And you will groan for two nights when you calculate the expense.'

'Well now, perhaps I won't. Despite your opinion, the dinner is to be on the most lavish scale.'

'Oh, I see.' She stared at him contemptuously. 'You are very friendly with these barbarians. Perhaps that is why I was not to be permitted to attend your conversation. Perhaps your little weazened soul is plotting to turn against my father.'

'Not at all.'

'Yes, I'd be likely to believe you, wouldn't I? If ever a poor woman was sacrificed for policy to an unsavoury marriage, it was myself. I could have picked a proper man from the alleys and mudheaps of my native world.'

'Well, now, I'll tell you what, my lady. Perhaps you would enjoy returning to your native world. Only to retain as a souvenir that portion of you with which I am best acquainted, I could have your tongue cut out first. And,' he lolled his head, calculatingly, to one side, 'as a final improving touch to your beauty, your ears and the tip of your nose as well.'

'You wouldn't dare, you little pug-dog. My father would pulverize your toy nation to meteoric dust. In fact, he might do it in any case, if I told him you were treating with these barbarians.'

'Hm-m-m. Well, there's no need for threats. You are free to question the man yourself tonight. Meanwhile, madam, keep your wagging tongue still.'

'At your orders?'

'Here, take this, then, and keep still.'

The band was about her waist and the necklace around her neck. He pushed the knob and stepped back.

The Commdora drew in her breath and held out her hands stiffly. She fingered the necklace gingerly, and gasped again.

The Commdor rubbed his hands with satisfaction and said, 'You may wear it tonight – and I'll get you more. *Now* keep still.'

The Commdora kept still.

7

Jaim Twer fidgeted and shuffled his feet. He said, 'What's twisting *your* face?'

Hober Mallow lifted out of his brooding, 'Is my face twisted? It's not meant so.'

'Something must have happened yesterday – I mean, besides that feast.' With sudden conviction, 'Mallow, there's trouble isn't there?'

'Trouble? No. Quite opposite. In fact, I'm in the position of throwing my full weight against a door and finding it ajar at the time. We're getting into this steel foundry too easily.'

'You suspect a trap?'

'Oh, for Seldon's sake, don't be melodramatic.' Mallow swallowed his impatience and added conversationally, 'It's just that the easy entrance means there will be nothing to see.'

'Atomic power, huh?' Twer ruminated. 'I'll tell you. There's just about no evidence of any atomic power economy here in Korell. And it would be pretty hard work to mask all signs of the widespread effects a fundamental technology such as atomics would have on everything.'

'Not if it was just starting up, Twer, and being applied to a war economy. You'd find it in the shipyards and the steel foundries only.'

'So if we don't find it, then—'

'Then they haven't got it – or they're not showing it. Toss a coin or take a guess.'

Twer shook his head, 'I wish I'd been with you yesterday.'

'I wish you had, too,' said Mallow, stonily. 'I have no objection to moral support. Unfortunately, it was the Commdor who set the terms of the meeting, and not myself.

And *that* outside there would seem to be the royal ground-car to escort us to the foundry. Have you got the gadgets?'

'All of them.'

8

The foundry was large, and bore the odour of decay which no amount of superficial repairs could quite erase. It was empty now and in quite an unnatural state of quiet, as it played unaccustomed host to the Commdor and his court.

Mallow had swung the steel sheet on to the two supports with a careless heave. He had taken the instrument held out to him by Twer and was gripping the leather handle inside its leaden sheath.

'The instrument,' he said, 'is dangerous, but so is a buzz saw. You just have to keep your fingers away.'

And as he spoke, he drew the muzzle-slit swiftly down the length of the steel sheet, which quietly and instantly fell in two.

There was a unanimous jump, and Mallow laughed. He picked up one of the halves and propped it against his knee. 'You can adjust the cutting-length accurately to a hundredth of an inch, and a two-inch sheet will slit down the middle as easily as this thing did. If you've got the thickness exactly judged, you can place steel on a wooden table, and split the metal without scratching the wood.'

And at each phrase, the atomic shear moved and a gouged chunk of steel flew across the room.

'That,' he said, 'is whittling – with steel.'

He passed back the shear. 'Or else you have the plane. Do you want to decrease the thickness of a sheet, smooth out an irregularity, remove corrosion? Watch!'

Thin, transparent foil flew off the other half of the original sheet in six-inch swaths, then eight-inch, then twelve.

'Or drills? It's all the same principle.'

They were crowded around now. It might have been a sleight-of-hand show, a corner magician, a vaudeville act made into high-pressure salesmanship. Commdor Asper fingered scraps of steel. High officials of the government tiptoed over each other's shoulders, and whispered, while Mallow punched clean, beautiful round holes through an inch of hard steel at every touch of his atomic drill.

'Just one more demonstration. Bring two short lengths of pipe, somebody.'

An Honourable Chamberlain of something-or-other sprang to obedience in the general excitement and thought-absorption, and stained his hands like any labourer.

And there was a single pipe! The new ends, with even atomic irregularities missing, formed one piece upon joining. Johannison blocks, at a stroke.

Then Mallow looked up at his audience, stumbled at his first word and stopped. There was the keen stirring of excitement in his chest, and the base of his stomach went tingly and cold.

The Commdor's own bodyguard, in the confusion, had struggled to the front line, and Mallow, for the first time, was near enough to see their unfamiliar hand-weapons in detail.

They were atomic! There was no mistaking it; an explosive projectile weapon with a barrel like that was impossible. But that wasn't the big point. That wasn't the point at all.

The butts of those weapons had, deeply etched upon them, in worn gold plating, the Spaceship-and-Sun!

The same Spaceship-and-Sun that was stamped on every one of the great volumes of the original Encyclopedia that the Foundation had begun and not yet finished. *The same Spaceship-and-Sun that had blazoned the banner of the Galactic Empire through millennia.*

Mallow talked through and around his thoughts: 'Test that pipe! It's one piece. Not perfect; naturally, the joining shouldn't be done by hand.'

There was no need of further legerdemain. It had gone over.

Mallow was through. He had what he wanted. There was only one thing in his mind. The golden globe with its conventionalized rays, and the oblique cigar shape that was a space vessel.

The Spaceship-and-Sun of the Empire!

The Empire! The words drilled! A century and a half had passed but there was still the Empire, somewhere deeper in the Galaxy. And it was emerging again, out into the Periphery.

Mallow smiled!

9

The *Far Star* was two days out in space, when Hober Mallow, in his private quarters with Senior Lieutenant Drawt, handed him an envelope, a roll of microfilm, and a silvery spheroid.

'As of an hour from now, Lieutenant, you're Acting Captain of the *Far Star*, until I return – or for ever.'

Drawt made a motion of standing but Mallow waved him down imperiously.

'Quiet, and listen. The envelope contains the exact location of the planet to which you're to proceed. There you will wait for me for two months. If, before the two months are up, the Foundation locates you, the microfilm is my report of the trip.

'If, however,' and his voice was sombre, 'I do *not* return at the end of two months, and Foundation vessels do not locate you, proceed to the planet, Terminus, and hand in the Time Capsule as the report. Do you understand that?'

'Yes, sir.'

'At no time are you, or any of the men, to amplify in any single instance my official report.'

'If we are questioned, sir?'

'Then you know nothing.'

'Yes, sir.'

The interview ended, and fifty minutes later, a lifeboat kicked lightly off the side of the *Far Star*.

10

Onum Barr was an old man, too old to be afraid. Since the last disturbances, he had lived alone on the fringes of the land with what books he had saved from the ruins. He had nothing he feared losing, least of all the worn remnant of his life, and so he faced the intruder without cringing.

'Your door was open,' the stranger explained.

His accent was clipped and harsh, and Barr did not fail to notice the strange blue-steel hand-weapon at his hips. In the half-gloom of the small room, Barr saw the glow of a forceshield surrounding the man.

He said wearily, 'There is no reason to keep it closed. Do you wish anything of me?'

'Yes.' The stranger remained standing in the centre of the room. He was large, both in height and bulk. 'Yours is the only house about here.'

'It is a desolate place,' agreed Barr, 'but there is a town to the east. I can show you the way.'

'In a while. May I sit?'

'If the chairs will hold you,' said the old man, gravely. They were old, too. Relics of a better youth.

The stranger said, 'My name is Hober Mallow. I come from a far province.'

Barr nodded and smiled. 'Your tongue convicted you of that long ago. I am Onum Barr of Siwenna – and once Patrician of the Empire.'

'Then this *is* Siwenna. I had only old maps to guide me.'

'They would have to be old, indeed, for star-positions to be misplaced.'

Barr sat quite still, while the other's eyes drifted away into a reverie. He noticed that the atomic force-shield had vanished from about the man and admitted dryly to himself that his person no longer seemed formidable to strangers – or even, for good or for evil, to his enemies.

He said, 'My house is poor and my resources few. You may share what I have if your stomach can endure black bread and dried corn.'

Mallow shook his head. 'No, I have eaten, and I can't stay. All I need are the directions to the centre of government.'

'That is easily enough done, and poor though I am, deprives me of nothing. Do you mean the capital of the planet, or of the Imperial Sector?'

The younger man's eyes narrowed. 'Aren't the two identical? Isn't this Siwenna?'

The old patrician nodded slowly. 'Siwenna, yes. But Siwenna is no longer capital of the Normannic Sector. Your old map has misled you after all. The stars may not change even in centuries, but political boundaries are all too fluid.'

'That's too bad. In fact, that's very bad. Is the new capital far off?'

'It's on Orsha II. Twenty parsecs off. Your map will direct you. How old is it?'

'A hundred and fifty years.'

'That old?' The old man sighed. 'History has been crowded since. Do you know any of it?'

Mallow shook his head slowly.

Barr said, 'You're fortunate. It has been an evil time for the provinces, but for the reign of Stannell VI, and he died fifty years ago. Since that time, rebellion and ruin, ruin and rebellion.' Barr wondered if he were growing garrulous. It was a lonely life out here, and he had so little chance to talk to men.

Mallow said with sudden sharpness, 'Ruin, eh? You sound as if the province were impoverished.'

'Perhaps not on an absolute scale. The physical resources of twenty-five first-rank planets take a long time to use up. Compared to the wealth of the last century, though, we have gone a long way downhill – and there is no sign of turning, not yet. Why are you so interested in all this, young man? You are all alive and your eyes shine!'

The trader came near enough to blushing, as the faded eyes seemed to look too deep into his and smile at what they saw.

He said, 'Now look here. I'm a trader out there – out toward the rim of the Galaxy. I've located some old maps, and I'm out to open new markets. Naturally, talk of impoverished provinces disturbs me. You can't get money out of a world unless money's there to be got. Now how's Siwenna, for instance?'

The old man leaned forward. 'I cannot say. It will do even yet, perhaps. But *you* a trader? You look more like a fighting man. You hold your hand near your gun and there is a scar on your jawbone.'

Mallow jerked his head. 'There isn't much law out there where I come from. Fighting and scars are part of a trader's overhead. But fighting is only useful when there's money at the end, and if I can get it without, so much the sweeter. Now will I find enough money here to make it worth the fighting? I take it I can find the fighting easily enough.'

'Easily enough,' agreed Barr. 'You could join Wiscard's remnants in the Red Stars. I don't know, though, if you'd call that fighting or piracy. Or you could join our present gracious viceroy – gracious by right of murder, pillage, rapine, and the word of a boy Emperor, since rightfully assassinated.' The patrician's thin cheeks reddened. His eyes closed and then opened, bird-bright.

'You don't sound very friendly to the viceroy, Patrician Barr,' said Mallow. 'What if I'm one of his spies?'

'What if you are?' said Barr, bitterly. 'What can you take?' He gestured a withered arm at the bare interior of the decaying mansion.

'Your life.'

'It would leave me easily enough. It has been with me five years too long. But you are *not* one of the viceroy's men. If you were, perhaps even now instinctive self-preservation would keep my mouth closed.'

'How do you know?'

The old man laughed. 'You seem suspicious. Come, I'll wager you think I'm trying to trap you into denouncing the government. No, no. I am past politics.'

'Past politics? Is a man ever past that? The words you used to describe the viceroy – what were they? Murder, pillage, all that. You didn't sound objective. Not exactly. Not as if you were past politics.'

The old man shrugged. 'Memories sting when they come suddenly. Listen! Judge for yourself! When Siwenna was the provincial capital, I was a patrician and a member of the provincial senate. My family was an old and honoured one. One of my great-grandfathers had been – No, never mind that. Past glories are poor feeding.'

'I take it,' said Mallow, 'there was a civil war, or a revolution.'

Barr's face darkened. 'Civil wars are chronic in these degenerate days, but Siwenna had kept apart. Under Stannell VI, it had almost achieved its ancient prosperity. But weak emperors followed, and weak emperors mean strong viceroys, and our last viceroy – the same Wiscard, whose remnants still prey on the commerce among the Red Stars – aimed at the Imperial Purple. He wasn't the first to aim. And if he had succeeded, he wouldn't have been the first to succeed.

'But he failed. For when the Emperor's admiral approached the province at the head of a fleet, Siwenna itself rebelled against its rebel viceroy.' He stopped, sadly.

Mallow found himself tense on the edge of his seat, and relaxed slowly. 'Please continue, sir.'

'Thank you,' said Barr, wearily. 'It's kind of you to humour an old man. They rebelled; or I should say, *we* rebelled, for I was one of the minor leaders. Wiscard left Siwenna, barely ahead of us, and the planet, and with it the province, were thrown open to the admiral with every gesture of loyalty to the Emperor. Why we did this, I'm not sure. Maybe we felt loyal to the symbol, if not to the person, of the Emperor – a cruel and vicious child. Maybe we feared the horrors of a siege.'

'Well?' urged Mallow, gently.

'Well,' came the grim retort. 'That didn't suit the admiral. He wanted the glory of conquering a rebellious province and his men wanted the loot such conquest would involve. So while the people were still gathered in every large city, cheering the Emperor and his admiral, he occupied all armed centres, and then ordered the population put to the atom-blast.'

'On what pretext?'

'On the pretext that they had rebelled against their viceroy, the Emperor's anointed. And the admiral became the new viceroy, by virtue of one month of massacre, pillage and complete horror. I had six sons. Five died – variously. I had a daughter. I *hope* she died, eventually. *I* escaped because I was old. I came here, too old to cause even our viceroy worry.' He bent his grey head, 'They left me nothing, because I had helped drive out a rebellious governor and deprived an admiral of his glory.'

Mallow sat silent, and waited. Then, 'What of your sixth son?' he asked softly.

'Eh?' Barr smiled acidly. 'He is safe, for he has joined the admiral as a common soldier under an assumed name. He is a gunner in the viceroy's personal fleet. Oh, no, I see your eyes. He is not an unnatural son. He visits me when he can and gives me what he can. He keeps me alive. And some day, our great and glorious viceroy will grovel to his death, and it will be my son who will be his executioner.'

'And you tell this to a stranger? You endanger your son.'

'No. I help him, by introducing a new enemy. And were I a friend of the viceroy, as I am his enemy, I would tell him to string outer space with ships, clear to the rim of the Galaxy.'

'There are no ships there?'

'Did you find any? Did any space-guards question your entry? With ships few enough, and the bordering provinces filled with their share of intrigue and iniquity, none can be spared to guard the barbarian outer suns. No danger ever threatened us from the broken edge of the Galaxy – until *you* came.'

'I? I'm no danger.'

'There will be more after you.'

Mallow shook his head slowly. 'I'n not sure I understand you.'

'Listen!' There was a feverish edge to the old man's voice. 'I knew you when you entered. You have a force-shield about your body, or had when I first saw you.'

Doubtful silence, then: 'Yes – I had.'

'Good. That was a flaw, but you didn't know that. There are some things I know. It's out of fashion in these decaying times to be a soldier. Events race and flash past and who cannot fight the tide with atom-blast in hand is swept away, as I was. But I was a scholar, and I know that in all the history of atomics, no portable force-shield was ever invented. We have force-shields – huge, lumbering power-houses that will protect a city, or even a ship, but not one single man.'

'Ah?' Mallow's under lip thrust out. 'And what do you deduce from that?'

'There have been stories percolating through space. They travel paths and become distorted with every parsec – but when I was young there was a small ship of strange men, who did not know our customs and could not tell where they came from. They talked of magicians at the edge of the Galaxy; magicians who glowed in the darkness, who flew unaided through the air, and whom weapons would not touch.

'We laughed. I laughed, too. I forgot it till today. But you glow in the darkness, and I don't think my blaster, if I had one, would hurt you. Tell me, can you fly through the air as you sit there now?'

Mallow said calmly, 'I can make nothing of all this.'

Barr smiled, 'I'm content with the answer. I do not examine my guests. But if there are magicians; if *you* are one of them; there may some day be a great influx of them, or you. Perhaps that would be well. Maybe we need new blood.' He muttered soundlessly to himself, then, slowly, 'But it works the other way, too. Our new viceroy also dreams, as did our old Wiscard.'

'Also after the Emperor's crown?'

Barr nodded, 'My son hears tales. In the viceroy's personal entourage, one could scarcely help it. And he tells me of them. Our new viceroy would not refuse the Crown if offered, but he guards his line of retreat. There are stories that, failing Imperial heights, he plans to carve out a new Empire in the Barbarian hinterland. It is said, but I don't vouch for this, that he has already given one of his daughters as wife to a Kinglet somewhere in the uncharted Periphery.'

'If one listened to every story—'

'I know. There are many more. I'm old and I babble nonsense. But what do you say?' And those sharp, old eyes peered deep.

The trader considered. 'I say nothing. But I'd like to ask something. Does Siwenna have atomic power? Now, wait, I know that it possesses the knowledge of atomics. I mean, do they have power generators intact, or did the recent sack destroy them?'

'Destroy them? Oh, no. Half a planet would be wiped out before the smallest power station would be touched. They are irreplaceable and the suppliers of the strength of the fleet.' Almost proudly, 'We have the largest and best on this side of Trantor itself.'

'Then what would I do first if I wanted to see these generators?'

'Nothing!' replied Barr, decisively. 'You couldn't approach any military centre without being shot down instantly. Neither could anyone. Siwenna is still deprived of civic rights.'

'You mean all the power stations are under the military?'

'No. There are the small city stations, the ones supplying power for heating and lighting homes, powering vehicles and so forth. Those are almost as bad. They're controlled by the tech-men.'

'Who are they?'

'A specialized group which supervises the power plants. The honour is hereditary, the young ones being brought up in the profession as apprentices. Strict sense of duty, honour, and all that. No one but a tech-man could enter a station.'

'I see.'

'I don't say, though,' added Barr, 'that there aren't cases where tech-men haven't been bribed. In days when we have nine emperors in fifty years and seven of these are assassinated – when every space-captain aspires to the usurpation of a viceroyship, and every viceroy to the Imperium, I suppose even a tech-man can fall prey to money. But it would require a good deal, and I have none. Have you?'

'Money? No. But does one always bribe with money?'

'What else, when money buys all else.'

'There is quite enough that money won't buy. And now if you'll tell me the nearest city with one of the stations, and how best to get there, I'll thank you.'

'Wait!' Barr held out his thin hands. 'Where do you rush? You come here, but *I* ask no questions. In the city, where the inhabitants are still called rebels, you would be challenged by the first soldier or guard who heard your accent and saw your clothes.'

He rose and from an obscure corner of an old chest brought out a booklet. 'My passport – forged. I escaped with it.'

He placed it in Mallow's hand and folded the fingers over it. 'The description doesn't fit, but if you flourish it, the chances are many to one they will not look closely.'

'But you. You'll be left without one.'

The old exile shrugged cynically. 'What of it? And a further caution. Curb your tongue! Your accent is barbarous, your idioms peculiar, and every once in a while you deliver yourself of the most astounding archaisms. The less you speak, the less suspicion you will draw upon yourself. Now I'll tell you how to get to the city—'

Five minutes later, Mallow was gone.

He returned but once, for a moment, to the old patrician's house, before leaving it entirely, however. And when Onum Barr stepped into his little garden early the next morning, he found a box at his feet. It contained provisions, concentrated provisions such as one would find aboard ship, and alien in taste and preparation.

But they were good, and lasted long.

11

The tech-man was short, and his skin glistened with well-kept plumpness. His hair was a fringe and his skull shone through pinkly. The rings on his fingers were thick and heavy, his clothes were scented, and he was the first man Mallow had met on the planet who hadn't looked hungry.

The tech-man's lips pursed peevishly. 'Now, my man, quickly. I have things of great importance waiting for me. You seem a stranger—' He seemed to evaluate Mallow's definitely un-Siwennese costume and his eyelids were heavy with suspicion.

'I am not of the neighbourhood,' said Mallow, calmly, 'but the matter is irrelevant. I have had the honour to send you a little gift yesterday—'

The tech-man's nose lifted. 'I received it. An interesting gewgaw. I may have use for it on occasion.'

'I have other and more interesting gifts. Quite out of the gewgaw stage.'

'Oh-h?' The tech-man's voice lingered thoughtfully over the monosyllable. 'I think I already see the course of the interview;

it has happened before. You are going to give me some trifle or other. A few credits, perhaps a cloak, second-rate jewellery; anything your little soul may think sufficient to corrupt a techman.' His lower lip puffed out belligerently. 'And I know what you wish in exchange. There have been others to suffice with the same bright idea. You wish to be adopted into our clan. You wish to be taught the mysteries of atomics and the care of the machines. You think because you dogs of Siwenna – and probably your strangerhood is assumed for safety's sake – are being daily punished for your rebellion that you can escape what you deserve by throwing over yourselves the privileges and protections of the tech-man's guild.'

Mallow would have spoken, but the tech-man raised himself into a sudden roar. 'And now leave before I report your name to the Protector of the City. Do you think that I would betray the trust? The Siwennese traitors that preceded me – perhaps! But you deal with a different breed now. Why, Galaxy, I marvel that I do not kill you myself at this moment with my bare hands.'

Mallow smiled to himself. The entire speech was patently artificial in tone and content, so that all the dignified indignation degenerated into uninspired farce.

The trader glanced humorously at the two flabby hands that had been named as his possible excecutioners then and there, and said, 'Your Wisdom, you are wrong on three counts. First, I am not a creature of the viceroy come to test your loyalty. Second, my gift is something the Emperor himself in all his splendour does not and will never possess. Third, what I wish in return is very little; a nothing; a mere breath.'

'So you say!' He descended into heavy sarcasm. 'Come, what is this imperial donation that your godlike power wishes to bestow upon me? Something the Emperor doesn't have, eh?' He broke into a sharp squawk of derision.

Mallow rose and pushed the chair aside. 'I have waited three days to see you, Your Wisdom, but the display will take only three seconds. If you will draw that blaster whose butt I see very near your hand—'

'Eh?'

'And shoot me, I will be obliged.'

'*What?*'

'If I am killed, you can tell the police I tried to bribe you into betraying guild secrets. You'll receive high praise. If I am not killed, you may have my shield.'

For the first time, the tech-man became aware of the dimly-white illumination that hovered closely about his visitor, as though he had been dipped in pearl-dust. His blaster raised to the level and with eyes a-squint in wonder and suspicion, he closed contact.

The molecules of air caught in the sudden surge of atomic disruption, tore into glowing, burning ions, and marked out the blinding thin line that struck at Mallow's heart – and splashed!

While Mallow's look of patience never changed, the atomic forces that tore at him consumed themselves against that fragile, pearly illumination, and crashed back to die in mid-air.

The tech-man's blaster dropped to the floor with an unnoticed crash.

Mallow said, 'Does the Emperor have a personal force-shield? *You* can have one.'

The tech-man stuttered, 'Are you a tech-man?'

'No.'

'Then – then where did you get that?'

'What do you care?' Mallow was coolly contemptuous. 'Do you want it?' A thin, knobbed chain fell upon the desk. 'There it is.'

The tech-man snatched it up and fingered it nervously, 'Is this complete?'

'Complete.'

'Where's the power?'

Mallow's finger fell upon the largest knob, dull in its leaden case.

The tech-man looked up, and his face was congested with blood. 'Sir, I am a tech-man, senior grade. I have twenty years behind me as supervisor and I studied under the great Bler at the University of Trantor. If you have the infernal charlatanry to tell me that a small container the size of a – of a walnut, blast it, holds an atomic generator, I'll have you before the Protector in three seconds.'

'Explain it yourself then, if you can. I say it's complete.'

The tech-man's flush faded slowly as he bound the chain about his waist, and, following Mallow's gesture, pushed the knob. The radiance that surrounded him shone into dim relief. His blaster lifted, then hesitated. Slowly, he adjusted it to an almost burnless minimum.

And then, convulsively, he closed circuit and the atomic fire dashed against his hand, harmlessly.

He whirled, 'And what if I shoot you now, and keep the shield?'

'Try!' said Mallow. 'Do you think I gave you my only sample?' And he, too, was solidly incased in light.

The tech-man giggled nervously. The blaster clattered on to the desk. He said, 'And what is this mere nothing, this breath, that you wish in return?'

'I want to see your generators.'

'You realize that that is forbidden. It would mean ejection into space for both of us—'

'I don't want to touch them or have anything to do with them. I want to *see* them – from a distance.'

'If not?'

'If not, you have your shield, but I have other things. For one thing, a blaster especially designed to pierce that shield.'

'Hm-m-m.' The tech-man's eyes shifted. 'Come with me.'

12

The tech-man's home was a small two-storey affair on the outskirts of the huge, cubiform, windowless affair that dominated the centre of the city. Mallow passed from one to the other through an underground passage, and found himself in the silent, ozone-tinged atmosphere of the power-house.

For fifteen minutes, he followed his guide and said nothing. His eyes missed nothing. His fingers touched nothing. And then the tech-man said in strangled tones, 'Have you had enough? I couldn't trust my underlings in *this* case.'

'Could you ever?' asked Mallow, ironically. 'I've had enough.'

They were back in the office and Mallow said, thoughtfully, 'And all those generators are in your hands?'

'Every one,' said the tech-man, with more than a touch of complacency.

'And you keep them running and in order?'

'Right!'

'And if they break down?'

The tech-man shook his head indignantly. 'They don't break down. They never break down. They were built for eternity.'

'Eternity is a long time. Just suppose—'

'It is unscientific to suppose meaningless cases.'

'All right. Suppose I were to blast a vital part into nothingness? I suppose the machines aren't immune to atomic forces? Suppose I fuse a vital connection, or smash a quartz D-tube?'

'Well, then,' shouted the tech-man, furiously, 'you would be killed.'

'Yes, I know that,' Mallow was shouting, too, 'but what about the generator? Could you repair it?'

'Sir,' the tech-man howled his words, 'you have had a fair return. You've had what you asked for. Now get out! I owe you nothing more!'

Mallow bowed with a satiric respect and left.

Two days later he was back at the base where the *Far Star* waited to return with him to the planet, Terminus.

And two days later, the tech-man's shield went dead, and for all his puzzling and cursing never glowed again.

13

Mallow relaxed for almost the first time in six months. He was on his back in the sun-room of his new house, stripped to the skin. His great, brown arms were thrown up and out, and the muscles tautened into a stretch, then faded into repose.

The man beside him placed a cigar between Mallow's teeth and lit it. He champed on one of his own and said, 'You must be overworked. Maybe you need a long rest.'

'Maybe I do, Jael, but I'd rather rest in a council seat. Because I'm going to have that seat, and you're going to help me.'

Ankor Jael raised his eyebrows and said, 'How did I get into this?'

'You got in obviously. Firstly, you're an old dog of a politico. Secondly, you were booted out of your cabinet seat by Jorane Sutt, the same fellow who'd rather lose an eyeball than see me in the council. You don't think much of my chances, do you?'

'Not much,' agreed the ex-Minister of Education. 'You're a Smyrnian.'

'That's no legal bar. I've had a lay education.'

'Well, come now. Since when does prejudice follow any law but its own. Now, how about your own man – this Jaim Twer? What does *he* say?'

'He spoke about running me for council amost a year ago,' replied Mallow easily, 'but I've outgrown him. He couldn't have pulled it off in any case. Not enough depth. He's loud and forceful – but that's only an expression of nuisance value. I'm off to put over a real coup. I need *you*.'

'Jorane Sutt is the cleverest politician on the planet and he'll be against you. I don't claim to be able to outsmart him. And don't think he doesn't fight hard, and dirty.'

'I've got money.'

'That helps. But it takes a lot to buy off prejudice – you dirty Smyrnian.'

'I'll have a lot.'

'Well, I'll look into the matter. But don't ever you crawl up on your hind legs and bleat that I encouraged you in the matter. Who's that?'

Mallow pulled the corners of his mouth down, and said, 'Jorane Sutt himself, I think. He's early, and I can understand it. I've been dodging him for a month. Look, Jael, get into the next room, and turn the speaker on low. I want you to listen.'

He helped the council member out of the room with a shove of his bare foot, then scrambled up and into a silk robe. The synthetic sunlight faded to normal power.

The secretary to the mayor entered stiffly, while the solemn mayor-domo tiptoed the door shut behind him.

Mallow fastened his belt and said, 'Take your choice of chairs, Sutt.'

Sutt barely cracked a flicking smile. The chair he chose was comfortable but he did not relax into it. From its edge, he said, 'If you'll state your terms to begin with, we'll get down to business.'

'What terms?'

'You wished to be coaxed? Well, then, what, for instance, did you do at Korell? Your report was incomplete.'

'I gave it to you months ago. You were satisfied then.'

'Yes,' Sutt rubbed his forehead thoughtfully with one finger, 'but since then your activities have been significant. We know a good deal of what you're doing, Mallow. We know, exactly, how many factories you're putting up; in what a hurry you're doing it; and how much it's costing you. And there's this palace you have,' he gazed about him with a cold lack of appreciation, 'which set you back considerably more than my annual salary; and a swathe you've been cutting – a very considerable and expensive swathe – through the upper layers of Foundation society.'

'So? Beyond proving that you employ capable spies, what does it show?'

'It shows you have money you didn't have a year ago. And that can show anything – for instance, that a good deal went on at Korell that we know nothing of. Where are you getting your money?'

'My dear Sutt, you can't really expect me to tell you.'

'I don't.'

'I didn't think you did. That's why I'm going to tell you. It's straight from the treasure-chests of the Commdor of Korell.'

Sutt blinked.

Mallow smiled and continued. 'Unfortunately for you, the money is quite legitimate. I'm a Master Trader and the money I received was a quantity of wrought iron and chromite in exchange for a number of trinkets I was able to supply him with. Fifty per cent of the profit is mine by hide-bound contract with the Foundation. The other half goes to the government at the end of the year when all good citizens pay their income tax.'

'There was no mention of any trade agreement in your report.'

'Nor was there any mention of what I had for breakfast that day, or the name of my current mistress, or any other irrelevant detail.' Mallow's smile was fading into a sneer. 'I was sent – to quote yourself – to keep my eyes open. They were never shut. You wanted to find out what happened to the captured Foundation merchant ships. I never saw or heard of them. You wanted to find out if Korell had atomic power. My report tells of atomic blasters in the possession of the Commdor's private bodyguard. I saw no other signs. And the blasters I did see are relics of the old Empire, and may be show-pieces that do not work, for all my knowledge.

'So far, I followed orders, but beyond that I was, and still am, a free agent. According to the laws of the Foundation, a Master Trader may open whatever new markets he can, and receive therefrom his due half of the profits. What are your objections? I don't see them.'

Sutt bent his eyes carefully toward the wall and spoke with a difficult lack of anger: 'It is the general custom of all traders to advance the religion of their trade.'

'I adhere to law, and not to custom.'

'There are times when custom can be the higher law.'

'Then appeal to the courts.'

Sutt raised sombre eyes which seemed to retreat into their sockets. 'You're a Smyrnian after all. It seems naturalization and education can't wipe out the taint in the blood. Listen and try to understand, just the same.

'This goes beyond money, or markets. We have the science of the great Hari Seldon to prove that upon us depends the future empire of the Galaxy, and from the course that leads to the Imperium we cannot turn. The religion we have is our all-important instrument toward that end. With it we have brought the Four Kingdoms under our control, even at the moment when they would have crushed us. It is the most potent device known with which to control men and worlds.

'The primary reason for the development of trade and traders was to introduce and spread this religion more quickly, and to insure that the introduction of new techniques and a new economy would be subject to our thorough and intimate control.'

He paused for breath, and Mallow interjected quietly, 'I know the theory. I understand it entirely.'

'Do you? It is more than I expected. Then you see, of course, that your attempt at trade for its own sake; at mass production of worthless gadgets, which can only affect a world's economy superficially; at the subversion of interstellar policy to the god of profits; at the divorce of atomic power from our controlling religion – can only end with the overthrow and complete negation of the policy that has worked successfully for a century.'

'And time enough, too,' said Mallow, indifferently, 'for a policy outdated, dangerous and impossible. However well your religion has succeeded in the Four Kingdoms, scarcely another world in the Periphery has accepted it. At the time we seized control of the Kingdoms, there were a sufficient number of exiles, Galaxy knows, to spread the story of how Salvor Hardin used the priesthood and the superstition of the people to overthrow the independence and power of the secular monarchs. And if that wasn't enough, the case of Askone two decades back made it plain enough. There isn't a ruler in the Periphery now that wouldn't sooner cut his own throat than let a priest of the Foundation enter the territory.

'I don't propose to force Korell or any other world to accept something I know they don't want. No, Sutt. If atomic power makes them dangerous, a sincere friendship through trade will be many times better than an insecure overlordship, based on the hated supremacy of a foreign spiritual power, which, once it weakens ever so slightly, can only fall entirely and leave nothing substantial behind except an immortal fear and hate.'

Sutt said cynically, 'Very nicely put. So, to get back to the original point of discussion, what are your terms? What do you require to exchange your ideas for mine?'

'You think my convictions are for sale?'

'Why not?' came the cold response. 'Isn't that your business, buying and selling?'

'Only at a profit,' said Mallow, unoffended. 'Can you offer me more than I'm getting as it is?'

'You could have three-quarters of your trade profits, rather than half.'

Mallow laughed shortly. 'A fine offer. The whole of the trade on your terms would fall far below a tenth share on mine. Try harder than that.'

'You could have a council seat.'

'I'll have that anyway, without and despite you.'

With a sudden movement, Sutt clenched his fist. 'You could also save yourself a prison term. Of twenty years, if I have my way. Count the profit in that.'

'No profit at all, unless you can fulfil such a threat.'

'It's trial for murder.'

'Whose murder?' asked Mallow, contemptuously.

Sutt's voice was harsh now, though no louder than before. 'The murder of an Anacreonian priest, in the service of the Foundation.'

'Is that so now? And what's your evidence?'

The secretary to the mayor leaned forward. 'Mallow, I'm not bluffing. The preliminaries are over. I have only to sign one final paper and the case of the Foundation versus Hober Mallow, Master Trader, is begun. You abandoned a subject of the Foundation to torture and death at the hands of an alien mob, Mallow, and you have only five seconds to prevent the punishment due you. For myself, I'd rather you decided to bluff it out. You'd be safer as a destroyed enemy, than as a doubtfully-converted friend.'

Mallow said solemnly, 'You have your wish.'

'Good!' and the secretary smiled savagely. 'It was the mayor who wished the preliminary attempt at compromise, not I. Witness that I did not try too hard.'

The door opened before him, and he left.

Mallow looked up as Ankor Jael re-entered the room.

Mallow said, 'Did you hear him?'

The politician flopped to the floor. 'I never heard him as angry as that, since I've known the snake.'

'All right. What do you make of it?'

'Well, I'll tell you. A foreign policy of domination through spiritual means is his *idée fixe*, but it's my notion that his ultimate aims aren't spiritual. I was fired out of the Cabinet for arguing on the same issue, as I needn't tell you.'

'You needn't. And what are those unspiritual aims according to your notion?'

Jael grew serious. 'Well, he's not stupid, so he must see the bankruptcy of our religious policy, which has hardly made a single conquest for us in seventy years. He's obviously using it for purposes of his own.

'Now *any* dogma, primarily based on faith and emotionalism is a dangerous weapon to use on others, since it is almost impossible to guarantee that the weapon will never be turned on the user. For a hundred years now, we've supported a ritual and mythology that is becoming more and more venerable, traditional – and immovable. In some ways, it isn't under our control any more.'

'In what ways?' demanded Mallow. 'Don't stop. I want your thoughts.'

'Well, suppose one man, one ambitious man, uses the force of religion against us, rather than for us.'

'You mean Sutt—'

'You're right. I mean Sutt. Listen, man, if he could mobilize the various hierarchies on the subject planets against the Foundation in the name of orthodoxy, what chance would we stand? By planting himself at the head of the standards of the pious, he could make war on heresy, as represented by you, for instance, and make himself king eventually. After all, it was Hardin who said: "An atom-blaster is a good weapon, but it can point both ways."'

Mallow slapped his bare thigh. 'All right, Jael, then get me in that council, and I'll fight him.'

Jael paused, then said significantly, 'Maybe not. What was all that about having a priest lynched? It isn't true, is it?'

'It's true enough,' Mallow said, carelessly.

Jael whistled. 'Has he definite proof?'

'He should have.' Mallow hesitated, then added, 'Jaim Twer was his man from the beginning, though neither of them knew that I knew that. And Jaim Twer was an eyewitness.'

Jael shook his head. 'Uh-uh. That's bad.'

'Bad? What's bad about it? That priest was illegally upon the planet by the Foundation's own laws. He was obviously used by the Korellian government as a bait, whether involuntary or not. By all the laws of common sense, I had no choice but one action – and that action was strictly within the law. If he brings me to trial, he'll do nothing but make a prime fool of himself.'

And Jael shook his head again. 'No, Mallow, you've missed it. I told you he played dirty. He's not out to convict you; he knows he can't do that. But he *is* out to ruin your standing with the people. You heard what he said. Custom *is* higher than law, at times. You could walk out of the trial scot-free, but if the people think you threw a priest to the dogs, your popularity is gone.

'They'll admit you did the legal thing, even the sensible thing. But just the same you'll have been, in their eyes, a cowardly dog, an unfeeling brute, a hard-hearted monster. *And* you would never get elected to the council. You might even lose your rating as Master Trader by having your citizenship voted away from you. You're not native-born, you know. What more do you think Sutt can want?'

Mallow frowned stubbornly. 'So!'

'My boy,' said Jael, 'I'll stand by you, but *I* can't help. You're on the spot – dead centre.'

14

The council chamber was full in a very literal sense on the fourth day of the trial of Hober Mallow, Master Trader. The only councilman absent was feebly cursing the fractured skull that had bedridden him. The galleries were filled to the aisleways and ceilings with those few of the crowd who by influence, wealth, or sheer diabolic perseverance had managed to get in. The rest filled the square outside, in swarming knots about the open-air trimensional 'visors.

Ankor Jael made his way into the chamber with the near-futile aid and exertions of the police department, and then through the scarcely smaller confusion within to Hober Mallow's seat.

Mallow turned with relief: 'By Seldon, you cut it thin. Have you got it?'

'Here, take it,' said Jael. 'It's everything you asked for.'

'Good. How are they taking it ouside?'

'They're wild clear through.' Jael stirred uneasily. 'You should never have allowed public hearings. You could have stopped them.'

'I don't want to.'

'There's lynch talk. And Publis Manlio's men on the outer planets—'

'I wanted to ask you about that, Jael. He's stirring up the Hierarchy against me, is he?'

'*Is* he? It's the sweetest set-up you ever saw. As Foreign Secretary, he handles the prosecution in a case of interstellar law. As High Priest and Primate of the Church, he rouses the fanatic hordes—'

'Well, forget it. Do you remember that Hardin quotation you threw at me last month? We'll show them that the atom-blaster can point both ways.'

The mayor was taking his seat now and the council members were rising in respect.

Mallow whispered, 'It's my turn today. Sit here and watch the fun.'

The day's proceedings began and fifteen minutes later, Hober Mallow stepped through a hostile whisper to the empty space before the mayor's bench. A lone beam of light centred upon him and in the public 'visors of the city, as well as on the myriads of private 'visors in almost every home of the Foundation's planets, the lonely giant figure of a man stared out defiantly.

He began easily and quietly: 'To save time, I will admit the truth of every point made against me by the prosecution. The story of the priest and the mob as related by them is perfectly accurate in ever detail.'

There was a stirring in the chamber and a triumphant mass-snarl from the gallery. He waited patiently for silence.

'However, the picture they presented fell short of completion. I ask the privilege of supplying the completion in my own fashion. My story may seem irrelevant at first. I ask your indulgence for that.'

Mallow made no reference to the notes before him.

'I begin at the same time as the prosecution did; the day of my meetings with Jorane Sutt and Jaim Twer. What went on at those meetings you know. The conversations have been described, and to that description I have nothing to add – except my own thoughts of that day.

'They were suspicious thoughts, for the events of that day were queer. Consider. Two people, neither of whom I know more than casually, make unnatural and somewhat unbelievable propositions to me. One, the secretary to the mayor, asks me to play the part of intelligence agent to the government in a highly confidential matter, the nature and importance of which has already been explained to you. The other, self-styled leader of a political party, asks me to run for a council seat.

'Naturally I looked for the ulterior motive. Sutt's seemed evident. He didn't trust me. Perhaps he thought I was selling atomic power to enemies and plotting rebellion. And perhaps he was forcing the issue, or thought he was. In that case, he would need a man of his own near me on my proposed mission, as a spy. The last thought, however, did not occur to me until later on, when Jaim Twer came on the scene.

'Consider again: Twer presents himself as a trader, retired into politics, yet I know of no details of his trading career, although my knowledge of the field is immense. And further, although Twer boasted of a lay education, *he had never heard of a Seldon crisis.*'

Hober Mallow waited to let the significance sink in and was rewarded with the first silence he had yet encountered, as the gallery caught its collective breath. That was for the inhabitants of Terminus itself. The men of the Outer Planets could hear only censored versions that would suit the requirements of religion. They would hear nothing of Seldon crises. But there would be further strokes they would not miss.

Mallow continued:

'Who here can honestly state that *any* man with a lay education can possibly be ignorant of the nature of a Seldon crisis? There is only one type of education upon the Foundation that excludes all mention of the planned history of Seldon and deals only with the man himself as a semi-mythical wizard—'

'I knew at that instant that Jaim Twer had never been a trader. I knew then that he was in holy orders and perhaps a full-fledged priest; and, doubtless, that for the three years he had pretended to head a political party of the traders, *he had been a bought man of Jorane Sutt.*

'At the moment, I struck in the dark. I did not know Sutt's purposes with regard to myself, but since he seemed to be feeding me rope liberally, I handed him a few fathoms of my own. My notion was that Twer was to be with me on my voyage as unofficial guardian on behalf of Jorane Sutt. Well, if he didn't get on, I knew well there'd be other devices waiting – and those others I might not catch in time. A known enemy is relatively safe. I invited Twer to come with me. He accepted.

'That, gentlemen of the council, explains two things. First, it tells you that Twer is not a friend of mine testifying against me reluctantly and for conscience' sake, as the prosecution would have you believe. He is a spy, performing his paid job. Secondly, it explains a certain action of mine on the occasion of the first appearance of the priest whom I am accused of having murdered – an action as yet unmentioned, because unknown.'

Now there was a disturbed whispering in the council. Mallow cleared his throat theatrically, and continued:

'I hate to describe my feelings when I first heard that we had a refugee missionary on board. I even hate to remember them. Essentially, they consisted of wild uncertainty. The event struck me at the moment as a move by Sutt, and passed beyond my comprehension or calculation. I was at sea – and completely.

'There was one thing I could do. I got rid of Twer for five minutes by sending him after my officers. In his absence, I set up a Visual Record receiver, so that whatever happened might be preserved for future study. This was in the hope, the wild but earnest hope, that what confused me at the time might become plain upon review.

'I have gone over that Visual Record some fifty times since. I have it here with me now, and will repeat the job a fifty-first time in your presence right now.'

The mayor pounded monotonously for order, as the chamber lost its equilibrium and the gallery roared. In five million homes on Terminus, excited observers crowded their receiving sets more closely, and at the prosecutor's own bench, Jorane Sutt shook his head coldly at the nervous high priest, while his eyes blazed fixedly on Mallow's face.

The centre of the chamber was cleared, and the lights burnt low. Ankor Jael, from his bench on the left, made the adjustments, and with a preliminary click, a scene sprang to view; in colour, in three dimensions, in every attribute of life but life itself.

There was the missionary, confused and battered, standing between the lieutenant and the sergeant. Mallow's image waited silently, and then men filed in, Twer bring up the rear.

The conversation played itself out, word for word. The sergeant was disciplined, and the missionary was questioned. The mob appeared, their growl could be heard, and the Revered Jord Parma made his wild appeal. Mallow drew his gun, and the missionary, as he was dragged away, lifted his arms in a mad, final curse and a tiny flash of light came and went.

The scene ended, with the officers frozen at the horror of the situation, while Twer clamped shaking hands over his ears, and Mallow calmly put his gun away.

The lights were on again; the empty space in the centre of the floor was no longer even apparently full. Mallow, the real Mallow of the present, took up the burden of his narration:

'The incident, you see, is exactly as the prosecution has presented it – on the surface. I'll explain that shortly. Jaim Twer's emotions through the whole business shows clearly a priestly education, by the way.

'It was on that same day that I pointed out certain incongruities in the episode to Twer. I asked him where the missionary came from in the midst of the near-desolate tract we occupied at the time. I asked further where the gigantic mob had come from with the nearest sizeable town a hundred miles away. The prosecution has paid no attention to such problems.

'Or to other points; for instance, the curious point of Jord Parma's blatant conspiciousness. A missionary on Korell, risking his life in defiance of both Korellian and Foundation law, parades about in a very new and very distinctive priestly costume. There's something wrong there. At the time, I suggested that the missionary was an unwilling accomplice of the Commdor, who was using him in an attempt to force us into an act of wildly illegal aggression, to justify, *in law* his subsequent destruction of our ship and of us.

'The prosecution has anticipated this justification of my actions. They have expected me to explain that the safety of my ship, my crew, my mission itself were at stake and could not be sacrificed for one man, when that man would, in any case, have been destroyed, with us or without us. They reply by muttering about the Foundation's "honour" and the necessity of upholding our "dignity" in order to maintain our ascendancy.

'For some strange reason, however, the prosecution has neglected Jord Parma himself – as an individual. They brought out no details concerning him; neither his birthplace, nor his education nor any detail of previous history. The explanation of this will also explain the incongruities I have pointed out in the Visual Record you have just seen. The two are connected.

'The prosecution has advanced no details concerning Jord

Parma because it *cannot*. That scene you saw by Visual Record seemed phoney because Jord Parma was phoney. There never *was* a Jord Parma. *This whole trial is the biggest farce ever cooked up over an issue that never existed.*'

Once more he had to wait for the babble to die down. He said, slowly:

'I'm goint to show you the enlargement of a single still from the Visual Record. It will speak for itself. Lights again, Jael.'

The chamber dimmed, and the empty air filled again with frozen figures in ghostly, waxen illusion. The officers of the *Far Star* struck their stiff, impossible attitudes. A gun pointed from Mallow's rigid hand. At his left, the Reverend Jord Parma, caught in mid-shriek, stretched his claws upward, while the falling sleeves hung half-way.

And from the missionary's hand there was that little gleam that in the previous showing had flashed and gone. It was a permanent glow now.

'Keep your eye on that light on his hand,' called Mallow from the shadows. 'Enlarge, that scene, Jael!'

The tableau bloated – quickly. Outer portions fell away as the missionary drew toward the centre and became a giant. Then there was only a head and an arm, and then only a hand, which filled everything and remained there in immense, hazy tautness.

The light had become a set of fuzzy glowing letters: K S P.

'That,' Mallow's voice boomed out, 'is a sample of tattooing, gentlemen. Under ordinary light it is invisible, but under ultra-violet light – with which I flooded the room in taking this Visual Record – it stands out in high relief. I'll admit it is a naïve method of secret identification, but it works on Korell, where UV light is not to be found on street corners. Even in our ship, detection was accidental.

'Perhaps some of you have already guessed what K S P stands for. Jord Parma knew his priestly lingo well and did his job magnificently. Where he had learned it, and how, I cannot say, but K S P stands for "Korellian Secret Police".'

Mallow shouted over the tumult, roaring against the noise: 'I have collateral proof in the form of documents brought from Korell, which I can present to the council, if required.

'And where is now the prosecution's case? They have already made and re-made the monstrous suggestion that I should have fought for the missionary in defiance of the law, and sacrificed my mission, my ship, and myself to the "honour" of the Foundation.

'*But to do it for an impostor*?

'Should I have done it then for a Korellian secret agent tricked out in the robes and verbal gymnastics probably borrowed of an Anacreonian exile? Would Jorane Sutt and Publis Manlio have had me fall into a stupid, odious trap—'

His hoarsened voice faded into the featureless background of a shouting mob. He was being lifted on to shoulders, and carried to the mayor's bench. Out the windows, he could see a torrent of madmen swarming into the square to add to the thousands there already.

Mallow looked about for Ankor Jael, but it was impossible to find any single face in the incoherence of the mass. Slowly he became aware of a rhythmic, repeated shout, that was spreading from a small beginning, and pulsing into insanity:

'Long live Mallow – long live Mallow – long live Mallow—'

15

Ankor Jael blinked at Mallow out of a haggard face. The last two days had been mad, sleepless ones.

'Mallow, you've put on a beautiful show, so don't spoil it by jumping too high. You can't seriously consider running for mayor, Mob enthusiasm is a powerful thing, but it's notoriously fickle.'

'Exactly!' said Mallow, grimly, 'so we must coddle it, and

the best way to do that is to continue the show.'

'Now what?'

'You're to have Publis Manlio and Jorane Sutt arrested—'

'What!'

'Just what you hear. Have the mayor arrest them! I don't care what threats you use. I control the mob – for today, at any rate. He won't dare face them.'

'But on what charge, man?'

'On the obvious one. They've been inciting the priesthood of the outer planets to take sides in the factional quarrels of the Foundation. That's illegal, by Seldon. Charge them with "endangering the State". And I don't care about a conviction any more than they did in my case. Just get them out of circulation until I'm mayor.'

'It's half a year till election.'

'Not too long!' Mallow was on his feet, and his sudden grip of Jael's arm was tight. 'Listen, I'd seize the government by force if I had to – the way Salvor Hardin did a hundred years ago. There's still that Seldon crisis coming up, and when it comes I have to be mayor *and* high priest. Both!'

Jael's brow furrowed. He said, quietly, 'What's it going to be? Korell, after all?'

Mallow nodded, 'Of course. They'll declare war, eventually, though I'm betting it'll take another pair of years.'

'With atomic ships?'

'What do you think? Those three merchant ships we lost in their space sector weren't knocked over with compressed-air pistols. Jael, they're getting ships from the Empire itself. Don't open your mouth like a fool. I said the Empire! It's still there, you know. It may be gone here in the Periphery but in the Galactic centre it's still very much alive. And one false move means that it, itself, may be on our neck. That's why I must be mayor and high priest. I'm the only man who knows how to fight the crisis.'

Jael swallowed dryly. 'How? What are you going to do?'

'Nothing.'

Jael smiled uncertainly. 'Really! All of that!'

But Mallow's answer was incisive. 'When I'm boss of this Foundation, I'm going to do nothing. One hundred per cent of nothing, and that is the secret of this crisis.'

16

Asper Argo, the Well-Beloved, Commdor of the Korellian Republic greeted his wife's entry by a hangdog lowering of his scanty eyebrows. To her at least, his self-adopted epithet did not apply. Even he knew that.

She said, in a voice as sleek as her hair and as cold as her eyes, 'My gracious lord, I understand, has finally come to a decision upon the fate of the Foundation upstarts.'

'Indeed?' said the Commdor, sourly. 'And what more does your versatile understanding embrace?'

'Enough, my very noble husband. You had another of your vacillating consultations with your councillors. Fine advisers.' With infinite scorn, 'A herd of palsied purblind idiots hugging their sterile profits close to their sunken chests in the face of my father's displeasure.'

'And who, my dear,' was the mild response, 'is the excellent source from which your understanding understands all this?'

The Commdora laughed shortly. 'If I told you, my source would be more corpse than source.'

'Well, you'll have your own way, as always.' The Commodor shrugged and turned away. 'And as for your father's displeasure: I much fear it extends to a niggardly refusal to supply more ships.'

'More ships!' She blazed away, hotly, 'And haven't you five? Don't deny it. I *know* you have five; and a sixth is promised.'

'Promised for the last year.'

'But one – just one – can blast that Foundation into stinking rubble. Just one! One, to sweep their little pygmy boats out of space.'

'I couldn't attack their planet, even with a dozen.'

'And how long would their planet hold out with their trade ruined, and their cargoes of toys and trash destroyed?'

'Those toys and trash mean money,' he sighed. 'A good deal of money.'

'But if you had the Foundation itself, would you not have all it contained? And if you had my father's respect and gratitude, would you not have more than ever the Foundation could give you? It's been three years – more – since that barbarian came with his magic sideshow. It's long enough.'

'My dear!' The Commdor turned and faced her. 'I am growing old. I am weary. I lack the resilience to withstand your rattling mouth. You say you know that I have decided. Well, I have. It is over, and there is war between Korell and the Foundation.'

'Well!' The Commdora's figure expanded and her eyes sparkled. 'You learned wisdom at last, though in your dotage. And now when you are master of this hinterland, you may be sufficiently respectable to be of some weight and importance in the Empire. For one thing, we might leave this barbarous world and attend the viceroy's court. Indeed we might.'

She swept out, with a smile and a hand on her hip. Her hair gleamed in the light.

The Commdor waited, and then said to the closed door with malignance and hate: 'And when I am master of what you call the hinterland, I may be sufficiently respectable to do without your father's arrogance and his daughter's tongue. Completely – without!'

17

The senior lieutenant of the *Dark Nebula* stared in horror at the visiplate.

'Great Galloping Galaxies!' It should have been a howl, but it was a whisper instead. 'What's that?'

It was a ship, but a whale to the *Dark Nebula*'s minnow; and on its side was the Spaceship-and-Sun of the Empire. Every alarm on the ship yammered hysterically.

The orders went out, and the *Dark Nebula* prepared to run if it could, and fight if it must – while down in the ultrawave room, a message stormed its way through hyper-space to the Foundation.

Over and over again! Partly a plea for help, but mainly a warning of danger.

18

Hober Mallow shuffled his feet wearily as he leafed through the reports. Two years of the mayoralty had made him a bit more housebroken, a bit softer, a bit more patient – but it had not made him learn to like government reports and the mind-breaking officialese in which they were written.

'How many ships did they get?' asked Jael.

'Four trapped on the ground. Two unreported. All others accounted for and safe.' Mallow grunted, 'We should have done better, but it's just a scratch.'

There was no answer and Mallow looked up. 'Does anything worry you?'

'I wish Sutt would get here,' was the almost irrelevant answer.

'Ah, yes; now we'll hear another lecture on the home front.'

'No, we won't,' snapped Jael, 'but you're stubborn, Mallow. You may have worked out the foreign situation to the last detail but you've never given a care about what goes on here on the home planet.'

'Well, that's your job, isn't it? What did I make you Minister of Education and Propaganda for?'

'Obviously to send me to an early and miserable grave, for all the co-operation you give me. For the last year, I've been deafening you with the rising danger of Sutt and his Religionists. What good will your plans be, if Sutt forces a special election and has you thrown out?'

'None, I admit.'

'And your speech last night just about handed the election to Sutt with a smile and a pat. Was there any necessity for being so frank?'

'Isn't there such a thing as stealing Sutt's thunder?'

'No,' said Jael, violently, 'not the way you did it. You claim to have foreseen everything, and don't explain why you traded with Korell to their exclusive benefit for three years. Your only plan of battle is to retire without a battle. You abandon all trade with the sectors of space near Korell. You openly proclaim a stalemate. You promise no offensive, even in the future. Galaxy, Mallow, what am I supposed to do with such a mess?'

'It lacks glamour?'

'It lacks mob emotion-appeal.'

'Same thing.'

'Mallow, wake up. You have two alternatives. Either you present the people with a dynamic foreign policy, whatever your private plans are, or you make some sort of compromise with Sutt.'

Mallow said, 'All right, if I've failed the first, let's try the second. Sutt's just arrived.'

Sutt and Mallow had not met personally since the day of the

trial, two years back. Neither detected any change in the other, except for that subtle atmosphere about each which made it quite evident that the roles of ruler and defier had changed.

Sutt took his seat without shaking hands.

Mallow offered a cigar and said, 'Mind if Jael stays? He wants a compromise earnestly. He can act as mediator if tempers rise.'

Sutt shrugged. 'A compromise will be well for you. Upon another occasion I once asked you to state your terms. I presume the positions are reversed now.'

'You presume correctly.'

'Then these are my terms. You must abandon your blundering policy of economic bribery and trade in gadgetry, and return to the tested foreign policy of our fathers.'

'You mean conquest by missionary?'

'Exactly.'

'No compromise short of that?'

'None.'

'Um-m-m.' Mallow lit up very slowly, and inhaled the tip of his cigar into a bright glow. 'In Hardin's time, when conquest by missionary was new and radical, men like yourself opposed it. Now it is tried, tested, hallowed – everything a Jorane Sutt would find well. But, tell me, how would you get us out of our present mess?'

'*Your* present mess. I had nothing to do with it.'

'Consider the question suitably modified.'

'A strong offensive is indicated. The stalemate you seem to be satisfied with is fatal. It would be a confession of weakness to all the world of the Periphery, where the appearance of strength is all-important, and there's not one vulture among them that wouldn't join the assault for its share of the corpse. You ought to understand that. You're from Smyrno, aren't you?'

Mallow passed over the significance of the remark. He said, 'And if you beat Korell, what of the Empire? *That* is the real enemy.'

Sutt's narrow smile tugged at the corners of his mouth, 'Oh, no, your records of your visit to Siwenna were complete. The viceroy of the Normannic Sector is interested in creating dissension in the Periphery for his own benefit, but only as a side issue. He isn't going to stake everything on an expedition to the Galaxy's rim where he has fifty hostile neighbours and an emperor to rebel against. I paraphrase your own words.'

'Oh, yes he might, Sutt, if he thinks we're strong enough to be dangerous. And he might think so, if we destroy Korell by the main force of frontal attack. We'd have to be considerably more subtle.'

'As for instance—'

Mallow leaned back. 'Sutt, I'll give you your chance. I don't need you, but I can use you. So I'll tell you what it's all about, and then you can either join me and receive a place in a coalition cabinet, or you can play the martyr and rot in jail.'

'Once before you tried that last trick.'

'Not very hard, Sutt. The right time has only just come. Now listen.' Mallow's eyes narrowed.

'When I first landed on Korell,' he began, 'I bribed the Commdor with the trinkets and gadgets that form the trader's usual stock. At the start, that was meant only to get us entrance into a steel foundry. I had no plan further than that, but in that I succeeded. I got what I wanted. But it was only after my visit to the Empire that I first realized exactly what a weapon I could build that trade into.

'This is a Seldon crisis we're facing, Sutt, and Seldon crises are not solved by individuals but by historic forces. Hari Seldon, when he planned our course of future history, did not count on brilliant heroics but on the broad sweep of economics and sociology. So the solutions to the various crises must be achieved by the forces that become available to us at the time.

'In this case – trade!'

Sutt raised his eyebrows sceptically and took advantage of the pause. 'I hope I am not of subnormal intelligence, but the fact is that your vague lecture isn't very illuminating.'

'It will become so,' said Mallow. 'Consider that until now the power of trade has been underestimated. It has been thought that it took a priesthood under our control to make it a powerful weapon. That is not so, and *this* is my contribution to the Galactic situation. Trade without priests! Trade alone! It is strong enough. Let us become very simple and specific. Korell is now at war with us. Consequently our trade with her has stopped. *But* – notice that I am making this as simple as a problem in addition – in the past three years she has based her economy more and more upon the atomic techniques which we have introduced and which only we can continue to supply. Now what do you suppose will happen once the tiny atomic generators begin failing, and one gadget after another goes out of commission?

'The small household appliances go first. After half a year of this stalemate that you abhor, a woman's atomic knife won't work any more. Her stove begins failing. Her washer doesn't do a good job. The temperature-humidity control in her house dies on a hot summer day. What happens?'

He paused for an answer, and Sutt said calmly, 'Nothing. People endure a good deal in war.'

'Very true. They do. They'll send their sons out in unlimited numbers to die horribly on broken space-ships. They'll bear up under enemy bombardment, if it means they have to live on stale bread and foul water in caves half a mile deep. But it's very hard to bear up under little things when the patriotic uplift of imminent danger is not present. It's going to be a stalemate. There will be no casualties, no bombardments, no battles.

'There will just be a knife that won't cut, and a stove that won't cook, and a house that freezes in the winter. It will be annoying and people will grumble.'

Sutt said slowly, wonderingly, 'Is that what you're setting your hopes on, man? What do you expect? A housewives' rebellion? A Jacquerie? A sudden uprising of butchers and grocers with their cleavers and bread-knives shouting "Give us Automatic Super-Kleeno Atomic Washing Machines".'

'No, sir,' said Mallow, impatiently, 'I do not. I expect, however, a general background of grumbling and dissatisfaction which will be seized on by more important figures later on.'

'And what more important figures are these?'

'The manufacturers, the factory owners, the industrialists of Korell. When two years of the stalemate have gone, the machines in the factories will, one by one, begin to fail. Those industries which we have changed from first to last with our new atomic gadgets will find themselves very suddenly ruined. The heavy industries will find themselves *en masse* and at a stroke the owners of nothing but scrap machinery that won't work.'

'The factories ran well enough before you came there, Mallow.'

'Yes, Sutt, so they did – at about one-twentieth the profits, even if you leave out of consideration the cost of reconversion to the original pre-atomic state. With the industrialist and financier and the average man all against him, how long will the Commdor hold out?'

'As long as he pleases, as soon as it occurs to him to get new atomic generators from the Empire.'

And Mallow laughed joyously. 'You've missed, Sutt, missed as badly as the Commdor himself. You've missed everything, and understood nothing. Look, man, the Empire can replace nothing. The Empire had always been a realm of colossal resources. They've calculated everything in planets, in stellar systems, in whole sectors of the Galaxy. Their generators are gigantic because they thought in gigantic fashion.

'But we – *we*, our little Foundation, our single world almost without metallic resources – have had to work with brute economy. Our generators have had to be the size of our thumb, because it was all the metal we could afford. We had to develop new techniques and new methods – techniques and methods the Empire can't follow because they have degenerated past the stage where they can make any really vital scientific advance.

'With all their atomic shields, large enough to protect a ship, a city, an entire world, they could never build one to protect a single man. To supply light and heat to a city, they have motors six storeys high – I saw them – where ours could fit into this room. And when I told one of their atomic specialists that a lead container the size of a walnut contained an atomic generator, he almost choked with indignation on the spot.

'Why, they don't even understand their own colossi any longer. The machines work from generation to generation automatically, and the caretakers are a hereditary caste who would be helpless if a single D-tube in all that vast structure burnt out.

'The whole war is a battle between those two systems; between the Empire and the Foundation; between the big and the little. To seize control of a world, they bribe with immense ships that can make war, but lack all economic significance. We, on the other hand, bribe with little things, useless in war, but vital to prosperity and profits.

'A king, or a Commdor, will take the ships and even make war. Arbitrary rulers throughout history have bartered their subjects' welfare for what they consider honour, and glory, and conquest. But it's still the little things in life that count – and Asper Argo won't stand up against the economic depression that will sweep all Korell in two or three years.'

Sutt was at the window, his back to Mallow and Jael. It was early evening now, and the few stars that struggled feebly here at the very rim of the Galaxy sparked against the background of the misty, wispy Lens that included the remnants of that Empire, still vast, that fought against them.

Sutt said, 'No. You are not the man.'

'You don't believe me?'

'I mean I don't trust you. You're smooth-tongued. You be-fooled me properly when I thought I had you under proper care on your first trip to Korell. When I thought I had you cornered at the trial, you wormed your way out of it and into the mayor's chair by demagoguery. There is nothing straight about you; no motive that hasn't another behind it; no statement that hasn't three meanings.

'Suppose you were a traitor. Suppose your visit to the Empire had brought you a subsidy and a promise of power. Your actions would be precisely what they are now. You would bring about a war after having strengthened the enemy. You would force the Foundation into inactivity. And you would advance a plausible explanation of everything, one so plausible it would convince everyone.'

'You mean there'll be no compromise?' asked Mallow, gently.

'I mean you must get out, by free will or force.'

'I warned you of the only alternative to co-operation.'

Jorane Sutt's face congested with blood in a sudden access of emotion. 'And I warn you, Hober Mallow of Smyrno, that if you arrest me, there will be no quarter. My men will stop nowhere in spreading the truth about you, and the common people of the Foundation will unite against their foreign ruler. They have a consciousness of destiny that a Smyrnian can never understand – and that consciousness will destroy you.'

Hober Mallow said quietly to the two guards who had entered, 'Take him away. He's under arrest.'

Sutt said, 'Your last chance.'

Mallow stubbed out his cigar and never looked up.

And five minutes later, Jael stirred and said, wearily, 'Well, now that you've made a martyr for the cause, what next?'

Mallow stopped playing with the ash-tray and looked up. 'That's not the Sutt I used to know. He's a blood-blind bull. Galaxy, he hates me.'

'All the more dangerous then.'

'More dangerous? Nonsense! He's lost all power of judgement.'

Jael said grimly, 'You're over-confident, Mallow. You're

ignoring the possibility of a popular rebellion.'

Mallow looked up, grim in his turn. Once and for all, Jael, there is no possibility of a popular rebellion.'

'You're sure of yourself!'

'I'm sure of the Seldon crisis and the historical validity of their solutions externally *and* internally. There are some things I *didn't* tell Sutt right now. He tried to control the Foundation itself by religious forces as he controlled the outer worlds, and he failed – which is the surest sign that in the Seldon scheme, religion is played out.

'Economic control worked differently. And to paraphrase that famous Salvor Hardin quotation of yours, it's a poor atom-blaster that won't point both ways. If Korell prospered with our trade, so did we. If Korellian factories fail without our trade; and if the prosperity of the outer worlds vanishes with commercial isolation; so will our factories fail and our prosperity vanish.

'And there isn't a factory, not a trading centre, not a shipping line that isn't under my control; that I couldn't squeeze to nothing if Sutt attempts revolutionary propaganda. Where his propaganda succeeds, or even looks as though it might succeed, I will make certain that prosperity dies. Where it fails, prosperity will continue, because my factories will remain fully staffed.

'So by the same reasoning which makes me sure that the Korellians will revolt in favour of prosperity, I am sure *we* will not revolt against it. The game will be played out to its end.'

'So then,' said Jael, 'you're establishing a plutocracy. You're making us a land of traders and merchant princes. Then what of the future?'

Mallow lifted his gloomy face, and exclaimed fiercely, 'What business of mine is the future? No doubt Seldon has foreseen it and prepared against it. There will be other crises in the time to come when money power has become as dead a force as religion is now. Let my successors solve those new problems, as I have solved the one of today.'

KORELL ... *And so after three years of a war which was certainly the most unfought war on record, the Republic of Korell surrendered unconditionally, and Hober Mallow took his place next to Hari Seldon and Salvor Hardin in the hearts of the people of the Foundation.*

ENCYCLOPEDIA GALACTICA

THE END

Isaac Asimov

The Caves of Steel

The classic robot novel

'One of the classic presentations of the womb-city, metropolis as mother, which has haunted imaginations ever since . . . *The Caves of Steel* and *The Naked Sun* are the best books Asimov ever wrote' *Guardian*

Detective Elijah Baley investigates the murder of an offworlder in Spacetown. In the opinion of the Spacers, the murder is tied up with recent attempts to sabotage the Spacer-sponsored project of converting Earth to an integrated human/robot society on the model of the Outer Worlds.

To search for the killer in the City's vast caves of steel, Elijah is assigned a Spacer partner named R.Daneel. That's Robot Daneel. And notwithstanding the celebrated Three Laws of Robotics, which should make such a murder impossible, R.Daneel is soon Elijah's prime suspect . . .

This is the first of Isaac Asimov's robot novels.

Isaac Asimov

The Rest of Robots

ROBOT TONY is the first robot designed to perform domestic duties by the U S Robots and Mechanical Men Corporation. Is it Tony's fault that the lady of the house where he's field-tested falls in love with him?

ROBOT AL was intended for shipment to a mining outfit on the moon. Instead, he's loose in the mountains of Virginia . . . building from scraps of junk his very own, very dangerous disintegrator. Goodbye, Virginia?

ROBOT LENNY answers workaday questions in babytalk. So why is Dr Susan Calvin, the world's top robopsychologist, fascinated by this messed-up specimen of an industrial robot?

THE REST OF THE ROBOTS is the second timeless, amazing and amusing volume of Isaac Asimov's robot stories offering golden insights into robot thought processes. Asimov's Three Laws of Robotics were programmed into real computers thirty years ago at the Massachusetts Institute of Technology – with surprising results. Readers of today still have many platinum-iridium surprises in store . . .

Isaac Asimov

The Complete Stories

VOLUME TWO

The definitive collection of short fiction by Isaac Asimov, supreme master of the science fiction genre, continues with Volume Two of the Complete Stories. The Good Doctor was always ahead of his time and his work stands today as the clearest expression of our collective hopes and fears for the future. But the ever-expanding popularity of his stories with young and old readers alike is explained by their wit, zest and human interest.

Herein are 23 compelling stories, ranging from the very surprising heart-tugger *The Ugly Little Boy* to the overwhelming vision of *Nightfall*, often voted the best science fiction story of all time. In these stories Asimov's vivid awareness of the potential of technology is translated into human dilemmas that are more relevant today than ever before.

'Asimov's career was one of the most formidable in science fiction' *The Times*

'Asimov displayed one of the most dynamic imaginations in science fiction' *Daily Telegraph*

'A publishing project that ranks with the building of the pyramids and summons proof, it was ever needed, that Asimov's stature in the field is richly deserved' *Locus*

Foundation and Empire

Isaac Asimov

The Seldon Plan guided the First Foundation safely through two centuries of chaos as the Galactic Empire disintegrated. Seldon's recorded holographic image appeared in the Council Chambers on Terminus at moments of crisis predicted by psychohistory, and his voice was heard. Even war between the Foundation and the remains of the Empire was foreseen – and planned for – by the great scientist.

But Seldon had no way of predicting the birth of the Mule, a mutant of uncanny power and unlimited ambition. The Mule's conquests are effortless and his subjects mind-controlled slaves.

The Foundation is powerless against the supernormal force the Mule exerts. The Seldon Plan is in tatters. Two men and a woman from Terminus flee to the ruins of mighty Trantor in an effort to discover where the mysterious Second Foundation was established. Its help is needed desperately against the mental powers of the Mule. But the Mule, using those same astonishing powers, is also looking for the Second Foundation.

Foundation and Empire is the story of first contact between the two Foundations of Hari Seldon.

'One of the most staggering achievements in modern SF.'
The Times